RADFORD PUBLIC LIB
30 WEST MAIN STF
RADFORD, VA 24141
540-731-3621

W9-ABE-772

WILD GIRLS

A NOVEL

Mary Stewart Atwell

SCRIBNER

New York London Toronto Sydney New Delhi

RADFORD PUBLIC LIBRARY
30 WEST MAIN STREET
RADFORD, VA 24141
540-731-3621

SCRIBNER

A Division of Simon & Schuster, Inc.
1230 Avenue of the Americas
New York, NY 10020

This book is a work of fiction. Names, characters, places,
and incidents either are products of the author's imagination or
are used fictitiously. Any resemblance to actual events or locales
or persons, living or dead, is entirely coincidental.

Copyright © 2012 by Mary Stewart Atwell

All rights reserved, including the right to reproduce this book
or portions thereof in any form whatsoever. For information, address
Scribner Subsidiary Rights Department, 1230 Avenue of the Americas,
New York, NY 10020.

First Scribner hardcover edition October 2012

SCRIBNER and design are registered trademarks of The Gale Group, Inc.,
used under license by Simon & Schuster, Inc., the publisher of this work.

For information about special discounts for bulk purchases,
please contact Simon & Schuster Special Sales at 1-866-506-1949
or business@simonandschuster.com.

The Simon & Schuster Speakers Bureau can bring authors to your
live event. For more information or to book an event, contact the
Simon & Schuster Speakers Bureau at 1-866-248-3049 or
visit our website at www.simonspeakers.com.

Book design by Ellen R. Sasahara

Manufactured in the United States of America

1 3 5 7 9 10 8 6 4 2

ISBN 978-1-4516-8327-1
ISBN 978-1-4516-8329-5 (ebook)

RECEIVED

MAR 06 2013

For Charlie

WILD GIRLS

PROLOGUE

My hometown, Swan River, could have been known for murder the way Chicago is known for pizza, Roswell for aliens. It was our thing, our trivia fact, and it occurs to me now that if the Chamber of Commerce had known what they were doing, people could have come to us the way they go to the Massachusetts town where Lizzie Borden axed her parents. Not that we had any murderers who were as famous as Lizzie Borden, but we did have a pattern: teenage girls, usually between the ages of sixteen and eighteen, who killed and pillaged with the abandon of lifelong criminals. There was Margaret Reid, burning her parents' farm in the 1890s; Angie Davenport, rolling a car full of her high school classmates into a ravine; Misty Greco, smashing up the hardware store in the heat of a midsummer day. You never knew when a teenage girl would take it into her head to shove a shiv into somebody's stomach, or cave in the back of their skull with a well-tossed brick.

In Swan River, we called these hellions the wild girls. I heard about them first from other kids, on the playground and at Girl Scout camp in the summer. With the hoods of sleeping bags pulled up over their heads, the older girls whispered about our homegrown terrors. The wild girls were reported to be able to fly. It was said that though their preferred weapon was fire, they could kill in any way they chose; some had strangled or drowned their victims, or bitten and torn their skin until they bled to death. Since people rarely saw a wild girl and survived, it wasn't exactly clear what they looked like, and no one knew what triggered the change of an ordinary teenager to one of these fierce creatures. There was no clear cause, no toxic sludge in the drinking water. It was just something about our town—the high wooded ridges, the valleys where abandoned farms slowly decayed to the earth. There was a spirit here, dark and uncontainable, and once it got into you it wouldn't let you go.

You had to talk to other kids about the wild girls, because the institutions of our town—the sheriff, the newspaper—preferred to act like they didn't exist. They pretended that when Misty Greco killed four people in half an hour, it was just a regular murder, comparable to a school shooting spree. But we knew that adults understood what was really happening, even if they never said so. As my sister Maggie said, when you turned sixteen everybody started to look at you as if you were the suicide bomber at the checkpoint, the enemy in disguise.

As a local, maybe I should have sympathized with the wild girls. I should have thought how terrifying it would be to lose control like that, your body conscripted by a force you couldn't possibly understand. I should have imagined the moment when they had to face responsibility for what they'd done, and pitied them for it. But I didn't feel sorry for them. I didn't try to see things from their point of view. When I thought about the wild girls, I just squeezed my eyes shut and swore to myself that it would never, ever, ever happen to me.

I didn't know exactly what the wild girls were, but I was pretty sure about what they were not. They were not the daughters of the few professional people in town, the doctors and ministers. They were not headed for college. They were bad girls, with reputations for doing things in the backs of pickups, and a lot of them came from the north side of town, from Bloodwort Road.

Flying over Swan River, you would have seen a town laid out in a straight line, north to south along the riverbank. The bluffs above the river supported the sprawling campus of the Swan River Academy for Girls, but most of the town clustered below, in the bluffs' long shadows. Downtown was one street with two stop-lights, one of which was used principally to control traffic onto the Swan River Bridge, an impressive arrangement of air and steel that made downtown look even uglier. North of downtown was the neighborhood called the Delta, a collection of shacks and trail-ers named for its habit of flooding every summer. At the end of the Delta, River Street became Bloodwort Road, where blacktop shaded to gravel and gravel to a dirt track that stretched, so I'd been told, through higher and higher mountains all the way to the Tennessee border.

Once Bloodwort Road must have been a flourishing part of the town, home to a mill that sent pallets of fine white pine down the river to Moorefield, but the mill had been closed since, in 1969, a girl named Luray Coulter set a fire in the main building, killing four workers trapped inside. The mill property belonged to Swan River Academy now, and aside from the signs proclaim-ing *Academy Property: Private*, the road showed few marks of human habitation. There were a handful of abandoned houses, burned or simply crumbling from age—windows broken, steps rotted, doors hanging open into thin air. There were rust-ing trailers, and shacks with half a dozen hungry dogs swirling around the front porch. For the most part, the people who lived on Bloodwort Road were the kind who didn't want to be around other people: drunks or old river rats who had washed up there and decided to stay. The children they raised were different from other children, and the landscape of Bloodwort was also different—bleaker, the slopes scalloped with exposed limestone. Though you sometimes saw vegetable patches along the road, the only thing that thrived around here was the flowering weed that gave the road its name, as endemic as kudzu was in other parts of the South.

It was the most depressing place I could imagine, and yet in the middle of this hopelessness and persistence was Bloodwort Farm, the commune run by back-to-the-land hippie types where my mom liked to buy produce in the summertime. The commune did a better job of farming than anyone else along the road, and they ran a stand where you could take whatever you wanted, leaving your money folded up in a little plastic box. Mom drove up here for asparagus and strawberries, black raspberries and tomatoes and pumpkins, and every October she took us to the equinox festival, which attracted visitors from as far away as Moorefield. Though my sister made fun of me for it, I still loved the pie-eating contest and the face painting. The festival was one of the highlights of my year, but the only visit worth telling about was the last one. That was the summer I turned fourteen, the one and only time that I was allowed to bring a friend.

That friend was Willow Becker, who had also grown up in Swan River but on the other side of the bridge, in the posh neighborhood that held the town's only bed-and-breakfast and a few out-of-staters' second homes. The Beckers' was an old Victorian, a wedding cake of a house decorated with wooden lace that seemed designed to be seen from afar. Though we had lived our whole lives not five miles from each other, I had never laid eyes on Willow until the first day of Orientation at the Academy, and there was a reason for that. Mr. Louis Becker owned a mail-order company and probably made more money than the dentist, the town's only doctor, and the mayor all put together. At the grocery store, I had once caught a glimpse of Mrs. Becker, a tall blonde woman with a pretty, vacant face, but I hadn't known that the family had a daughter until I met Willow. Since kindergarten, she had attended the Waldorf school in Moorefield, where the students learned math on an abacus and practiced the recorder. Waldorf school was stupid, she said, but her parents would have driven her to Knoxville every morning rather than send her to the public school in Swan River.

Within a few days of meeting, Willow and I had pricked our fingers with a safety pin and sworn ourselves blood sisters. We had so much in common, even beyond the fact that we were the only Swan River locals enrolled at the Academy. We both liked strawberry lip gloss. We hated chicken nuggets and boys who tucked their shirts in and anything that was made especially for teens: movies, magazines. I liked her better than anybody I'd ever met, but at the same time I couldn't help recognizing all the ways that we were not alike. I was medium height with a medium build, and thought of myself as exactly halfway between ugly and pretty. Willow was tall and near-beautiful, with an inborn confidence that made people look up when she walked into a room. She had a sharp but not pointy face, red hair that fell in waves to her shoulders, and fragile-looking skin that held on to marks and bruises. She wore colored contacts that she changed every week or so, the colors varying from fern green to storm gray to wildflower blue. Willow also had a wicked talent for caricature, and she was already well-known among the girls in our dorm for drawing a cartoon of our housemother sniffing at the crack of a door for cigarette smoke, her big bottom stuck up in the air.

After the first week of school, I invited Willow to come home with me for a weekend, but it didn't take long for me to realize that our two days away from the Academy were not going to be the one-hundred-percent good time I'd anticipated. Willow seemed more subdued than usual, and I came to see that some of the things I thought were cool were not cool, and that other things that seemed neutral to me were actually deeply embarrassing. There was Travis, for instance, my mother's longtime boyfriend. Of course I knew that he was funny-looking, slouched on the couch in his police uniform, his drooping mustache foamy with beer. He was a thin, small man with a perpetual look of friendly belligerence, and I knew, because my mom said so, that he was lazy and spent most of the time when he should have been on patrol sitting in the parking lot of the River House, smoking pot and listening to classic rock. Still, he had always been nice to me, and it wasn't until I saw Willow stifle a laugh at the sight of him hopping on one foot while he emptied gravel out of his cowboy boot that I wondered if I ought to be ashamed of him.

"Kate," Travis said on the way to the festival. "If those girls give you any trouble this year, you can send them to me. I know that Antoinette Lemons believes in letting kids work things out on their own, but that was a nasty-looking bump you got last time."

I wished he'd keep his mouth shut in front of Willow. I didn't want her to know about Crystal Lemons and Tricia Jo Leggett hitting me on the head with a tree branch. It was humiliating to think of how I'd bawled as I limped into the yard where the grown-ups were drinking and dancing, a knot the size of a golf ball rising under my fingers. "Crystal Lemons is a total deadneck," I said, sliding down in my seat.

Travis laughed. He had a short laugh, sudden as a gunshot. "Deadneck, huh? I like that."

"It's somebody who's half-hippie and half-redneck," I explained to Willow. "Like their parents used to follow the Grateful Dead, but then they bought land and decided to be squash farmers or whatever." Willow grinned, but Maggie was giving me a look. Most of her friends were deadnecks, and her boyfriend too.

After a long pause Mom spoke dreamily, as if the words had taken that long to penetrate to her brain. Probably she and Travis had split a joint before the drive. "Kate, I wouldn't say that word to their faces if I were you."

"It's not a slur," I said. "It's not like I called them white trash."

"Seriously, though." Maggie twisted the silver stud high on her ear between thumb and forefinger. "Those girls will take you out."

"Take you out how?" Willow asked, leaning around me. "You mean like beat you up?"

"I mean they're dangerous," Maggie said, leveling Willow with a stare. Willow turned away, tugging at her bottom lip with her teeth, and I kicked Maggie in the anklebone.

When Bloodwort Road looped back toward the river, we turned onto an even rougher track, passing between bushes that scraped both sides of the car. Just after the entrance was a sign that read *Welcome to Bloodwort Farm!*, a dippy-looking sun suspended over the double *o*. Brief gaps between oaks and poplars showed fields fringed with the rotting stalks of late-summer corn. Travis parked with the left tires sloping up onto the grass, and we walked through a lane of trees toward the field. Every twenty feet or so a clearing disclosed one of the family cabins, constructed out of whatever scraps of wood and metal the builder had been able to lay his hands on and painted in garish shades of blue, pink, or green. To me each one looked like a different species of fungus, absurd and at the same time completely suited to the place where it had sprouted.

At the end of the path, a larger space opened, the cleared field crowded with picnic tables, croquet sets, obstacle courses, and booths selling sweet potato pie and roasted chestnuts. Through all these distractions, what drew my eye was the fire, and what was in the fire. I have no idea where Mrs. Lemons got a pig like that—whether, as the commune kids said, it was a wild boar hunted in the high mountains or whether she'd had it shipped from some boutique farm where they bred pigs that size. From her son, Mason, years later, I heard that the men of Bloodwort Farm butchered the pig themselves, cutting its throat and letting it bleed to death to keep the meat tender. They stuck it through with a spit and hoisted it above the fire, where it turned all day, its skin blistering to a crackling rose-pink. When it turned upside down, the folds of skin over its eyes fell back and for a moment it met my gaze, making me jump.

I could never stand the thought of eating that pig, so Willow and I loaded our plates with squash casserole and black bean tamales before taking them to a table at the edge of the fire. Groups of men stood outside the circle of heat, voices raised as if they were competing to see who could talk the loudest. A lot of them were already drunk; you could tell by the way they favored one leg, leaning hard and then, when their knees locked, nearly toppling. They were red-faced and braying with laughter, and I saw that life at the commune was one big party for the grown-ups. They drank and ate and did whatever else grown-ups did for fun, and while they were occupied, their kids amused themselves. Tonight this freedom extended to us, but I couldn't think of anything exciting enough to suggest to Willow.

I was still eating, but Willow had rested her head on her hand, a long strand of red hair trailing over her wrist. "Where did the rest of your family go?"

"Maggie likes to hang out with the band. Sometimes when the guys get loaded, they let her sit in on banjo. Mom and Travis are probably smoking pot."

Willow looked up with a flicker of interest. "They do drugs? I thought Travis was a policeman."

"He's the deputy." Embarrassed, I pretended to be distracted by my apple pie. Willow had shared my room for the past two nights, and I'd assumed she'd noticed the smell of the sage that Travis burned to cover the smell of marijuana, and the high-pitched laughter that rose up from the living room in the middle of the night. "It's not like they're crackheads or something," I mumbled around a mouthful of ice cream.

"I'm not judging them," Willow said. "My mom takes every kind of pill in the world. So have you ever tried it?"

"Smoking pot?" I sounded shocked, I knew—I couldn't help it. But I thought of the night in the dorm when Willow had asked if I was still a virgin, and seemed mildly surprised when I told her I'd never even kissed a boy. It was better to be casual about these things. "I don't really want to," I said. "I'm kind of into having a healthy lifestyle, I guess."

"I took one of my mom's Vicodin once." She poked her salsa-stained fork into my pie. "It's supposed to relax you, but it made me really tense."

I sat back and let her finish the pie. "Hey," I said, kicking at the table leg. "Please don't tell anybody at school that my mom smokes pot."

"Oh my God, I wouldn't," Willow said. "She could lose her job."

An ice-water shiver ran up my spine. I was only able to attend the Academy because my mom, the headmaster's secretary, got a break on tuition. If she ever got fired, I would have to go back to public school.

The picnic table jolted suddenly to the right. Seated at the opposite end, her arms folded on the table, Crystal Lemons tipped me a wink. Behind her stood Tricia Jo Leggett, a girl whom I had never seen smile. "Hey Kate," Crystal said. "I just wanted to apologize for giving you that boo-boo last year. My mom said you were really upset."

"Whatever," I muttered.

"Are you refusing to accept my apology?" she drawled. "That hurts, you know."

Crystal Lemons was not a pretty girl—she was short and a little heavy, with frizzled black hair and a cartoonishly wide mouth—but there was an interesting ripeness about her, an early voluptuousness that she shared with a lot of the girls from Bloodwort Road. *Grown up too soon,* my mom said about those girls. Tricia Jo was clearly a sidekick, stolid and quiet, with long brown dreadlocks and eyebrows that grew together. I hadn't seen either of them since school let out, and I noticed a new snake tattoo on the side of Tricia Jo's neck. I guessed that Willow had never met either of them, and I wished I could have kept it that way.

Sighing heavily, Crystal turned to Willow and sketched a lazy wave. "Who are you?"

As Willow gave her name, I felt my shoulders rise to my ears. I knew that Crystal's dislike of me had something to do with the fact that we were people who bought stuff from the commune, rather than people who lived there. If a secretary's daughter like me could seem like a stuck-up snob to her, how much more would she dislike Willow, with her designer jeans and her sprawling house atop the river bluff? But Crystal didn't slam her with a put-down like I'd expected. She just sat there, blinking a little, like a sleepy lizard sunning itself on a rock.

"You guys seem cool," she said finally. "You want to give us a hand with a little prank we're planning?" As Willow and I glanced at each other, Crystal pulled a long tube from her pocket and waggled it in the air between us. It was heavy cardboard, like a paper towel tube, with the words *Roman Candle* printed on the wrapper.

Of course I wanted to say no to any plan that involved fireworks. Though Crystal and Tricia Jo were being nice enough now, I felt that we had every reason to suspect a double cross. Probably they wanted to hit us with branches, or throw poison ivy leaves at us, or something even worse. But Willow wanted to go with them, and they seemed to sense that Willow's opinion trumped mine.

Silently, gripping the Roman candles in their fists, the commune girls led us through the woods to a ridge overlooking a clearing. In the clearing was a cave, but it wasn't what people normally pictured when they thought of a cave—not a breach in the side of a rock but an open hole in the ground. Caves like this were common in these hills, formed by the river tunneling through the earth until it collapsed in on itself. This one was unusually big, perhaps ten by twenty feet, with bloodwort and mountain laurel knitted around the rim and a cold yawning hole in the middle. Any responsible landowner would have fenced it off, but it didn't surprise me that they didn't care about that sort of thing at the commune.

Along one edge of the cave was a makeshift shooting range built from tiered orange crates, with glittering bottles balanced on the highest levels. Two men and two boys crouched at the end of the range, the men passing a bottle between them.

One of the men I'd seen in the crowd of drinkers by the roasting pig, and I was pretty sure that he lived at the commune, though he never helped out with the three-legged races or the pony rides. He was bald, with a neatly pointed gray mustache and a disreputable face. Maggie and I had named him the Birdman for the tattoos that covered every inch of his bare upper body—blue jays, blackbirds, and screaming eagles fluttering the muscles of his arms and chest. He was always smiling, and I would have thought of him as friendly if it hadn't been for something strange about his eyes, a shallow deadness to them, as if they were backed with tinfoil just behind the iris.

The other man I'd never seen before, but I could tell that he didn't belong to the commune. He was tall, black-bearded, broad-shouldered, and wore the preppy uniform of polo shirt and khakis. Head tilted, he watched the target practice in front of him from a critical distance. In his hand was a thick leather-bound notebook in which he occasionally scribbled, opening it in his palm, as if he didn't want the others to pay too much attention to what he was doing.

The boys were familiar, though I'd never spoken to either of them. Mason Lemons, Crystal's older brother, was hands down the best-looking guy at the high school, with a dark, moody face and goldy eyes that seemed to look all the way down into you. I had heard that his IQ ranked at Mensa levels, and that the principal had made him take the test again to be sure there hadn't been a mistake. Though a certified genius, Mason was always getting in trouble for stupid stuff that other boys would have gotten away with—breaking windows, throwing condoms filled with water at a float in the Christmas parade. The younger boy, Clancy Harp, had been a year ahead of me when I went to public school. An orphan, he was tall and awkward, with hands and feet too big for the rest of him. His light hair swung into his eyes, and his skin was so deeply freckled that he looked permanently tanned. He was holding a rifle, the Birdman kneeling down to help him aim it.

"Hey," Crystal hissed, pointing her Roman candle at my nose, "try not to fling it all over the place. You want to level it right at them, understand?"

Once we'd passed the lighter around, everything seemed to speed up. Fireworks fizzing from our outstretched hands, we leaped out of the rhododendron and raced down the crumbling slope, screaming at the top of our lungs. Red, green, and yellow fireballs were popping on every side, and for a few moments I forgot about how much the commune girls scared me and had fun. I had never set off fireworks before. Maggie and I begged for them every Fourth of July, but Mom said they were a waste of money. I twirled in a circle, the air sharp with the smell of black powder, and Tricia Jo punched me in the shoulder. "At *them,* moron," she growled. "Aim it at them."

Then a purple fireball whizzed by Clancy's ear. The two boys were crouched behind the orange crates, threatening, pleading. When Clancy had stuck his head up to holler about a truce, his face went white, and he clapped a hand to the side of his head. It looked to me like he was checking to make sure that he wasn't on fire, and I felt guiltily certain that it was my Roman candle that had almost taken his ear off. It was fizzling out anyway. Willow's had already gone dead, and when I looked around I saw the strange man walking fast up the ridge toward the fire road, the leather notebook making a fat bulge in his back pocket.

At that moment I heard a crackling behind me and turned to see Crystal advancing on the Birdman, the Roman candle trained on him like a gun. He was crab-walking back toward the cave, and on his face was an expression of pure terror. Distorted by his posture, the birds on his upper body looked more grotesque than ever, a mad aviary of elongated, clawlike beaks and distended feathers.

"*Je*-sus, Crystal," he shouted. He said something else, but I couldn't make out the words. He was at the very edge of the cave now. One of his hands broke through the latticework of mountain laurel, and he lurched backward before regaining his balance. Crystal's face shone with triumph. A spark hit the Birdman's leather vest, and he let out a howl that echoed against the ridge.

I told myself that Crystal wasn't really trying to kill him. It was a prank, like she'd said, and pranks depended on convincing the other person that you meant business. That was why she timed it so the Birdman was right on the verge of the abyss—his head shiny with sweat, his lips bloodless, his right hand lifted as if in plea for mercy—when her Roman candle finally sputtered and died. In half a second the Birdman was on his feet, twisting her arm behind her back. "What the hell, girl," he whispered, with a tricky sweetness that made me sick to my stomach.

He looked up at Tricia Jo and winked showily. She still held the dead candle, pointed straight out in front of her. "Don't you touch me," she said, her voice trembling a little even as her hand held steady.

"Did I start this?" the Birdman asked. "I don't believe I did. But if you want me to go easy on your friend, you best get in line."

A shimmer of rage passed across her face, and my fingertips tingled as the blood rushed to my head. Tricia Jo could not be a wild girl, I told myself firmly. I knew this, because if she and Crystal *had* gone wild, the rest of us would have already been dead.

They filed up the hill, the Birdman driving Crystal, her hands bound with a bandanna, and Tricia Jo following behind them.

"You can do what you want with those other ones," the Birdman called back to Mason and Clancy. "Just don't hurt them where it shows."

I smiled vaguely before I realized how weird that must look and made my face go blank. I didn't really see the humor in what the Birdman had said, but I knew it had to be a joke. *Don't hurt them where it shows?* My mom and Travis were right up the hill. Travis was a police officer—not a good one, but still, he wore a badge and carried a pistol.

Mason kicked over one of the orange crates and sat down, facing us. He had picked up the rifle and held it cradled in his arms like a pet snake. "Sit down," he said. I lowered myself onto a butt-size patch of bloodwort in the middle of the range, but when I looked back at Willow she was still standing, lip curled.

"I don't want to sit on the *ground*," she said.

"Christ's sake," Mason murmured, disdain mixing with a tinge of boredom. He nodded at Clancy, who stripped off his windbreaker and spread it on the dirt before settling back on his crate, a good lieutenant. Still frowning, Willow sat, neatly folding her ballet flats under her body.

"Everybody comfortable?" Mason said. "Everybody copacetic? Now here's how this is going to go. We're going to have an interrogation, and the first question is—what are you doing here?"

His attention flustered me more than the gun. "I—" I coughed, started again. "Your sister brought us. We didn't know what was going to happen. I mean, we kind of did, but—"

Mason shook his head and leaned forward, balancing his elbows on his knees. "I mean what are you doing on Bloodwort Road?"

"Everybody comes to the festival," I said. When he didn't dispute this, I felt emboldened to ask a question of my own. "What is he going to do to her? Your sister, I mean." I didn't care about

Crystal Lemons being punished, but the syrupy cruelty in the Birdman's voice had made me uneasy. Adults administered discipline, that was a given, but they weren't supposed to enjoy it like that.

Mason shrugged, and would have moved on if Clancy hadn't spoken first. "He'll probably lock her in the cabin or something," he said. "No one's going to get hurt." I saw that he was trying to sound like a man, as if he could pledge our safety with his strength, and suddenly I felt much older than him, even though he was in tenth grade and I was only in ninth.

Laying the gun at his feet, Mason pulled a pouch from his jeans and, with the same fixed attention that had made my face heat up and my palms go slick, set about rolling a cigarette. When he was still, there was a heavy blankness about him—a shutdown quality that I'd observed in the other commune kids—but when he moved, even in an action as simple as this, it was hard to keep your eyes off him. His big, thick-fingered hands worked slowly but with an appealing deftness. His gold-brown eyes shuttled between my face and Willow's, pausing, I noticed with mixed feelings, more often on hers.

"See that?" he asked, nodding at an old trailer halfway up the slope. Grown over with vines that covered the windows, it looked as if it had been abandoned for years. I had noticed it, but in the negligent way that you notice things that seem to have no human purpose. "That's my mom's trailer. You know about my mom, right?"

He was looking at me again, and as I nodded I could feel my face turning red. "Why is she so far away from everyone else?" I asked.

"She has a cabin up the hill too," he said. "But she works better down here."

"Works?" Willow repeated indifferently; I suspected she'd spoken only to direct Mason's attention back to her. "What kind of work can you do in the woods?"

"She's a witch," Mason said. "She can tell the future. She can do about anything you can think of. Her granny was a witch too, and she learned it all from her. I thought that might have been why you girls were here. I thought you might have been looking for a love potion or something."

Embarrassed, I pulled a bloodwort leaf from its stem and shredded it to pieces. I had heard the stories about Mrs. Lemons, of course. She could sell you one bottle to cure a headache, another to take the sting out of a sunburn, still another to bring back a lost love. I believed that what Mason said about his mother was true, but never in a million years would I have mentioned any of this in front of Willow. We had talked about the wild girls once, and she seemed to believe that they were a quaint myth, our local Bigfoot. Shut in behind a wrought-iron fence, shuttled back and forth to school in Moorefield, she had probably never even heard of Mrs. Lemons.

Looking between Willow and Mason, I could tell that she wanted to laugh. Her pale eyebrows were lifted, one side of her mouth jerking as if tugged by a string. Mason kept his cool, a faraway squint in his eye as he dragged on his cigarette. "We could give you a tour," he said, looking at a spot to the right of Willow's head. "You can pick out anything you want. Like a candy store." No one said anything. A deep stillness had settled over the clearing, and Clancy licked his dry lips. For a moment I thought I could smell the cave—sulfur, stone, running water.

Then something moved in the corner of my eye. If I hadn't known better, I could have sworn that a blind had twitched in the trailer's front window. "Mason," Clancy said uneasily.

Mason ignored him. "Come on," he said to Willow with a smile that made my stomach flip. "Let me show you around."

The silence was split by the loud clang of metal on metal. The boys took off like flushed rabbits, Mason in one direction and Clancy in the other. The last we saw of them was their shirttails flying as they leaped over the fallen trees and crashed through the brush, Mason with the rifle pressed against his leg.

I had jumped to my feet too, and the only thing that kept me from running was my confusion about which path led back to the festival. Willow had stayed where she was, and as I looked back she reached for Mason's dropped cigarette, pinched it between her fingers, and took a deliberate drag. "Don't you think we should get out of here?" I asked.

"It was the gutter," she said. "It fell off and hit the side. Look."

I followed her gaze to the trailer roof, a section of rusted gutter dangling off like a broken arm. Willow was on her feet, dusting the back of her jeans. With a sneer, she kicked Clancy's windbreaker into the cave. "Ready?" she asked. "Let's check it out."

"I don't think we're supposed to be in there," I said. "With Mason it would have been different, but—"

Willow sighed. "Don't be such a wuss."

When we got closer, the trailer below the ridge looked even less like the trailers you saw in town. Those were practically regular houses, with wooden siding and shutters and bikes on the front lawn. Manufactured homes, some people called them, but this manufactured home looked like it had fallen out of a cargo plane and been set up any which way, without plans or tools. Like most things at the commune it was slightly off-level, and the tilt-edness gave me an uncomfortable feeling, as if the whole thing might collapse any moment in an explosion of sawdust and rust.

Pokeweed like blood-tipped needles thrust up beside the front steps.

"This might not be a good idea," I whispered. "I think I saw a snake in the foundation."

"Why are you whispering?" Willow said. "There's nobody here." The knob stuck when she tried to turn it, but she nipped her lip between her teeth and set her shoulder against the door. One shove and we were in, my elbow catching Willow between the shoulder blades.

We had stepped through the door of a trailer in the woods, but now we were in another kind of place altogether, a witch's den out of a fairy tale. The metal shelves against the walls were stocked with bottles. One seemed to contain dried peach halves, while another looked to be full of chili powder. Some were clear as water, others dark and clotted like blood. There were scales, and measuring cups, and jugs of filtered water. Nothing was too disturbing or too unfamiliar, but I was reluctant to take what I saw at face value. What if the marbled pebbles were actually eyeballs? What if the black paste was bat guano? There were jars of powdered leaves, and brown moss, and unstrung golden beads. Animal heads had been nailed above the shelves—not the obvious bear and buck but squirrels, and rabbits, and what looked like a yellow dog with its tongue hanging out.

I wanted to turn around again, but Willow picked up a bottle of greenish liquid even as I backed toward the door. "Who is Mrs. Lemons anyway?" she asked.

"Who is she?" I said. "She's the head of the commune, I guess. She's Crystal and Mason's mom."

"And she's supposed to have magical powers or something?"

I shrugged. "Kids say stuff."

"What kind of stuff?"

"Like they say she turned Mason and Crystal's father into a pig." I thought of the pig on the spit and felt queasy.

"Why did she turn him into a pig?"

"*I* don't know. I guess he left her and—"

I never made it to the end of that sentence. A door that I was sure hadn't been there a minute ago had opened in the far wall. Light poured through the opening, and standing there, backlit and gleaming like silver, was Antoinette Lemons.

"Hello, girls," she said. "Is there something I can help you with?"

At the summer festival Mrs. Lemons looked like all the other hippie women—carefree and joyful, with friendly, heavy-lidded eyes—but here, in the woods by Bloodwort Ridge, she seemed different. I had never noticed how tall she was, for one thing. She wore her blonde hair as long as mine, and had long skinny arms and legs. Though she was probably no older than my mom, her skin was webbed all over with wrinkles like fine cracks in porcelain. She wore a white linen robe with a capacious hood, the hem trailing the ground behind her. To me she looked like an ice queen who had come from the north with the glacier that rucked and buckled these mountains and stayed, ice-stranded, when it retreated. "Looking for something in particular?" she asked.

I shook my head dumbly. Mrs. Lemons seemed friendly enough now, but did she know what we had done with the fireworks? The air inside the trailer felt thick, warm and sweet. Behind the open door was a bed that filled the room, the sheets mussed and bunched at the foot.

Willow kept looking over as if she expected me to have an escape plan, but Mrs. Lemons had positioned herself in front of the outside door, and she seemed to be in no hurry to let us go. "I know you," she said to me. "Kate Riordan. I know your parents."

Bumping into an adult I knew downtown or at the River House Coffeeshop, I would have expected this comment, but here it seemed as out of place as Willow's designer jeans. "Yeah," I muttered, tugging at my braid. "Well, Travis isn't really my—"

"Your mother used to ask me to read her palm," Mrs. Lemons interrupted. "She stopped coming around years ago—I guess she didn't like what she was hearing. But I'll do yours for free if you want, for old times' sake."

Trembling, I put out my hand and let her trace her fingertips from wrist to knuckle. My heart beat so fast I could hear its hollow roar in my ears. "Oh," she said, her hand tightening around my wrist. "Well, I can tell you one thing. What you're afraid of isn't going to happen. You're different."

"Different than what?"

"Different than what you think you are."

"Umm," I said. "What am I then?"

Instead of answering, Mrs. Lemons closed my fingers and grabbed Willow by the wrist. Willow threw her head back, bright hair rolling over her shoulders, as calm and self-possessed as if Mrs. Lemons were doing her nails.

"Well?" Willow demanded. "Am I supposed to offer you silver or something?"

"I'm not a gypsy."

"I just want to know what you see."

Hissing as she scanned the lines and creases, Mrs. Lemons looked as mad as any wild girl, and I wondered if it was possible to live so close to the dark side of Swan River without being driven at least a little crazy. "You're going to get what you want," she said, pressing down with her long fingernails until Willow flinched. "You're going to get exactly what you want."

By the time we got back to the festival, the food booths had been packed up and the parking lot was half-empty. For the locals, this was when the party really started. The bluegrass band had moved onto a low wooden stage and were sawing away at "Foggy Mountain Breakdown." Sweat flung off the mustache of the fiddle player every time he drew his bow across the strings.

We sat on top of a picnic table, drinking homemade root beer, not speaking. Temporary floodlights had been set up at the corners of the stage, and people flitted in and out of the beams like ghosts. There was Travis, headed for the beer tent, stumbling a little. There was Mason Lemons in a hooded sweatshirt, glancing over whenever he thought we weren't looking. There was Mrs. Lemons, not a witch now but just a regular hippie woman, swinging the skirts of her robe as she danced in and out of the light. Willow and I didn't talk about what had happened down in the trailer. The fortune I'd been given felt too private for analysis, and I guessed that she felt the same way.

It was dark and silent when Travis shook us awake. He wasn't weaving as badly now, but his shirt was untucked and there was a barbecue stain on his chin. The field was empty except for a woman in a man's leather jacket passed out at the edge of the stage, and the light was turning predawn gray as we climbed into the backseat. Crowded with early shadows, the underbrush that rocked the car seemed bloated and grotesque. Willow slept or pretended to sleep. The heart-shaped locket I'd given her fell out of her collar and jittered in the hollow of her throat.

I thought everything was settled now. The witch had told me

that what I feared most was not going to happen. I would choose neither the fierce madness of the wild girls nor the dull unhappiness of my mother, who had disliked the thought of her own future so much that she'd refused to hear any more of it. Making friends with Willow was the first step toward getting out of Swan River, the Academy itself a kind of way station between one world and the next. But what I didn't realize, as we bounced and jostled up the rough road out of Bloodwort, was that Willow had her own ambitions. Mrs. Lemons had told her that she'd get what she wanted, and she was right about that. Girls like Willow always got what they wanted, no matter what.

CHAPTER ONE

As I'd expected, life at the Academy was different than life as a Swan River local—so different that I sometimes almost forgot to worry about becoming a wild girl. But at the beginning of my senior year, something happened that made me question whether Mrs. Lemons could be trusted to predict the future.

Until then, I'd expected my last year to be relatively uneventful. I didn't love the Academy like I'd thought I would, but I didn't hate it the way I'd hated public school. I had a single room overlooking the river from the top floor of Fallis Hall. I had friends, though they were not Willow's friends, not the popular girls who went skiing together over the holidays and hired drivers to whisk them off to the Grand Hotel in Moorefield on the weekends. I got mostly A's, and one of my favorite things to do was to pull out the folder of college brochures that I kept in my desk drawer and leaf through them when I should have been studying. In one, a smiling couple in Fair Isle sweaters bent their heads together across a library carrel. In another, a group of friends gathered on a winter-bare lawn, staring up at the Frisbee that rotated above them like a planet. Pritchard College in Tanner, Minnesota, was my favorite because they had the best-looking boys, soulful long-haired guitar players with gentle eyes. I knew my mom couldn't afford any of those schools unless I got a full scholarship, but I couldn't stop myself from dreaming about Vermont, Minnesota, Michigan—those cold, spare climates, all black and white with no shadowy spaces in between.

That August, Swan River was the opposite of Minnesota, hot and swampy, threatened by a growling thunderstorm that stayed just over the crest of the mountains. On the night of the twentieth, I was awakened by the scream of sirens, and I imagined that the fire at a backyard cookout had gotten out of hand. But in the morning I could see smoke hanging over Bloodwort Road, and its bitter taste was in my mouth when I brushed my teeth.

By noon everyone knew what had happened, but the story would be told in two different ways. There was the official story, the one reported by Sheriff McClellan and the newspaper, and then there was the real story, the one that all locals knew to read between the lines. The stories agreed that a man named Rondal Clark, whom Maggie and I had called the Birdman, had been found in the ruins of Bloodwort Farm, his body so bloodied and burned that no one thought he could live. A fire had raged through the cabins, and in one of them the firefighters found the remains of Crystal Lemons. The Birdman and the Lemons family were the only people left at the commune by then, the other members having left in a slow exodus as Mrs. Lemons's behavior became stranger and more erratic, the Birdman took over more responsibility, and the farm failed.

This is where the stories began to diverge. The sheriff claimed that the Birdman had been attacked by wild animals, though he was vague about what kind of animals they could have been: coyote, or bear, or possibly one of the catamounts that had been sneaking back into the region for the past few years. They wouldn't know for sure until they got the lab tests back. He never even tried to explain how a bear, coyote, or catamount had managed to start a fire that would send up flames that could be seen all the way from downtown.

Travis spent the day after the fire at the commune, and at home that evening he hunched over a bowl of soup and a beer, gray-faced and exhausted. He wouldn't talk to me about what he'd seen, but that night I heard him and Mom whispering, giving voice to the local certainty that the coyotes and catamounts had been unfairly blamed. We all knew that the sheriff's lab tests would come back inconclusive, if they came back at all. No experts would ever examine the Birdman, and whatever he remembered about that night, he wasn't talking.

Except for Crystal's family, the people who were most upset by what happened at the commune were probably the Academy parents. August twenty-first was the day of Convocation, when the moms and dads piled into the outdoor amphitheater to hear Dr. Bell talk about the Academy's illustrious past and bright future. Walking around campus that afternoon, I saw a handful of dads frowning down at the paper. They didn't know how to read between the lines of the *Riparian*'s coverage. They didn't believe in supernatural possession, and if their daughters had repeated the local stories, they would have replied with some smug commonplace, citing the rich tradition of Appalachian folklore. Still it was plain to see that the gruesome details of the Birdman's mauling had them spooked. How could they be sure that coyotes weren't slinking around campus in the middle of the night, blending into the tree-thickened shadows, turning their yellow eyes hungrily up to the glowing windows?

The students had to go to Convocation too, and we had to sit in the unshaded part of the amphitheater, where the slanting sun struck the stone benches at full strength. I sat with my friend Caroline Potts way up at the top, as far as we could get from the stage where Dr. Bell was summarizing the life of Charles Arkwright, founder and first headmaster of the Swan River Academy for Girls.

"But why did Crystal die?" Caroline asked me in a whisper. "The wild girls don't always die, do they?"

"Not always," I said. "Sometimes they just go back to their normal selves the next day, and it's like nothing ever happened."

"Like a fit." Caroline chewed her bottom lip. "Or a twenty-four-hour flu."

"I guess." I tried to act like I was listening to Dr. Bell, but with the sun in my eyes and the bench scratching my calves above my kneesocks, it was hard to pretend. Three rows ahead, Willow turned to say something to the girl beside her, long silver earrings brushing her SRA-crested blazer. I shifted inside my own ill-fitting blazer, bought secondhand from a graduating volleyball player whose shoulders had nearly split the seams.

"But sometimes they die?" Caroline persisted.

"Yeah, sometimes."

"I bet it just burns you up. All that energy, it's got to go somewhere. I bet it turns back on you, like an explosion."

"Maybe," I said uneasily.

Clicking through his slides, Dr. Bell ran down the list of the accomplishments of Academy graduates, which weren't actually all that amazing. There was a treasurer general of the DAR, and the volunteer of the year at the High Museum in Atlanta. The locals called the Academy a finishing school, where southern girls of a certain class were sent to learn the social graces, and certainly it had been that sort of place in the old days. Civil War–era portraits of girls doing embroidery still hung on the walls of the post office. I guessed that one reason why Dr. Bell had been promoted to headmaster after only a year on the faculty was that he promised to make the Academy famous for doing something besides turning out perfectly mannered young ladies, and supposedly SAT scores were up. Still, there were plenty of the old kind of Academy girls hanging around—Willow's best friend Tessa Cochran, for instance.

"It must be so weird for you to grow up in the same town with the wild girls," Caroline said. "I mean, you knew Crystal Lemons from way back, right?"

"*Shh,*" I whispered. I stared hard at the flat, grainy face of Leola Mackey, the former director of marketing at the Emily Post Institute.

The sun dipped behind the trees, stretching cool shadows across the white marble seats. Dr. Bell had moved on to slides of recent building projects, first the renovations to Fallis Hall, and then the new multimillion-dollar John P. and Jane S. Cochran Fitness Center and Natatorium. The Cochrans, plump and moneyed, sat in special cushy chairs at the edge of the stage, their daughter beside them. Not all the Academy parents were as fancy as the Cochrans, but most of the adults seated on the darkened side of the amphitheater had the self-satisfied look of people who never had to worry about how much they had in the bank. My mom didn't come to Opening Convocation, which was fine by me. I was used to seeing her here on weekdays, leaning over her messy desk in the administration building, but she didn't belong with these other parents—elegant and worldly, and almost entirely ignorant of the danger that lurked outside the school gates.

Dr. Bell switched off the slide projector and took a drink from the tiny water bottle at his elbow. Without the slides to look at, my eyes shifted to the opposite side of the amphitheater, where a group had lined up behind the rows of seated parents. This was the staff—not the secretaries like my mom, but the old man from the bookstore, and the maintenance guys, and the women who worked

at the dining hall. I didn't understand why they had to come to
the assembly, unless they were there to demonstrate to the parents
how many people were involved in the business of serving the students' daily needs. I picked out Clancy Harp from the landscaping
crew, clutching a baseball cap at his waist as if he were waiting for
"The Star-Spangled Banner."

When I looked back, Dr. Bell was rolling up his sleeves and
balancing his forearms on the podium. I never understood it when
girls said that he was hot, but he was definitely handsomish for a
middle-aged guy, with pale eyes and dark hair that he wore just
a little longer than the Academy dads wore theirs. He had the
right to be different because he was a great scholar, the author of
books on mythology and folklore, who had left some hoity-toity
college in New England to take the job at Swan River. The first
time my mom pointed him out to me as he strode down the hall of
the administration building, she had gushed about how lucky the
school was to have him. That might have been true, but as soon as
I saw him I knew that he was the man I'd seen on the firing range
at the commune, and it gave me an uneasy feeling, like a fingernail
scratch down the back of my neck.

From what I'd heard from my mom, the headmaster was
expected to spend all his time schmoozing with donors, but Dr.
Bell taught one class, a Greeks-to-superheroes survey course
called Myths and Mysteries, which Caroline had finally convinced me to sign up for this fall. I'd taken some persuading,
because Dr. Bell still made me uncomfortable. On the night of
the festival, he had run away from the firing range as if he didn't
want to be seen. Now that Crystal Lemons had burned Bloodwort Farm, I felt more strongly than ever that the world of the
wild girls and the world of the Academy should not intersect;

could not, for the sake of my peace of mind, come anywhere near each other.

"Some of you may have heard of the sad events that occurred in Swan River earlier this week," Dr. Bell said. "Though this is a joyous occasion, I couldn't let the opportunity go by without saying a few words about it. I want each of you to know that protecting the safety of our students is my highest priority. Our campus is secure, and the only wild animals we have to worry about are the squirrels that get into the trash cans." Turning to the student section, he made his eyes twinkly and said, "Keep the lids down, girls." A small ripple of laughter swept through the parents' side of the amphitheater.

That was smart, I thought. Instead of speculating on what had happened to Crystal Lemons and the Birdman, he was making it about the students. He was telling the parents to ignore the mountains, towering at an angle that threw the sports fields into shadow by three o'clock in the afternoon. There might be bear and catamount and God knows what all up in those ravines and high rocky meadows, but they could not get at us down here.

"I just wonder what it feels like," Caroline whispered. "Not that I want to kill people, obviously. But, I mean, girls aren't supposed to have any power. That's the whole thing about being a girl."

I looked over at her, her river gray eyes wide behind round glasses. For a long time I'd thought that Caroline's interest in the violence of my hometown was a kind of slumming. I thought that she was gawking at the wild girls, the way tourists in a Mercedes might rubberneck a pickup pasted all over with Confederate decals steaming at the side of the road, its driver slumped on the bumper picking his teeth. There were plenty of girls like that at the Academy, who thought the most interesting thing about Swan River was how hilariously backward it was. But Caroline never did anything just because other people were doing it. She had figured out on her own that there was more to the stories of the wild girls than met the eye. She had asked me to make a list of the names I'd heard from kids at school and Girl Scout camp and had researched them all, from Margaret Reid to Sharon Englehard. She had been to the newspaper archives, the historical society, and had found the reports that spawned the legends I had grown up with—girls seen flying over the tops of hundred-foot trees, girls setting buildings on fire with the tips of their fingers. In college, Caroline wanted to major in folklore and ethnography. Later, after she got her doctorate, she planned to write a book on the wild girls of Swan River. She would prove to a skeptical world that these high dark mountains harbored a strangeness that could not be explained by rational means.

I tolerated Caroline's research, but I got annoyed when it sounded like she was trying to make the wild girls into something mysterious and romantic. They were murderers, and after they murdered they either died or went to prison. There was nothing about them to envy, nothing to celebrate. "You don't get it," I said.

"Don't get what?"

"The whole thing. You're not *from* here, Caroline."

The girls to her left were staring at us. I tugged at a thread that hung off the hem of my skirt. "Forget it," I muttered. "Look, do you want to go down to the River House after this is over? We could get that gelato you like."

"Oh my God, I've been craving it," Caroline whispered. "I know it sounds weird, but the stuff I had in Rome this summer wasn't nearly as good."

The speakers stuck up on poles around the stage crackled to life. The staff passed out copies of the school song to all the parents, but there weren't enough for the students. The title was "Swan River, My Swan River," and it was something about mountains high and bygone days and always being true. I moved my lips obediently, but I was thinking about the last time I'd seen Crystal Lemons.

It was mid-October, almost a year earlier, and I was walking back to the Academy after a Saturday morning of studying at the River House. Crystal was sitting on a bench outside an empty storefront. Her legs stuck straight out into the sidewalk, and I might have tripped over them if she hadn't called my name. "I know you," she said. "You're the kid who goes to the Academy." She scanned me from braids to kneesocks and saddle oxfords, and broke out in a grin that made me blush. I knew that the uniform was stupid, but Crystal didn't look so great herself. Her long tangled hair looked dirty, and one of her front teeth was chipped.

"Are you okay?" I asked, since I had to say something.

"Oh yeah," she said, drawing back her lips to reveal the chipped tooth. "Yeah, I'm peachy keen." Then, for just a second, something flickered in her eye—something white and hot, like the spark from a wayward flame.

I'd felt a premonition then, a sense that Crystal might become one of them, and I'd almost tripped over my own feet trying to get away from her. Now that I knew I'd guessed right, I should have been grieving for her and the family she'd left behind. But whenever I thought of Mrs. Lemons, my mind went back to the day that Willow and I had broken into the trailer. If Mrs. Lemons could tell the future, why hadn't she known that her daughter was going to turn into a wild girl? And if she had been wrong about Crystal, wasn't it possible that she was also wrong about me?

CHAPTER TWO

I'd made it sound as if by taking her to the River House Coffeeshop, I was doing Caroline a favor, but the truth was that I had an ulterior motive. I wanted to know what had happened to Mrs. Lemons and Mason when the commune burned, and I knew that Maggie would have heard any news that was going around. Over the summer, I had seen that my sister was tied in to the daily life of my hometown in a way I would never be.

If you were a girl in your late teens or twenties, the big weekly social event in Swan River was the Friday night party at the Tastee-Freez. In other towns, women had book clubs or Mother's Day Out; in Swan River, local girls congregated here to laugh, pass cheap wine in brown paper bags, and swap stories of no-good husbands and boyfriends. The husbands and boyfriends tolerated the convention and stayed away, perhaps believing that this was a harmless way for the women in their lives to let off some necessary steam. If I'd been by myself, I would have grabbed my sundae from the counter and made a speedy exit, but Maggie could talk to anyone: the anxious-looking middle-class girls who had moved home after college to take jobs as bank tellers or managers at the grocery store, the deadnecks who had never considered leaving Swan River in the first place. She pulled me from one group to another, sipping at a bottle when it was passed to her, admiring the children curled sleeping in the backseats.

Her friends accepted me, and I was grateful for the company, but I found the whole thing sort of depressing. A lot of Maggie's friends were out of work. A lot of them were living with their parents, and sometimes their parents were out of work too. There was a sense of desperation, as if everyone knew but hadn't yet admitted that things were broken here.

The last time we'd gone to the Tastee-Freez, things had been weirder than usual. Maggie and I had just sat down to split our sundae when a girl named Donna Higgins dropped her wine cooler. For a moment everyone around us fell silent, looking at the starburst pattern on the pavement. "Well, shit," someone said, "that's about the prettiest thing I've seen all day," and soon half a dozen girls were throwing their bottles against the wall of the outdoor bathroom, cheering when they smashed.

The owner, who normally ignored the crowd in his parking lot no matter how loud they got, came out and shouted that he had called Sheriff McClellan. A few minutes later the cruiser coasted by, lights flashing, before circling and passing a second time. The sheriff was Travis's boss, a solid, slow-spoken man whose white whiskers and broad face made me think of a sheep. According to Maggie, Sheriff McClellan spent his time handing out citations for jaywalking and drunk in public, ignoring the real crimes (burglary, domestic assault) and trying his best to ignore the wild girls too. "Y'all ladies go on home," he called through his megaphone. "I want this lot cleared in ten minutes or I'm going to write up every damn one of you."

The air thickened as the crowd pushed toward the shoulder of the road, hissing and jeering. "Why don't you get out of that car, fat man," Donna shouted, a bottle exploding against the rim of the sheriff's rear tire. The sheriff tapped his brakes, but the heckling got louder and he sped off toward the bridge. My sister made a raspberry noise, and Donna threw her arm around Maggie's shoulders.

"What was *that*?" I asked as we walked home through the dark. "Everybody got so pissed off all of a sudden."

"Of course they're pissed off," Maggie said. "Half the girls I knew in middle school are divorced, Kate. They've got little kids, the men are all morons or assholes, and they can't make a living. Everything's going out of business. Most of the houses in the Delta are for sale."

"But that's not Sheriff McClellan's fault."

Maggie tossed the sundae cup at the mouth of an overflowing trash can. When we were younger, the streets behind downtown had been as well-lit as a skating rink, but a couple years ago the mayor, to save money, had taken out every other streetlight. We were in a dark spot now, and I could hear rather than see Maggie's impatience as she turned to me. "It's not any one person's fault," she said. "It's bigger than that. Something's wrong with this place. You see all these rich people coming into town when the Academy is starting up, and it just makes me sick. The people who live here, the *real* people—they're barely getting by."

There was no point in trying to argue with Maggie when she was mad. She loved to make speeches, and when she was in that mode she would just talk over you. Besides, I knew she was right. We lived in a dying town. On days of strong winds, loose shingles from the downtown buildings floated over the river like awkward flat-winged birds. For me, these were all good reasons to get out of here as quickly as possible, but for Maggie they seemed to be reasons to stay. After two years of traveling around the country, she had come home to Swan River and gotten back together with her high school boyfriend, and showed no signs of wanting anything more than what she already had.

On the way to the River House Coffeeshop, I filled Caroline in on Maggie's plan to move into the new cabin that her boyfriend was building on Bloodwort Road. "She went down to the liquor store last weekend and got a bunch of boxes," I said. "They were supposedly for me, so I could get ready to go back to school, but then she took half of them and started packing up her own stuff. She took this sheepskin rug that used to belong to my dad, and my mom accused her of stealing it. She hates it that Maggie doesn't want to go to college—she thinks she's settling."

Caroline hung her elbow out the window, the breeze ruffling her straight bangs. "Did your mom go to college?"

"She got her associate's degree when she was like thirty. That's her whole point."

"So your mom's trying to fix her own life through her kids."

I shrugged. Caroline's parents were psychiatrists, and she was prone to this sort of analysis.

"I stay out of it," I said. "I'm Switzerland."

But it was hard to be Switzerland when for the last month of the summer Mom and Maggie had gotten into it almost every night. Mom yelled at Maggie about working in a coffee shop and not caring about her future; Maggie yelled at Mom about smoking pot and never cleaning the house. Then they both yelled at Travis, who was always sitting on the couch in sweatpants and no shirt, a copy of *Sports Illustrated* upside down on his lap. By then I was usually out of there and up to my room, where I spent my time lying on the bed with a pillow folded behind my neck, diving into one book after another.

I should have had a job that summer—I could have used the money—but no one seemed to care that I was hanging around the house, and I couldn't motivate myself to put in applications at the grocery store and the Tastee-Freez. When Maggie wasn't around, I read, checking out books by the stack and plowing through them in order—mostly novels, but sometimes a book on archaeology or World War I. I tried to read Freud because I'd heard he wrote about dreams and sex, two things I wanted to know more about, but I couldn't get past the first paragraph. I read *Lolita;* I read *Beowulf* and *The Arabian Nights.* Each book was like an underwater cave, and when I rose again to the surface I was pale and grumpy, resentful of everyone who hadn't been where I'd been.

When I tired of reading, I palmed the keys to Maggie's Volkswagen van and drove endless circles around the town—through our boring neighborhood of sad peeling ranch houses, to the boggy muddle of the Delta, then for a fast skim down Bloodwort Road until the silence and the thick woods freaked me out and I turned around again. I always ended up at the gates of the Academy, where I sat staring at the blank windows of Fallis Hall and wishing for school to start. My life at the Academy wasn't perfect, but summer in Swan River was no life at all.

"You know what I just realized?" I said to Caroline. "I might never have to live in my mom's house again. Except for Christmas vacation. I could find a summer job and just move wherever."

Caroline pressed the soles of her shoes against the glove box. "But I think it's really hard to get a job if you haven't been to college."

"I don't mean a *good* job. I mean like at a bookstore, or waitressing. Or an internship or something."

"You should be a companion to an old lady," Caroline said. "You know how in books, girls who don't have money are always companions to old ladies?"

"That was a hundred years ago," I said. "Nobody does that anymore."

I turned onto Jessup Avenue, which ran north-south all the way to the Swan River Bridge. The businesses—florists that seemed to sell only plastic flowers; a dusty, failing shoe store—had all gone dark for the night, and as I looked at their black windows, I felt a flash of hatred. I wasn't unemployed or divorced, but I thought I could give any of Maggie's friends a run for their money when it came to resenting the state of things in Swan River.

At the one stoplight, a car pulled up next to us in the turning lane. It was the navy blue BMW that Willow called Jean-Luc, after a boy she'd met on a summer enrichment trip to Toulouse. In the passenger seat, Tessa Cochran waved and gestured for me to roll down my window.

"Excuse me," Tessa said, flashing a peace sign, "could you tell me how to get to Haight-Ashbury?"

My face burned. It was bad enough that the only car I had access to was a 1972 Volkswagen van. I didn't know why Maggie wouldn't at least let me scrape off the bumper stickers—dancing skeletons, *Love Your Mother, Coexist.* "It's not *mine*," I managed to say, but the light had already changed. Jean-Luc zipped in front of me, Tessa wiggling her fingers in the rearview.

"Thanks a lot, Tessa Cockroach," I muttered under my breath. This was my preferred nickname for her, though because she was a champion equestrian with a long chin, we also called her Tessa Horse-Face.

"She's going to be even worse now with her name on a building," Caroline said. "But you can't get rid of her."

"Right," I said. It was our usual joke. "She'd survive a nuclear apocalypse."

The River House was two levels, with a stage downstairs where

Maggie played with the Bluegrass Jamboree on Saturdays, and a deck upstairs that ran over the edges of the roof like crust off a pie plate. It had been decorated with junk store treasure: uneven-legged chairs and antique marble-top tables, and some things that were deliberately absurd—a cooler filled with feather boas, a coat tree with watering cans stuck upside down on the hooks. Maggie's boyfriend, who ran the place, had wanted to be an artist, and now the coffee shop was his canvas. On a regular summer night it would have been full of locals, but tonight it was just booth after booth of Academy girls abusing their free refills and splitting scones four ways. They had packed their parents off to the Cedar Tree Inn for the night, and they were ready to catch up on summer vacations and summer boyfriends. Each booth was so stuffed that the last girl on the bench sat half on the wood and half on nothing, bracing herself on her outside foot.

At the counter, Maggie was picking at the polish on her thumbnail, ignoring a rabbit-toothed sophomore meekly try-ing to order a chai latte. I was hoping that I'd be able to shuffle Caroline off to one of the tables, because as much as I wanted to know what had happened to the Lemons, I didn't necessarily want Caroline to hear Maggie talking about the wild girls. Now that the Academy had started again, Maggie's familiarity with the news of Swan River seemed slightly embarrassing, like the but-terfly tattoo that showed above the waist of her lowrider jeans. But Maggie waved us behind the counter and pulled up two stools beside the espresso machine, and it was clear that I wouldn't have to ask her anything. Like everyone else in town, she had only one subject on her mind.

"Travis said that Mrs. Lemons won't leave," Maggie told us. "The sheriff tried to clear her out—some of the cabins that burned are still standing, and he's afraid they might come down—but it's her property, so they can't force her. She says she was passed out that night and slept through the fire. When they told her about Crystal, Travis said that she was just totally calm, like she didn't even understand what was happening."

I chewed at the skin beside my thumbnail. It was possible Mrs. Lemons was straight-up crazy, and if that was the case, I probably couldn't believe what she said about anything. "What about Mason?" I began, but there was a loud clang from the kitchen, and Maggie jumped, rolling her eyes.

"Kate, take the register," she said.

"I don't want to," I protested. It was one thing to sit behind the counter, eating broken brownies, half-hidden by the bakery case, but I didn't want anyone to think I actually *worked* at the River House. "I don't know how to use a register," I said to Caroline as Maggie disappeared through the swinging doors. "As far as I'm concerned, for the next five minutes everything's free."

"I'll take a carrot cake," said the boy at the counter.

It was Clancy Harp. He had changed out of his uniform and, in jeans and a new Carhartt jacket, looked cleaner than I had ever seen him. His wet hair was pulled into a ponytail at the base of his neck. "Hi," I said, forgetting to laugh. "Listen, I'm sorry about what happened at Bloodwort Farm. I know you used to live out there, and—"

"Yeah," Clancy said. "Well, I didn't exactly keep in touch with them or anything. Except for Mason."

I caught Clancy's eye and looked away again, uncertain of how much sympathy would be welcome. "How is Mason?" I asked. "Did he actually see—"

Clancy shook his head. "He hasn't been at the farm all summer. He had a construction job in Glen City, and he's been staying up there. But he's back now, and I think he's going to crash with me for a little while. I just came by to pick up a sandwich for him, actually."

"Oh," I said. "Well, tell him— I mean, if it doesn't seem weird, tell him that I'm sorry and everything."

"I'm sure he'll appreciate that." Clancy caught my gaze and held it, and I could tell that he was trying to put me at my ease. "You know, I worked here a couple summers ago," he said. "Do you want some help with the register?"

As it turned out, using a cash register wasn't as hard as it looked. All you had to do was put in the amount, press Total and then Cash. I felt stupid then, and to make up for it I pretended to be helpful, rearranging the pastries so they were centered on their little doilies. I started to introduce Clancy to Caroline, but they already knew each other. Apparently Caroline liked to chat with the landscaping crew while they worked on the flower beds outside our dorm.

The girls lining up for coffee were watching Clancy too. There were tiny, timid freshmen; juniors talking loudly about the summer parties at their beach houses; and Willow's friends, snooty seniors with single-strand pearls around their necks—all of them staring at him from under their eyelashes, checking out his butt when he worked the espresso machine. Probably they would have looked at any teenage boy; Academy girls were desperate like that, but their interest made me see Clancy in a new light. In a lull between customers he turned to me, wiping imaginary sweat from his brow. "You girls shouldn't drink so much coffee," he said. "It'll stunt your growth."

"You shouldn't tell people what to do," I said. "It makes you sound like a jerk."

"Almost forgot." Grinning, he pulled a piece of paper from his pocket and waved it in the air between us. "Somebody gave me a note for you."

He put the paper in my hand, where it uncurled from its folds like an origami bird. "For me?" I said. "Who's it from?"

"That red-haired girl, the one you brought to the farm." He snapped his fingers, pointed at me with a smile. "Willow."

Upstairs, Willow and Tessa Cochran sat at a table topped by a ragged-looking palm tree, a group of their minions clustered around them. Willow and Tessa were the two most popular seniors and the other girls fawned on them like they were rock stars. To all appearances they were best friends, but I had been around them long enough to learn that there was an undercurrent of rivalry to their friendship.

To understand the competition between Tessa and Willow, you had to understand the kind of place that the Academy had been in the old days. One Sunday when I was hanging around the library with nothing to do, I had pulled down *The History of Swan River Academy* by Clementine Reynolds Ledbetter and flipped through the pictures of girls in soft dresses playing badminton and reading on the riverbank. When Dr. Arkwright had founded the Academy, in the decade before the Civil War, it had been a haven for the daughters of plantation families, sent to learn a few genteel parlor tricks before they were married off to their cousins in the next county. Even under Dr. Bell's new leadership, there were still plenty of girls like those antebellum belles. According to Willow, one of Tessa's ancestors had ridden in the dragoons with Light-Horse Harry Lee; another had surrendered to Grant at Appomattox. At seventeen, Tessa had the sculptured pageboy of a senator's wife and a face that only an unshakable sense of privilege could save from ugliness.

The school belonged to Tessa by rights, and Willow should have been one of her followers. Owning a mail-order company might have made Louis Becker a big deal in Swan River, but among people like the Cochrans, it made him a joke. I had seen his catalog, which included a Christmas tree topper shaped like Rudolph's head that rotated and sang, vibrating socks that massaged your feet while you slept. I couldn't believe that anybody could get rich selling stuff like that, but Willow said that insomniacs would buy a turd if you advertised it on TV at three in the morning. The Beckers' money was so new you could smell the ink on the bills, but that hadn't stopped Willow from rising to the top of the social food chain. The other popular girls, who were mostly lesser versions of Tessa, copied everything about Willow, from the low bun at the back of her neck to the polka-dotted kneesocks she wore with her uniform. It was like she gave off some kind of coolness pheromone, or a high-pitched whistle that only teenagers could hear.

The note read simply *Come upstairs. Have to talk.* I sat down alone at the table with the least bird shit, folding and unfolding the paper in my hand. Willow stood and made a path through the circle of her admirers, who looked at me like I was a commoner singled out by the prince for a dance as she beckoned me to follow her. At the railing, she offered me her pack of Balkan Sobranies. Nested in tissue paper, each a different pastel, they looked more like petits fours than cigarettes. I didn't smoke, but I had to restrain myself from picking up a handful and stuffing them into my mouth.

Willow picked out a blue cigarette that almost matched her contacts and tapped it on her palm. "Kate, I want to apologize to you," she said. "I thought that what Tessa said was really mean. I told her that it isn't even your car."

"Honestly, I don't care a whole lot what Tessa thinks of me."

Willow sighed, her heart-shaped locket slipping out of the collar of her uniform blouse. When I'd given it to her, it had held a picture of the two of us in the Moorefield Mall photo booth, tongues out, fingers waggling in our ears. It made me cringe now—what could be more pathetic than giving a Best Friends Forever locket to a girl you'd known only a month? But did it mean something that she was still wearing it? Or had she replaced the picture with another, Tessa Cockroach or some summer boyfriend, this year's Jean-Luc?

"I know you don't care," she said. "That's what's so great about you. You really don't give a shit what anybody thinks."

I wasn't sure this was true, but I liked the idea that Willow saw me that way. Echoing her sigh, I braced my forearms on the railing. The deck was built over the edge of the bluff, which meant that we were leaning all the way out over the river. Though you couldn't tell in the dark, I knew that there was nothing but this flimsy piece of wood between us and a hundred-foot drop. "Anyway," I said, "how was your summer and all that?"

Willow grimaced, the dainty-looking cigarette hanging from the corner of her mouth. "Oh, fabulous as usual. I'd be home for a day and then they'd pack me off again. I took a monthlong Mandarin immersion class and don't remember a single word. I wish I could just hang out on the beach like a normal person."

"It'll look good on your college apps."

She smiled, a polite get-down-to-business smile that made it clear she had no intention of asking about my summer. That was fine with me—I didn't want to talk about being stuck in Swan River, driving in circles and failing to read Freud.

45

"I have a favor to ask," she said. "I want you to set me up with a boy. A boy who you introduced me to. Who also happens to be the best-looking guy in Swan River."

"Who?" I asked, but then, before she could answer, I guessed. "Mason Lemons?" Willow must have kept track of him as I had, watching out of the corner of my eye as he tooled around Swan River in his gold El Camino. Clancy said that Mason had worked construction in Glen City this summer, but before that he'd been hanging around town, doing odd jobs and getting in trouble for the same stupid stuff as in high school. Usually he had a girl in his passenger seat, and during the school year, it was usually a girl from the Academy. He had a thing for the ones who should have been most out of his league, haughty, pedigreed beauties with names like Wesley or Emerson, and they seemed to have a thing for him too—maybe because they were slumming, or maybe because he was just too handsome to say no to. "But don't you know what happened to his family?" I asked.

She nodded. "We could see the fire from our gazebo. I know he probably doesn't want to talk to me right *now*. But give him a couple weeks, and then—" She must have seen disapproval in my face, because she drew closer, slinging her arm across my shoulder. "What, do I not seem sad enough? I don't know those people, Kate. I only met his sister that one time."

I looked down, pretending to be interested in the graffiti on the railing. Was it her lack of sympathy that shocked me, or only her failure to pretend that she mourned for Crystal Lemons? Was I really more compassionate than Willow, or just more hypocritical?

"Hey, check it out," I said, pointing to a graffiti line enclosed by a border of red hearts. "I never knew that John Lennon was the one who said 'Life is what happens to you while you're busy making other plans.'"

Willow put her arm around my shoulders. "I have to be hon-est," she said. "It's been a dry summer for me, guy-wise."

It had been a dry life for me, guy-wise. "First of all," I began, "I never even see Mason, and even if I did—"

"I told you, I'm not asking you to talk to him today," she said. "Come on, Kate. I just want you to soften him up for me."

I traced the line of hearts with my fingertip. When we'd first met, I had thought I needed Willow to be my passport to the mys-terious grown-up world outside Swan River. I didn't think like that anymore, but I still felt that she and I were linked in some way—that we had something in common that I couldn't share with Caroline or anyone else. I knew there was a part of me that was not good, not nice. There was a part of me that wanted to misbehave, to make my own rules, and that part of me admired Willow's confidence. Maybe I would have been like that myself, if my life had been different from the beginning.

I didn't want Willow to think I was one of her minions, ready to drop everything to do her a solid, but I knew I would help her in the end. I had known when I came up here that she would probably ask me a favor and that, whatever it was, I would probably say yes.

Caroline and I didn't talk as we walked out to the parking lot, and I knew that she wasn't going to ask why Willow had wanted to see me. Caroline didn't try to wheedle things out of you. She believed in respecting other people's privacy, which, when you lived in a boarding school with two hundred and fifty other girls, was as bizarre as believing in Zoroaster.

I was happy to be quiet, since I hadn't decided how I felt about what had happened upstairs. I didn't care if Willow went out with Mason Lemons; that was her business. But how was I supposed to hook her up exactly? And why was I willing to do her a favor in the first place, when she had only ever been a lukewarm friend to me? As I patted my pockets for my keys, I heard footsteps pounding on the gravel. Clancy ran up behind us, my knitted purse swinging from his fist.

"You left this under the counter," he said. "I wouldn't have seen it, but some girl spilled tea into the tip jar and I was looking for paper towels."

I grabbed for the purse, feeling more flustered than ever. "I'm always forgetting things. Mrs. Brush in fourth grade used to say that I'd forget my head if it wasn't attached to my shoulders."

"Yeah, Mrs. Brush was mean," Clancy said. When he passed me the bag, he reached out and touched the crease of my neck, as if to assure himself that my head was still there.

I was glad that it was too dark for him to see how the blood had rushed to my cheeks. Clancy looked as if he wanted to say something else, but the River House was closing and the Academy girls were streaming out into the lot, doors slamming all around us. Somehow I got in the van and started the engine, and to drown Caroline's careful silence I turned the radio up as loud as it would go.

CHAPTER THREE

L ights out was at eleven, and Caroline was not supposed to be in my room after that. Theoretically you could get suspended for wandering around late at night, but the housemother, Mrs. Putnam, was about eighty years old and had so much hair in her ears that you wondered how she could hear at all. When Caroline plopped down on my bed like she planned to stay all night, I dug an old bag of gummy frogs out of my sock drawer and we passed it back and forth, lying head to heel in my too-small single bed.

Caroline pulped a gummy frog between her fingers. "You know what I noticed?"

"You probably notice a lot of things."

As usual, she ignored my sarcasm. "After you went up to the deck, I was watching Maggie with the customers, and I think she acts kind of weird with the Academy girls. Sarah VanDexter stood at the counter for like two minutes, and Maggie just pretended she didn't see her."

"Well, she hates the Academy," I said. "But she's extra-weird with the girls from our class. She says that they give her funny looks."

Using her longest fingernail, Caroline decapitated the frog and popped head and body into her mouth. "Why would they give her funny looks?"

I didn't have to see Caroline's face to know that she was sincere. It was kind of hard to believe that she wouldn't have heard about my sister, but then again, Caroline didn't pay attention to gossip. I had never truly appreciated this, because I'd never kept a big secret from her before.

But I had a secret now, and I couldn't help feeling that I owed her something to make up for my silence about Willow. The story of what had happened to Maggie would be my gift to Caroline, a selfish and partial compensation for everything she'd done for me.

Maggie hadn't wanted to go to the Academy in the first place. At Amos T. Harding Junior High she'd been one of those girls who gets along with everybody, from jocks to deadnecks to drama nerds. You could hear her laugh from across the cafeteria, loud and bright as the call of a gull. She belonged to clubs, and though she was only five-foot-seven, she was the second-highest scorer on the girls' basketball team. She wanted to graduate from Swan River High, but Mom kept asking why she'd want to stay at an underfunded country school when she could go for half tuition to one of the best boarding schools in the state.

My sister was a senior at the Academy when I was a freshman, and when Willow stopped eating lunch with me to move to Tessa Cochran's table, Maggie was the one I went to for sympathy. I hoped that her friends would take me in, but it didn't take me long to see that Maggie didn't really have any friends. Not that she was exactly unpopular. She walked the Academy halls like they belonged to her, head thrown back, long dark hair swinging around her shoulders. But at four o'clock every afternoon, when the other girls were on their way to Madrigals or softball practice, Maggie was standing at the delivery truck entrance waiting for her boyfriend to show up in his pickup with the psychedelic paint job. She had promised me that if I kept her afternoon getaways a secret from our mom, she would give me the vintage Dylan poster that hung above her bed.

My sister never told me where they went on those autumn afternoons between the end of classes and six o'clock dinner. Probably, like all the other local teenagers, they drove out to the trailheads off Bloodwort Road and fooled around until the windows steamed. I worried about Maggie being caught sneaking off campus, but about the boyfriend himself I felt mostly neutral, at least at the beginning. His name was Kevin, but I called him Kayak Boy. He played fiddle at the Bluegrass Jamboree at the River House, and on weekends took his homemade boat down the county's white water runs. He made oversize sculptures out of junk from salvage yards that Maggie said were amazing, though they all looked like giant metal spiders to me. He was the sort of guy who would never leave Swan River, but for a deadneck he wasn't bad, not dumb or mean. He sometimes brought me weird old books from the secondhand store in Moorefield, and I would have liked him just for that.

But then Maggie began to change. Sometimes she passed me in the hall like she didn't know me. She would be jittery, almost manic for a few days, and then subside into a gloom that nothing could penetrate. She was flunking two of her classes, Spanish III and Dr. Bell's lit class called Myths and Mysteries, but when I asked her what was going on, she just sighed and looked depressed. "You know Kevin's uncle Jasper, who owns the River House? He says I should move to Nashville. He says I'm the real thing, but Kevin doesn't get it."

"Kevin doesn't want you to play music?"

"He doesn't want me to play professionally. His idea is that when we're married, we'll get a bunch of friends together and jam, and that should be enough for me."

"But can't you figure it out after college?"

"I don't know if I'm even going to college."

I chewed on the end of my braid, something I usually did only when I was alone. If Maggie wasn't going to college, I was pretty sure that Mom hadn't heard about it. Our mother had married young and moved here from her own small town in Tennessee, and she had made it clear that we were supposed to do more with our lives than she had done with hers. As slack as she was about things like housecleaning, she was fanatical about us getting into good schools, getting scholarships, and getting out of our hometown.

That was right around the time Maggie started on her kick about how the Academy was the symbol of everything that was wrong with Swan River. Now every time I went by my sister's room to borrow a ponytail holder or cadge a quarter for a pack of ramen, she went on about how the Academy was a rotten place, full of phonies with nothing better to do than waste their parents' money. It was easy to put it all together—Kayak Boy didn't want Maggie to be ambitious, and he was turning her against anything that promised a larger experience than what she could expect in our hometown. How else could you get a smart, talented girl to stay with you in Hicksville, other than by convincing her that the world outside was no place worth traveling to?

By then I was thinking that maybe I ought to talk to Mom. I didn't like the feeling of being alone with this problem, and what if Maggie did run off and get married at age seventeen? What if she just disappeared one day, and I had to live with the fact that I had known and hadn't done anything? Twice I went over to Mom's office in the administration building and sat in the uncomfortable plastic seat beside her desk, chattering aimlessly about my classes and waiting for the words to come out of my mouth: *Something's going on with Maggie.* But Maggie would hate me for going behind her back, and in the end I left without saying anything.

On Fridays after lights out, Maggie always helped me with my Geometry homework. Friday was the night Kayak Boy worked at the River House, so they couldn't talk on the phone for hours like they did every other day of the week. It felt a little weird to be doing work at the beginning of the weekend, but I was glad for the company and the help. I usually got better grades than Maggie did, but certain subjects came naturally to her. She could just look at the angles, cylinders, and spheres, and see what you were supposed to do with them. For me the figures lifted off the page, swimming around and turning into familiar things—the sphere a basketball, the cylinder a trash can—and I'd realize that I was thinking about how you could tell when a basketball was worn out instead of doing the problem. I'd gotten a B- on the last test, and I was already worrying that the Pythagorean theorem would strand me in Swan River like a high flood unless I fought it as hard as I could.

On the Friday before midterms, I waited for the dorm to go quiet before clutching my textbook to my chest, feeling my way to the staircase and down one flight to Maggie's hall. The housemother was doing her rounds, and I barely had time to duck into the bathroom to avoid her. The coast clear, I peeked out again, and almost made it to the water fountain when I bumped into someone slinking along the wall in the opposite direction. I cried out, and a cold ring bit into the skin of my lip.

When I'd swallowed my scream, the figure stepped back, the

glow of the Exit sign turning her hair pale orange. I tasted metal and smelled a disinfectant odor that I was pretty sure was vodka. "Kate?" Willow whispered. "What are you doing out here?"

I wished that I had an interesting lie, but I didn't, so I explained about my Geometry difficulties. "What are *you* doing?" I asked. "No offense, but your breath kind of stinks."

She put her hand over her own mouth now, eyes widening above the shadows of her fingers. "Tessa's cousin sent her a care package with a bottle in it. She needed some grapefruit juice from the vending machines."

For a moment I wanted to let Willow continue to the stairwell, right into the housemother's arms, but I decided that that would be too mean. "Mrs. Putnam's doing rounds," I said. "You can hide out in Maggie's room for a minute if you want."

Things went all right at first. Willow nestled into the papasan, and Maggie answered her questions about the bands that played at the River House in bored but tolerant monosyllables. I lit a cone of lemongrass incense and put on a Willie Nelson CD. It wasn't really my thing, but I knew that the girls Willow was hanging out with these days listened mostly to country.

I could see now that she was actually sort of drunk. Her cheeks were pink, and her eyes had the droopy look that Travis's got after four or five beers. "What a kickass Friday night," she said, rolling her eyes at the tapestry-draped ceiling.

"I know," Maggie said. "I'm so bored it's like a coma."

Using my thumbnail for leverage, I picked at a hard ridge of plastic on the back of the chair. Not many miles from here, on a mountain farm or one of the river beaches, the local kids were surely gathering around a bonfire that shot blue sparks up to the cold sky. The boys were crushing beer cans underfoot, talking about the Homecoming game against Glen City and the start of deer season, while the girls smoked and gossiped, legs hung over the lowered truck gates. When regular high school life was that boring, how could anybody complain about the Academy?

"I was up in Tessa's room," Willow said to Maggie, "and they're all talking about their horses. Tessa's is named Taffy—she has his picture on her desk and I swear she thinks he's a person. They go on about the competitions that the team is going to this year, and I don't even know what the acronyms mean."

"Princesses," Maggie agreed. "I don't know how you can stand those girls."

Willow tucked her elbows into her sides and sank farther into the chair. "Well, it's not like I have a choice."

"What do you mean?" I said. "Of course you have a choice about who your friends are."

"You'd think, wouldn't you?" she said. "It's my mom that's the problem. My dad grew up in Glen City, and my mom's always been mad at him for bringing her back here. She thinks she should be in Atlanta or Charleston, shopping at Neiman's all day while they photograph her house for *Southern Living*. My dad would never go for it, but now that I'm at the Academy they both think I'm her meal ticket. I'll make the right sort of friends, and then we'll all get invited to somebody's place on Hilton Head for Christmas." Willow rubbed the skin of the beanbag between her thumb and forefinger.

"That's sick," Maggie said. "You should rebel."

Willow smirked. "Rebel how?"

"They're your parents. You should be able to figure out what's going to piss them off the most."

"Maybe," Willow said. "All I know is I'm not going back up there. I've learned enough about dressage for one damn night."

A drowsy beat pulsed through the speakers, and the room

RADFORD PUBLIC LIBRARY
30 WEST MAIN STREET
RADFORD, VA 24141
540-731-3621

fell into an underwater calm. When I looked over again, Willow was asleep. Maggie stared at the empty bunk above her. Her skin looked strangely luminous, kindled by the red glow of the shaded lamps.

I curled up in the beanbag chair and closed my eyes, thinking about the time I'd seen Willow's mom at the grocery store, wandering from aisle to aisle as if she'd forgotten why she'd come there in the first place. It made me sad to think about the pressure she was putting on her daughter, but I still had to wonder why Willow had chosen to tell this story tonight. Was she trying to offer some sort of indirect apology for choosing Tessa over me?

At times I dropped below the surface into sleep, and fought my way up only to see that it still wasn't morning. In my dreams, Willow turned into Dr. Bell, who offered me a Roman candle while sparks flew from his hand. One o'clock. Two o'clock. In the hazy interludes between dreams, I felt my heart beating hard against my rib cage.

When I woke for the third time, I thought at first that the sun was coming up. Though the windows were still dark, the room was filled with a soft glow—not focused like a flashlight beam but diffused, sourceless. It took me a minute to realize that it came from Maggie. She was sitting backward in the desk chair, reading a magazine while light leaked from under the cuffs of her nightgown.

Trembling, I shook Willow by the shoulder. "What's going on?" she said. Her voice, groggy and annoyed at first, thinned to alarm as she noticed Maggie blazing as if she'd swallowed a lightbulb.

I couldn't say anything. My eyes kept going back to the water glass on the desk, imagining it splintered, each shard sharp enough to slice the skin or pierce an artery. Maggie laid her magazine on

RADFORD PUBLIC LIBRARY
30 WEST MAIN STREET
RADFORD, VA 24141
540-731-3621

the desk. "Kate, don't freak out," she said. "Just go sit on the top bunk and pull the ladder up behind you. Then I wouldn't be able to hurt you if I wanted to—which I don't, by the way."

"*Hurt* us?" Willow said, and I shook my head, warning her not to speak. I understood that Maggie couldn't guarantee anything. She didn't really know what was going to happen, and if she did decide she wanted to murder us, a missing ladder was not going to get in her way. Still, disagreeing with her did not seem like a good idea either, and she was blocking the door. I nudged Willow up to the top bunk. We sat with our backs braced against the wall, holding hands under the sheet.

"What's going *on*?" Willow asked again. "Is she one of those— is she really—" I nodded, and her eyes got even wider.

"So how does it feel?" I asked Maggie. I was trying to sound casual, but my breath was short, my hand so clammy that I would have wiped it on the bed if Willow had loosened her grip.

"I don't really feel anything. I only knew it was happening because of this." Maggie held her arms out, light filtering through the sleeves of her nightgown. "It might not be that bad actually."

She sounded more intrigued than anything, but suddenly she seemed to notice how scared we were, our hands squeezed so tightly together that I could feel Willow's pulse. "Look, you guys can relax," Maggie said. "I'll probably float around for a while and then things will go back to normal." But then a shudder went through her, and it started for real.

The room got hot as a sauna. Maggie knocked over the bookcase, smashed the CD player, and grinned up at us from the wreckage, hands on hips. Footsteps thudded down the hall; someone was shaking the doorknob. Maggie hissed, her long hair floating out behind her like the smoke trail from a cigarette.

"You know I could get to you," she said, and her voice was

different too—deeper, harsher. "You know I could hurt you if I wanted to." Then, before I could nod, she jumped out the window.

I tumbled off the bed and raced across the room, half-expecting to see her flattened on the Lawn, but she had disappeared. A white layer of mist floated above the privet hedges. I knew I should do something—call our mother, call Kayak Boy, answer the people screaming outside the door—but I couldn't stop staring at the window glass that held the outline of Maggie's body, the lines clean as if cut by a torch.

As I sat in Mrs. Putnam's office, shivering under a fleece blanket, I tried to imagine Maggie's journey over the high pines of the state forest. Where was she right now? What was she doing? Would she end up like the other wild girls, dead or on trial for her life? I felt sick with anxiety, but a tiny part of me had moved on to worrying about my own future. I knew that my life at the Academy would never be the same. The administration could spin this incident however they wanted; they could blame the damage that Maggie had caused on a freak gust of wind or a poltergeist, but Willow knew the truth, and what was to stop her from telling her friends?

On our way out to the parking lot, my mom and I ran into Dr. Bell. Two weeks had passed since the board had forced out the old headmaster, the nice old septuagenarian Dr. Coyne, and appointed Dr. Bell in his place. Though my mom had liked Dr. Coyne, she was already slightly nutso on the subject of her new boss. She knew every detail of Dr. Bell's biography, from the Harvard BA to the seven years teaching Greek, Latin, and folklore studies at a college in Massachusetts, and I'd seen her check her teeth in a hand mirror as he approached her desk. I couldn't miss the flustered hitch in her breath as he stepped out of the shadows of the elms, a cigarette cinched between his thumb and forefinger.

Mom fumbled apologies, but he waved them away. "None of this is your fault, Ellen," he said, in a gentle voice. "No one was hurt, thank God."

"But if there's damage," Mom stammered. "I know I'm responsible—"

Dr. Bell patted her on the shoulder, turning her toward our car. "It's nothing—a broken window, a little fire in the library. We had it out in no time."

"She burned the *library*?" I said. "Shit."

I'd thought I'd been speaking under my breath, but from my mom's pinched brow I knew that I'd misjudged. Dr. Bell's pale eyes settled on me, and I wondered, not for the first time, whether he recognized me from the festival at Bloodwort Farm. "A bibliophile, are you?"

My mom put her hands over her face. "Kate, for God's sake—"

Dr. Bell raised his chin, looking amused. "I know Maggie, and she's a good girl. She'll get home safe, and then we'll make sure that the library is back in order for Kate here."

"Thank you," Mom whispered. Dr. Bell could not have been better, more generous and comforting. But when I looked back he was pacing again, his steps sure and quick, his eyes trained on the sky above the rooftops. He was looking for my sister, I realized. He was wondering if she was coming back to finish what she'd started.

I'm not sure when Maggie came home, but I do know that she slept until dinnertime the next day. Mom went to work, giving me permission to stay home and rest. She had seen Maggie that morning, before I got up, but all she would tell me was that everything was fine; nothing had been broken that couldn't be fixed. I went limp with relief. My sister would not go to prison like Jenny Stockton and Sharon Englehard. She would not be one of the most unlucky, so obviously implicated in murder or arson that even Sheriff McClellan would be unable to explain it away.

Three times that morning, I crept up to Maggie's room and knocked softly at the door. Despite what Mom had said, I knew I wouldn't relax until I saw Maggie with my own eyes and was sure that she was herself again. I wanted to be reassured, and I was also curious. Where had she gone when she flew out the window? What had it felt like to have that power, that violence inside you? Why hadn't she hurt people like the other wild girls did? "Go away!" Maggie shouted, and when I tried the knob, it was locked.

After the third time, I gave up and napped in front of the TV until five. I watched the Moorefield news, which didn't say anything about Maggie, and then fixed myself a second bowl of cereal and flopped down on the couch to eat it, surveying the disorder around me with dull disgust. There were piles of magazines and newspapers in the corners, a set of unused free weights under the coffee table, everything thick with dust. It hadn't always been like this, but in recent years Mom had gotten lazy, or tired. I wondered if it was this house, more than our strange experience at Bloodwort Farm, that had made Willow change her mind about wanting to be my friend.

The front door wheezed open, and I set my bowl on top of last month's *Southern Fishing*. "Cómo estás?" Travis called. "Hola, señoritas? Anybody home?"

"You don't understand what you're saying," I shouted back. Travis stuck his head around the living room wall, looking at me expectantly. "Cómo estás? means 'how are you?'" I said. "Why would you open a door and say 'How are you?' before you even know if anybody's home?"

Travis pointed a finger at me as he fell into the recliner. "Watch your mouth, smart mouth. Maggie up yet?"

"No," I mumbled. "I guess going apeshit for no reason makes you tired."

"Language," Travis said, in the same tone Mom used on the rare occasions when she remembered that she didn't like us to curse.

"Jesus, Travis—if I know any cusswords, it's your fault. Besides, I don't even know if *apeshit* counts."

"It's got the word *shit* in it," he said. "What's up your ass, Kate? All I did was walk in here and say hello."

I studied him through narrowed eyes. He was wearing his uniform, a scaly mustard stain drying just below the left collar. His black hair was greasy, and his mustache was long enough for him to bite the ends without trying. All our lives Maggie and I had treated him as Dad-*like*, Dad-*ish*, but he was not our dad. If our real dad hadn't died in a head-on collision with a logging truck, we wouldn't have had to live like this, in a house full of discarded mail and bags of beer cans that never made it to the recycling center. I might have been like the other girls at the Academy, with spending money in my school account and summer vacations to brag about when I came back in the fall. Travis had a few good points, of course; he made a killer barbecued brisket, and last year had spent two weekends patiently teaching me how to drive stick. Still, I was sure that my mom could have found someone who didn't keep a spit cup in the drink holder if she'd only bothered to try.

"I bet you and the sheriff were hiding under your desks all night," I said. "Couldn't you have at least tried to stop her? Isn't that your job?"

Travis stared at me with mounting impatience. "Look, she's fine, isn't she? Nobody got hurt. What's the problem?"

He dug a cigarette from a flattened pack of Camels, curling his spine into a C as he brought the tip closer to the lighter. A strand from his ponytail strayed into the flame, and the room filled with the carbon scent of singed hair. Because Travis was generally liked in Swan River, he didn't get blamed for the lack of policing like Sheriff McClellan did. It was like the town, as well as my mother, had given him a free pass, and the more I thought about it, the angrier I got. "You can't just decide not to do your job because you're scared. What if a real cop had that attitude—*Oh, I better wait until this criminal calms down before I try to catch him?*"

He bristled. "Are you saying I'm not a real cop? Little girl, I've seen things that would make your eyes fall right out of your head. I've been places where you'd never set foot. I've—"

"And you placed second in the chili dog–eating contest that one time. I know you're awesome, Travis. Can we talk about something else now?"

He took a breath that seemed to inflate him like a balloon, bugging his eyes, turning his skin tomato red. Before he could explode, the door opened and closed, and my mom walked in, her shoulders slumped beneath her long, shapeless coat. "How is she?" Mom asked, looking at me.

"I don't—" I began, but she didn't wait for my answer. She turned for the stairs, and I followed.

Though Mom knocked with even less force than I had, Maggie opened the door immediately. She was wearing a T-shirt with *Niagara Falls* scripted along the side, her snarled hair falling to her elbows. Her lip trembled, and in a second Mom stepped forward and folded her into her arms. Maggie was the tallest of the three of us, but she seemed to shrink then, as if something propping her up from the inside had let go.

"I'm *sorry*," she gasped, her tears darkening the collar of Mom's ugly coat.

"Shh," Mom said. "It's all over now."

I sat on the carpet, which smelled like the powder that Maggie sprinkled when she vacuumed. With most of her stuff at the Academy, she kept her room at home as clean and bare as a hotel, a private comment on the disorder of the rest of the house. "Has Kevin called?" she asked, and I shook my head.

"He may not know," Mom said. "Travis is trying to keep it quiet. I talked to David Bell before I left work, and he has a whole story worked out for the parents. There's so little damage, Maggie—people might never find out that—"

Maggie closed her eyes, shaking her head rhythmically from side to side. "I'll get Kevin to go and pack up my stuff on Sunday. Would it be okay with you if I took a week off before I go back to school?"

"Of course," Mom said, reaching over to pat her hand.

"Could you call Principal Leonard just to let him know that I'm coming back?" Maggie said. "I shouldn't be behind or anything. I've read all the books on the twelfth-grade reading list."

Mom's face went still—lips pursed, mouth furrowed by a single line. I was watching her, so I understood the problem before Maggie did. Mom was talking about going back to the Academy, while Maggie had taken it for granted that she'd be going to Swan River High. "Well, I don't see any reason for you to transfer to the public school," Mom said in her most soothing voice.

Maggie raised her head, her face heart-attack white. "I can't go back to the Academy," she said, and I could tell that she too was trying to be reasonable, trying to keep calm. "Don't ask me to go back there."

"Why should you be embarrassed?" Mom said. "Dr. Bell certainly isn't going to hold this against you. When I talked to him this afternoon, he said that he was anxious to have you back in class." Her voice was still mild, still composed, her face gentled by sympathy. This had hurt her too, but Maggie and I had always known that there were certain things our mother wouldn't budge on. She came off like a pushover until you ran up against something hard and solid, something that wouldn't be moved.

Maggie watched her, her chest rising and falling, and I knew that she was calculating whether it was worth trying again. She must have seen that it wouldn't do any good, because she stood up and began dragging clothes out of her dresser, tossing them to the floor without paying attention to where they landed. A pair of underwear fell on my head, and I threw them back at her, but she still wouldn't look at me. She pulled on jeans and a clean T-shirt, and then pushed past us and down the stairs.

"Maggie," I called, clattering down behind her. "Maggie!" I thought about trying to block the front door, but she already had her hand on the knob, so I threw myself on the floor and grabbed her ankles. It felt silly, but I couldn't help myself. "Stop!" I shouted, so loudly that for a moment she actually did stop, looking down at me with blank eyes. She pulled one foot free, drew it back, and kicked me hard in the chest.

I was rolling on the floor, howling with self-pity more than pain, when the door slammed shut behind her. Mom sat me on the couch and brought me a pack of frozen peas for the boot-shaped bruise. Travis walked up and down the hall muttering under his breath. They left me with a set of solemn instructions: Do Not Leave The House. Keep The Doors Locked. Do Not Let Anyone

In Until We Get Back. "What if Maggie comes back before you do?" I asked, and Mom turned to Travis with the kind of panicked confusion that makes you wonder if adults really know what they're doing.

"We'll bring her back with us," Mom promised, kissing the top of my head.

I never knew where Maggie went after she left our house. She didn't go to any of her usual hangouts—not to the Tastee-Freez, not to the River House. Kayak Boy, who joined in the search, swore that he hadn't heard from her since the day before. At some point that night, she returned to the Academy and cut through the police tape over her door, taking her guitar, her banjo, and a duffel bag full of clothes; at six the next morning, she was on the bus to Moorefield. The man at the station said that she had leaves in her hair and looked as if she'd slept outside.

A month went by before we got a postcard from Knoxville, then another from Nashville. Maggie must have made a rule to send the postcards just as she was leaving town, because when Mom drove out to Nashville and asked around in the bluegrass bars, they said that Maggie had just left. In Northern California she put a band together with a few guys and they began touring the state as the Swan River Ramblers. Travis flew out to try to catch her in Fresno, but by then she was picking raspberries in Tanner, Minnesota. From Minnesota she sent the first postcard that was addressed just to me, and I taped it up above my desk in my dorm room. *There's a college here. You'd like this town,* she wrote next to a cartoon of stick figures reading books by the side of an O-shaped lake.

Willow and I never talked about what had happened. There were whispers about Maggie, a vague sense that she had left the Academy for some scandalous reason, but no one seemed inclined to connect her to the fire. It was obvious Willow wasn't gossiping, and I felt grateful for that, if perplexed about her reasons for keeping quiet. Was she trying to spare me embarrassment, or was it that she understood that there was no point in talking about the wild girls, since outsiders would never believe the truth?

That winter I noticed a change in Willow. She joined the equestrian team and the tennis team, and spent all her time with the girls who were into that sort of thing—not just Tessa, but Rosa Slater, Elise Seidel, Lucie Yates; girls whose mothers, aunts, and grandmothers had attended the Academy and then gone home to Savannah, Macon, and Birmingham, to country clubs and charity work. The Beckers' plan had succeeded beyond all reckoning; Willow was not only one of that group but the most popular, the prettiest, the most admired. As for me, I felt cheated. It seemed that our paths had diverged again, for good this time, but every once in a while I would catch Willow watching me with a strange look on her face, as if she wanted something from me, but couldn't say for certain what it was.

CHAPTER FOUR

It didn't surprise me that Caroline wanted to take notes on Maggie's story. She wrote down every bit of it, from my run-in with Willow in the hallway to Maggie's flight on the early-morning bus, and had a bunch of questions too, including why I thought Maggie was different from the other wild girls. "Well, there's the obvious thing," I said, chewing on the second-to-last gummy frog. "I mean, she doesn't come from Bloodwort Road."

Caroline tapped her lip with her pen, making a blue comma at the corner of her mouth. "But Bloodwort Road is part of Swan River, isn't it? You think it can only happen to girls who live in that specific area?"

"That's not what I meant." But it was hard to explain what I did mean. Bloodwort was more than the old mill village; it was an attitude, a state of mind. You could always tell a Bloodwort kid in the school hallway because they all had a habit of looking down, as if the mountains had circumscribed their vision. It made a kind of sense for girls like that to go wild, and when they were the only ones, I'd been able to tell myself that my fear of becoming a wild girl was all out of proportion. But if it could happen to a not-especially-poor, non-trashy girl like my sister, it could happen to anyone.

We were quiet for a while. I felt myself dropping under the surface of a dream, but then Caroline spoke again. "Do you still want to be friends with Willow?"

"I don't know," I said. "I don't hate her, I guess."

"Because I thought I was your best friend."

"You are." I had become friends with Willow because we'd sat near each other at an Orientation meeting, but I'd become friends with Caroline by deliberate choice. We'd met in French class, where day after day I'd watched her watching our teacher, Monsieur Barnes. Monsieur was tragically clumsy, and while he stalked around the classroom, reading passages from Maupassant, he sometimes forgot to look where he was going and stumbled over chairs, desks, and, one memorable time, a lamp cord that somehow tangled itself around his ankles. Caroline never laughed at Monsieur, but she watched him and I watched her, until the day she turned her head and caught me. Before I could get awkward, she leaned between the aisles and said in a whisper, "J'ai un crotte de nez. Est-ce que vous avez un mouchoir en papier?" *I have a booger. Do you have a tissue?* "Oui," I said.

I knew that Caroline was a better friend for me than Willow could have been. Instead of country, Caroline and I both listened to Dylan and Joni Mitchell. We both loved the texture of elaborate words like *bailiwick* and *vociferous,* and looked for excuses to use them in sentences. She had read everything, and as we walked around the campus, we talked about all kinds of topics: why adolescence was an artificial stage of life, and why a girls' school like the Academy always had male headmasters, and why God let bad things happen when he was supposedly good. Caroline's mom and stepdad were intellectuals, and I imagined that these were the kinds of things they talked about around the dinner table.

Caroline was her own person, as my mom liked to say. She

read journal articles on folklore for fun. She wore rainbow-striped kneesocks and John Lennon glasses, and if anybody made fun of the way she looked, the sarcasm passed right over her without making an impression. Her father lived in Rome, and traveling with him had given her faith in her ability to move in the world that I envied. She was the one who had encouraged me to apply to my dream colleges in Minnesota, Maine, and Vermont when my mom said that maybe I should look for a backup—something less expensive, and closer to home.

Caroline shook out the last gummy frog, glowing alien green in the palm of her hand. "You know it could happen to you at any time," she said. "It's like being possessed, I guess—one minute you're fine, and the next you're a completely new person. I mean, we could just be lying here and then suddenly you could—"

"Sure, I know that," I said grimly. "I know all that already."

Maybe the fact that my sister had been an unusual kind of wild girl should have been reassuring to me. Maggie had proven that it was possible to come out on the other side of the wildness without any major baggage. In this she was not just different from Crystal Lemons, dead in the ruins of Bloodwort Farm, but different from the girls who went to prison, who always came back changed, degraded. I had seen Sharon Englehard, drunk at ten a.m., talking to herself at a bus stop, and Angie Davenport was rumored to work as a prostitute at the travel plazas on Route 19. Given the track records of the other ex–wild girls, Maggie's choice to settle for a deadneck life with Kayak Boy didn't seem so bad. Still, I couldn't help noticing that the one thing the wild girls had in common was that they were all stuck in Swan River—stuck under six feet of dirt like Crystal, or stuck with a man so uncurious that he would have been happy to stay this side of the river bridge for the rest of his life.

It wasn't what Maggie deserved, but when she invited me over to the new cabin where she was living with Kayak Boy, I wanted to be supportive. She was making Sunday dinner, and she told me that I was supposed to bring a dessert. It seemed like the kind of thing that the whole family should have done together, but Mom, who was still mad at Maggie for moving out, hadn't even been invited.

Travis offered to pick me up in the cruiser and drive me over there, but he seemed nervous and stayed just long enough to eat two carrot sticks with hummus and ask Kayak Boy a few semi-pointless questions about carpentry. When he was gone, the three of us sat at a picnic table next to one of the giant metal sculptures. This one looked like a plunger with tentacles.

"What is that?" Maggie asked, poking at the box I'd brought as if it were some rare and probably disgusting kind of bug.

I pointed at the words on the lid. "Umm, chocolates. Or else I really got robbed."

"Kate, when people say bring a dessert, they mean a dish," Maggie said. "Like a pie, or at least cupcakes. Not that we care, but if you go over to someone's house for dinner, you ought to know that—"

I rolled my eyes. "I live in a dorm, Maggie. What was I supposed to do, use my Easy-Bake oven? You took the Volkswagen back, so it's not like I could go to the—"

"Peace, ladies," Kayak Boy said, holding up hands ornamented by half a dozen bandages. After building the cabin with the help of a high school friend and a cousin or two, he had decorated the rooms on a classical elements theme: fire for the kitchen, water for the bedroom, earth for the living room, air for the bathroom.

"Look, we've got good friends, good wine—" He tried to top off my glass of sparkling cider with chardonnay, but Maggie caught his wrist and guided his hand away.

Though I agreed with my mom that Kayak Boy was the reason Maggie had curtailed her ambitions, I would have had to be a class A bitch to begrudge him the happiness that shone from his face as he set down the bottle and captured my sister's hand. He had suffered more than anyone from her absence. I had run into him once or twice when she was gone, at the movie theater or the grocery store, and he'd looked beyond depressed. I knew that this odd little cabin with its cedar-sawdust smell was the manifest expression of his gratitude that she'd returned to him, and it was a pretty nice place. You reached the property by turning off Bloodwort Road onto a windy gravel path that bottomed in a boggy, tannin-stained creek and climbed an eighty-degree hill before coming out on a clearing with a jaw-dropping view of the river and mountains. If this property had been twenty minutes south, where the tourists built their vacation homes, Kayak Boy never would have been able to afford it.

I could have taken a cue from Travis and asked polite questions about how you built a cabin and whether they were going to plant a vegetable garden, but I didn't feel like it. After the chocolate dispute, Maggie was clearly annoyed with me and didn't try to make conversation either. She and I knew how to make the silent treatment a competitive event, but Kayak Boy couldn't stand it for very long. He asked me about my classes, and I recited my schedule, ticking off each class on my fingers: Environmental Science, Calc, PE, French IV, and Myths and Mysteries with Dr. Bell. "But PE is actually an independent study," I explained. "I was supposed to take it as a freshman and I didn't, so now I run on the track twice a week and they give me credit for it."

"I can't believe you're taking that b.s. with Dr. Bell," Maggie said, stabbing a baby carrot into the cratered hummus. "He should call it the listen-to-me-be-brilliant class. When he reads out loud, it's like an orgasmic experience for him."

I tried to interpret Maggie's face, but her hair had fallen over her eyes. "Isn't that the guy who's supposed to get freaky with his students?" Kayak Boy said.

"That's just crap," I said. Though I had my own reasons for being wary of Dr. Bell, I'd never believed the stories that Becca Hochschild had come back from his office at midnight, lipstick bitten off and her blouse buttoned wrong, or that Kyra Baker had been spotted getting out of his car at the roadhouse on the other side of the Swan River Bridge. Becca and Kyra, both graduated now, had been National Honor Society types, pretty but serious, not at all the sort to get involved with a teacher. I had always supposed that their air of superiority had been the reason for the rumors, the linking of their names with Dr. Bell an appropriate insult for girls who seemed to think themselves above the intrigues of adolescence.

I looked at Maggie for confirmation, but she was twisting one of her long curls around her finger. If the rumors had been true, there would still be the fact that Maggie was not Dr. Bell's type. She was pretty in a messy way, with freckles and a gap between her front teeth that had never seen braces; still, I felt uncomfortable all of a sudden. "You don't think—" I stammered. "I mean, those are just stupid stories, right?"

Maggie pulled her curl out as long as it would go and, cross-eyed, checked for split ends. "Well, I didn't sleep with him if that's what you're asking. But he's a weird guy."

"What do you mean?"

She laid her palms facedown on the table. "I just think you should stay away from him. He's a middle-aged dude who's not married, and where there's smoke—"

"It's a boarding school," I said. "Where there's smoke there's probably a curling iron."

Kayak Boy snorted and got up to light the grill. It was getting dark. The trees on the ridge across the river had disappeared, and the fire cast a warm glow on his face as he poked at the coals. If Caroline had been there, she would have whipped out her notebook and started talking about the wild girls; I wished I had the guts to be as blunt as she would have been. I wanted to know why Maggie had chosen to come back to live in the very heart of wild-girl territory, mere miles from the ashes of Bloodwort Farm. But Maggie poured me another glass of cider, and Kayak Boy set down a platter that dripped blood through the slats in the picnic table, and I didn't mention the wild girls at all.

Whether or not Dr. Bell had gotten freaky with Becca and Kyra, I was certain that he knew something about the subject that both fascinated and repelled me. On the night Maggie jumped out the window, he had understood right away what was happening to her. At Convocation, he had known enough about Crystal Lemons to spin a smooth story for the parents. Perhaps, for him as for Caroline, the wild girls were an academic interest, a topic to discuss with men with beards and PhDs.

After the dinner with Maggie and Kayak Boy, I began to notice a pattern in the readings for Myths and Mysteries. We'd started out with *Macbeth*, discussing the witches' role as truth tellers. Then we'd moved on to a book about the Salem witch trials, pausing along the way to read selections from Greek myths about maenads and trance-struck sibyls. According to Dr. Bell, we were studying the myths of our subconscious, learning about our most primitive selves. In his lectures there was a lot of talk about Jung, whom I didn't understand any better than Freud but seemed to be all about archetypes and one thing standing for another thing. The assumption was that our readings were variations of myth and fairy tale, and that the creatures that populated them were fantasies thought up to fill some primitive need. That was fine, but I didn't understand why Dr. Bell was dancing around the subject of the wild girls, talking about things that were sort of like them but not quite the same. There was a black hole at the center of the syllabus, a hole that only Caroline and Willow and I knew was there.

Myths and Mysteries was first thing in the morning, and afterward it was always a relief to walk across campus to the Environmental Science room in the basement of the old library. In Environmental Science I was never confused, never on the lookout for buried references or hidden meanings. The teacher was Mr. Hightower, prematurely gray at twenty-five, his long name suited to his lanky body. He was only a few years out of some West Virginia college where he'd led a triple A football team to the regional championship, and he still suffered from a hick accent that made the girls smirk behind their hands. On the first day of class I felt sorry for him, but as soon as he started lecturing I forgot that he pronounced *eyewash* as *eyewarsh* and just paid attention. Mr. Hightower told us that environmentalism was not a trend but a way of life. He told us that country people often made the best conservationists, because they knew how to have a positive and respectful relationship with the land. He told us that it was our obligation, as temporary residents in a place of great natural beauty, to be conservationists too. A lot of what he said made sense to me, though I questioned the part about Swan River locals being natural environmentalists. We might have had some thrifty, canny country people back in the hills, but we also had the wild girls, whose philosophy was less Save the Planet than slash and burn.

Caroline and I agreed that there should be a term besides *teacher's pet* for a student the teacher likes more than others, not for sucking up but because the student and the teacher actually have something in common. If there had been such a word, it would have described what I was to Mr. Hightower. He liked me, but in a completely appropriate sort of way. I sometimes stayed after class to talk to him about water pollution and mountain-top removal mining, and he told me once that I had an unusual social consciousness for someone my age. Instead of just getting mad, he said, I should make up my mind to do something about the problems that bothered me. "Like what?" I said. "I'm only seventeen."

He'd been rolling up a topographical map that we'd used in class, and as he looked at me he tapped it thoughtfully against his palm. "Well," he said, "you won't be seventeen forever."

Mr. Hightower's class was my favorite by a mile, but as soon as September rolled around, I started dreading the overnight trip to the bunkhouse. The Environmental Science class always spent at least one night a semester at the old mill property on Bloodwort Road, collecting edible plants and observing soil erosion along the riverbank. Mr. Hightower called the property our outdoor classroom, and I knew that I was supposed to be excited about the chance to actually see all the things we were studying, but I just wished we could have done it somewhere else. Academy girls didn't belong in those dark woods.

At least that was what I thought before that weekend. Before Dr. Bell told us the story of Victoria Duvalier, and I began to wonder if the world of Bloodwort and the world of the Academy were really that far apart after all.

CHAPTER FIVE

*H*ave *you ever heard of Victoria Duvalier?*
That was the way the stories always started. Have you ever heard of Sophia Peabody, Misty Greco, Crystal Lemons? On the back of the bus, or behind the jungle gym at Cornelius Mickelson Elementary, a girl would lean forward and whisper the shocking details into your ear. I was used to these stories; I knew them by heart, but I never imagined that I would hear one from Dr. Bell.

He had come along on the trip as an extra chaperone. He was always stopping by Mr. Hightower's office to ask him about some plant he'd found in the woods, and I assumed that he'd be pretty into the collecting of edible flora, but during the dinner of boiled cattails and turkey dogs he hardly said a word. He'd brought his own vinyl camping chair, and while Mr. Hightower crouched on the ground with us, Dr. Bell sat a little apart, silhouetted by the leaping flames of the campfire. He had his feet crossed at the ankles, his hands folded on his belly; all I could see of his face was a partial beard, left sideburn, the outline of a nose. When Willow brought up the murders at Bloodwort Farm, Lucie Yates was yawning, and Frances Ortega was picking at her nails.

"I don't understand why you're letting us spend the night out here," Willow said, her eyes fixing on Dr. Bell. "I mean, at Convocation you made it sound like we'd be eaten up by bears or coyotes as soon as we set foot outside the gates." Though her tone was light, a collective shiver ran through the minions and I knew that they weren't bored anymore. Mr. Hightower was washing the pots and plates at the pump by the outhouse, and Rosa Slater started at every screech of the rusty pipe.

The girls might have been shocked by Willow's words, but Dr. Bell didn't seem to be. "I had to say those things," he said. "I had to tell the parents something they'd understand."

Willow drew closer to the fire. "So that guy who got mauled—you don't really think it was an animal? What was it, then?"

"Nobody knows."

"Oh my *God*," Matilda Peebles drawled, "it was an insane person, wasn't it? Some kind of country serial killer."

She grabbed Rosa's hand and they broke into hysterical laughter, but Dr. Bell and Willow didn't seem to notice. They kept their eyes on each other, Willow with her lips slightly parted, the locket on her neck moving with her breath. And then Dr. Bell said the words that I knew right away could only signal the beginning of a wild girl story: *Have you ever heard of Victoria Duvalier?*

In 1864, he told us, Swan River Academy had been requisitioned as a Union armory. General Stephen Burbridge was out to destroy the Confederate saltworks at Glen City, and he had settled on Swan River as his base of operations. The few students who were left at the Academy so late in the war had no way of getting home, if they still had homes to go to. The school arranged for them to board with local families, and a Widow Barfield on Sixth Street took in five of the girls. One was Victoria, who had grown up in Swan River, her father the part owner of the saltworks. In the last year of the war he had joined a cavalry battalion, leaving Victoria behind.

Dr. Bell paused, rubbing his beard. "I learned this from a diary I found in the archives at the Museum of the Middle Appalachians," he said. "The author was another of the students at Widow Barfield's boardinghouse. She writes about Victoria in the most glowing terms, as a lovely and charismatic young woman. All her friends seemed to agree that she would live a fortunate life, marrying well and taking her place in high society. Even the long war hadn't dimmed their hopes for her. But one night, all the Union sentinels at the Academy were slaughtered at their posts— ripped to pieces, an arm over here, a head over there. Confederate marauders were blamed, naturally, but the historians agree that there were no Confederates in the area that night."

A wind rustled through the laurel along the ridge, and I tucked my hands between my knees for warmth. Dr. Bell changed the cross of his ankles.

"In the diary, the date of October eleventh, 1864, is marked by a drawing of five girls suspended in the air, flying over a thick forest. The next few pages are scribbled all over in black, but under the marks you can make out the name Victoria repeated over and over. The written account ends there, but when I asked the curator about it, he told me a very strange story. When the author went home to Richmond, she told her family that *she* had murdered the sentinels—she and her friends, including Victoria Duvalier. Not only that, but she claimed that, on the night of the murders, they had acquired supernatural powers that allowed them to fly, to set fires without light or tinder, et cetera. In the parlance of the day, she called it witchcraft, and insisted that she and her friends, particularly Victoria, required exorcism. As the young woman came from a family of some standing, the case attracted attention. She became a patient of a celebrated neurologist, a student of Duchenne de Boulogne. According to the doctor's account, published privately after the girl had been committed, she swore that Victoria had made them kill the sentinels—that she was the instigator, the head of the coven, so to speak."

It was so quiet that we could hear the water sloshing in Mr. Hightower's basin. "Of course stories like this aren't unknown in Swan River," Dr. Bell said. "There's a folkloric tradition of girls committing these sorts of crimes, these seemingly motiveless murders and maulings."

His face was in shadow now, but I could have sworn he was looking straight at me. "What happened to Victoria Duvalier?" I whispered.

"I was curious about that too," Dr. Bell said, "so I did a bit of research. She went to stay with family in Charleston, married a Manigault. Died in childbirth in 1869."

In the center of the fire, a strip of bark rose in blue flame and collapsed into ashes. Willow stretched out her legs and leaned forward, hands on knees. "But how did Victoria make those girls do what she wanted? According to the doctor, I mean."

"The details are rather vague," Dr. Bell said. "Apparently the patient told him that Victoria had taken control of their minds. He interpreted this as referring to her personal charisma, as if she'd simply accustomed them to doing her will, but it could also refer to a more formal process. In other traditions, the sort of violent frenzy that is reported in Swan River is usually stimulated by ritualized behavior. As you'll remember from your readings, the maenads incited their madness through a combination of drinking and ecstatic dancing."

Rosa whispered, "Friday night in Willow's room, y'all," but nobody laughed. The night wind had kicked up again. From behind us we heard a muffled clanging sound, and Matilda Peebles had already started shrieking when Mr. Hightower stepped into the light, the tin basin he'd used for washing dishes thumping against his leg.

Probably the minions didn't know quite what to make of Dr. Bell's story, but there was no doubt that it had stirred them. As we got ready for bed, the air inside the bunkhouse felt charged with excitement. The narrow room full of knotty-pine bunk beds seemed small and imperiled, like the cabin of a ship on the high seas. The new atmosphere should have made me more a part of the group, but I felt self-conscious and wanted to get to bed as quickly as possible. Why had Dr. Bell been looking at me? Had he noticed the connections between me and Victoria Duvalier—both Academy students, both Swan River natives? Eyes lowered, I was on my way to brush my teeth when Frances Ortega grabbed a handful of my pajama pants. "We're going to play Truth or Dare," she said.

"Who's we?" I asked.

Frances half-closed her eyes. "Everybody. Willow, you're playing, aren't you?"

Willow looked up from the pad she'd been doodling on. Before she covered it with her hand, I caught a glimpse of a caricature of Frances, her big nose enlarged to baguette proportions. Though technically one of the minions, Frances was always the odd man out. She came from Abilene and was Texas-pretty, with too much eye makeup and long red nails. When called on in class, she always tried to give a funny answer instead of the right one, and she didn't seem to notice that no one else ever laughed. Worst of all, she imitated Willow's style but got everything subtly wrong. Her ballet slippers were crocodile instead of velvet. Instead of Balkan Sobranies she smoked a brand called Piccolo Sam's, which had the same pastel paper but smelled of bubble gum. The minions tolerated her because her father was the lieutenant governor of Texas and the family owned a vacation house on the other side of the bridge, but they never tried very hard to include her, and Willow was least likely of all to go out of her way to make Frances happy.

"Oh, why not," Willow said, surprising me. "God knows there's nothing else to do around here."

The game started with Lucie Yates, who dared Matilda to hang her butt out the bathroom window for five seconds. Matilda dared Elise Seidel to knock on the flap of Mr. Hightower's tent and ask to borrow a cup of sugar. Elise asked Rosa how many guys she'd slept with (four, or seven if you counted oral sex), and Rosa asked Frances if it was true that her dad had had a fling with an adult film star named Lulu Styx (yes, but they were just friends now). By the time it was my turn, I'd decided that I'd rather be in bed with a sweatshirt tied around my ears. "This is stupid," I said. "Give me a dare, I guess."

Glowering, Frances stared at me down the line of her nose. "Sorry we bored you," she said. "All right. Did you see the notebook that Dr. Bell kept taking out during the hike?"

I nodded. As we'd hunted among the bracken of the Bloodwort wilderness, I had seen Dr. Bell lean against a red oak, pen cinched between his fingers, absently watching Willow bend over to nab a fern. In a flash he pulled a wallet-size notebook from his pocket, scribbled a note or two. "You know what I think?" Frances said, dropping her voice to a dramatic whisper. "I think he's taking notes about Willow. Y'all saw how he was looking at her when he told that weird story. He's writing down something about her— something personal."

We all turned at once to Willow, who was thumbing a deck of cards, a red spot centered high on each of her cheekbones. "So your dare," Frances said to me, "is to go out there and get the notebook."

"No," I said. "You want me to climb in the tent with the head-master? That's ridiculous."

"He's asleep! Just grab his pants. It'll take five seconds."

"No," I said. "First of all, I don't care if he's asleep. And second, he's not writing secret information about Willow, because what would that even mean?"

"Sure, fine," Frances snapped. "I guess he was writing down the Latin names of trees or something."

I looked away. Maybe she was trying to fake me out, or maybe she'd guessed that I actually did have my own theory about what Dr. Bell was doing with that mysterious notebook. The minions had treated the story of Victoria Duvalier as nothing more than a creepy campfire tale, but I knew better. This was the wild girls' habitat, and to someone as versed in their mythology as Dr. Bell seemed to be, every detail of the Bloodwort landscape must speak of a past crime. Was the rubbled farmhouse we'd passed, roof caved and tangles of kudzu spilling out the windows, the home of Margaret Reid, who had cut her siblings' throats before setting them on fire? Did a crumbling brick wall belong to the sawmill that Luray Coulter had burned to the ground? The truth was that I wanted to see the inside of that notebook badly enough to do almost any dumb thing.

"I don't know if you play this way," Willow said, "but at my summer camp, if someone refused a dare, it went to the whole group."

The minions hadn't been paying much attention to the conflict between Frances and me, but now Rosa Slater put down her hair-brush, and Matilda Peebles took a break from filling in the block-letter *MP* she'd drawn on the floor. "Obviously Kate's right about getting in the tent," Elise said. "But back at school, it wouldn't be *such* a big deal. I've seen him take the notebook out of his pocket and leave it on his desk during class. All you'd have to do is just knock it into your bag on the way out the door."

Lucie nodded. "He swims at the fitness center every morning. You could sneak in and get it out of his locker."

I suspected that one of the minions really would find a way to steal Dr. Bell's notebook, because that's how they were about Willow. I had seen Matilda at the basement vending machines at one in the morning, buying both cherry and strawberry Pop-Tarts since she wasn't sure which ones Willow liked better. Rumor had it that Lucie had walked through six inches of snow to catch a bus to the one tobacco shop in the county that would sell you Balkan Sobranies without checking your ID. Since I'd already refused to steal the notebook, I figured that Willow wouldn't have much use for me for a while, but then she came and knelt by my bunk in the dark. "Hey," she whispered. "Come out with me so I can have a cigarette."

With the bunkhouse lights extinguished, the woods were as black as the inside of a cave. Willow led me past the tents where Dr. Bell and Mr. Hightower were sleeping to the far end of the wooden walkway. Though I couldn't see them, I could picture the rusty water pump to our right and the bristling branches of wild mountain laurel that Mr. Hightower had had to cut away from the handle before we could use it. Swaying, breathing night sounds came from the thicket below us.

At the River House Willow had asked me if I wanted a cigarette, but this time she just handed me one without asking. I slid the foil filter between my lips and, when she held the flame to the tip, inhaled tentatively. A warm, restless wind swept through the thicket, stirring my braid between my shoulder blades, touching the mosquito bite that burned just below my hairline. It blew Willow's hair back from her neck, and I saw the silver feather earrings that she'd worn the night we talked about Mason Lemons. "I like those," I said, pointing.

"They're from my dad. You can have them if you want." As I shook my head, she unhooked one of the earrings and held it up to my bare lobe. "No, you're right," she said. "You have your own style."

I looked down at the fisherman's sweater I'd thrown over my pajamas. "I can't wear big earrings because of my hair. It ends up in this crazy snarl. I look like Medusa."

"I can cut it for you if you want," Willow said. "My dad used to have a girlfriend who cut hair. He'd drop me off at her apartment in Moorefield sometimes, and she'd let me practice on her mannequin heads."

"Girlfriend?" I repeated. "I thought your parents were still married."

"Sometimes people have girlfriends when they're married. I believe it's called cheating."

"But does your mom know?"

"It's hard to tell what my mom knows. She'll be calm for a month or two and then she'll have this insane explosion about nothing. Mrs. Cochran just invited her to go to Canyon Ranch with her for New Year's, so at the moment she's pretty happy."

I scraped the toe of my shoe through the grass and weeds. "Your dad must trust you a lot," I said. "To take you along on his dates or whatever."

"He likes people to know that he's messing around, actually. It's a status symbol for him. Like, you know you're a big man when you can introduce your girlfriend to people who know your wife and they act like it's totally normal." Willow exhaled, smoke unrolling from her lips. "In a weird way, he's just as obsessed with social climbing as my mom is. Freshman year, he got a list of all the other incoming girls and circled the ones who he wanted me to make friends with—the ones who had money or important families or whatever. He said, 'Willow, those are the girls you want to cultivate. They're good contacts for you.'"

She always used the same voice to imitate her dad—deep and rough, with just enough drawl to sound politician-folksy. "A good *contact*," I said. "What does that even mean? We're in high school."

Willow smiled, affectionate and condescending at the same time. "Half the girls at the Academy have their whole lives planned out already. Not just where they're going to college but where they're going to live, who they're going to marry. If you want to live like that, you need to know the right people."

High grass tickled my ankles below the hems of my pajama pants, which were embarrassingly old, covered in cartoons of polar bears bouncing beach balls off their noses. "Well, you did better than make contacts," I said. "Forget Dr. Bell's notebook—those girls would steal third base if you told them to."

"I know. But it's kind of boring—having followers instead of friends."

I hadn't expected her to be so honest about it. My eyes had adjusted to the dark, and I could see that she was looking at me, her cigarette poised by her chin. I had forgotten all about mine, and I raised it to my lips for a drag that made my eyes water.

"That story Dr. Bell told," I said, lowering my voice to a whisper. "That's crazy shit, right?"

Willow stretched her arms above her head, curling and uncurling her fingers. "I guess. I mean, if you believe all that stuff."

"If you believe all that stuff," I repeated. "You saw what happened to Maggie. If there's another wild girl before we graduate—if one of them attacked the school—"

"Kate, you shouldn't freak yourself out so much." She picked up my braid and studied it critically. "You've got to be practical. I'm sure a lot more people die in car accidents in Swan River than get killed by wild girls."

This was a local's attitude. This was what my mother said about the wild girls, and Travis, and almost everyone else who had to live with the threat of their violence day in and day out. It was the only way to survive in Swan River without going cuckoo, and to hear this practical advice coming from Willow filled me with a kind of grudging admiration.

"I know you're right," I said. "I know I shouldn't obsess, but sometimes I can't help it. When Frances was talking about Dr. Bell's notebook, I kept thinking, What if he's writing down stories like the one he told us tonight? What if he knows more about them than he's telling?"

Willow shrugged. "I figured that Frances was right about him writing down pervy stuff. Christine Fox told me that she'd seen a drawing of a naked woman in the margin of a book he loaned her."

She gave my braid a last little tug before replacing it on my shoulder. "How about I make you a deal? I'll cut your hair, and in exchange, you can talk to that Mason guy for me."

I'd hoped that Willow had given up on her plan to get with Mason Lemons. "What would your parents think about you going out with a guy like that?"

"They never have to know," she said. "Just ask him what he thinks of me. I need some kind of intro."

I sighed. "I feel like your pimp."

"But it's more like you're his pimp, actually. Since I'm the one paying."

Though it had been a hot summer and half the state was under a drought watch, I flicked the embered butt into the mountain laurel. I would do what Willow had asked me, but I didn't have to like it. Bloodwort was a haunted place, rotted-out and desolate, and Mason Lemons, handsome as he was, was still the son of a witch.

CHAPTER SIX

Probably everybody has a time—a week, or month; a year if you're lucky—that sears itself into your memory, imprinting with such vividness that you can play it back at will, a personal film. I had been nervous about reintroducing Willow to Mason, but it turned out that the month I spent with them, driving around in Mason's beat-up El Camino, was one of the best times of my life.

It was October and the leaves were changing: first the aspens and poplars to shades from dry lemon to police-tape yellow; next the oaks and maples to crimson and heat-seeking orange. I don't even have to close my eyes to feel the wind in my face as we rolled down Bloodwort Road, or to taste the sweet wine that Mason bought at gas stations and passed to us in a paper bag. I think I was more alive then than I've ever been since, and I can picture the hectic skittering leaves on the side of the road, the bobble-head Jesus suction-cupped to Mason's pebbled dashboard, better than the faces of people I saw yesterday.

After careful consideration, I'd decided not to approach Mason in the dining hall. He had taken a job there after Crystal's death, and I knew that everyone would be watching us if I tried to chat him up while he served macaroni casserole. I waited for a good opportunity to catch him off duty, and one Thursday evening, I thought I'd found it. I was heading over to the track for my twice-weekly run when I saw Clancy lacing up his sneakers in front of Calhoun Hall, a basketball under his arm. I knew that a bunch of guys from the staff played basketball together one night a week, and I decided to jog over to say hello.

Seeing me, Clancy looked edgy and alert, and I felt suddenly powerful. I had never made anyone nervous before. "You know, that's about the weeniest track I've ever seen," he said when I told him where I was headed. "What is it, like, a quarter mile around? Why don't you run on the fire road instead?"

I didn't want to admit that I was scared of the fire road, which wound from the back gates of the Academy down a heavily wooded ridge to an intersection with Bloodwort Road. "The track's flat. I don't want to run up mountains—I have a bad knee."

"Okay," Clancy said, smiling. We'd almost made it to the old library, and I started to ask him if Mason would be there tonight, but Clancy began talking at the same time. We both paused, I looking down at his long knobbly hands bracing the basketball, then up at the windows. Three years after Maggie had burned her way through the Dewey decimals from history and geography to arts and recreation, sheets of plastic still covered the holes where the glass used to be.

"You first," I said.

"Oh well, I—" he stammered in a voice that was louder than it needed to be. "I was just wondering if you wanted to hang out sometime, go see a movie or something."

We locked eyes, and I felt a heat that started in my stomach, spreading fast through the rest of my body. "Sure. You should call me. I don't actually have my own extension, nobody does, but you just call the switchboard and they'll connect you to the hall phone." I was babbling now, and I bit my tongue to make myself shut up.

We had reached the stairs that led down to the old gym, and I knew that in a second he'd expect me to turn off toward the track. "How is Mason doing these days?" I asked. "I've seen him in the dining hall, but I haven't gotten a chance to—"

Clancy looked down, bouncing the basketball between his feet. "It was hard for him, what happened to Crystal, but he's doing okay."

"Is he still living with you?"

"No," he said, more guardedly. "He went back to the farm to take care of his mom."

"And, umm—" I stumbled. "Does he play basketball with you guys? I didn't want to bother him, you know, when he was grieving, but that friend of mine wanted me to talk to him, and—"

As I rambled, I saw a brief flash of disappointment cross Clancy's face. He started down the stairs to the basement, talking over his shoulder. "Yeah, he should be down here already. I'll get him for you."

Waiting outside the double doors to the gym, I cursed Willow in my head. I wasn't sure whether or not I wanted to go out with Clancy, but I definitely didn't want him to think that I was the one with the crush on Mason. Clancy seemed to take a long time, and I inhaled the smell of sweat and old paper, listening to the balls thudding against the wood floor. Finally I bent down for a drink, keeping my eyes on a cutout of a blobby ghost taped to the cinder-block wall. "Hey," said a voice behind me. "I like your tights."

"They're not tights," I said. "They're running pants."

"Clancy said you had some kind of message for me." Mason

tilted his head back and grinned, the cocky grin of a guy who would never be surprised to hear that a girl was waiting for him. A ball had rolled through the door behind him, and he kicked it up into his hands.

I smoothed the stray hairs that had fallen out of my braid. "It's for a friend of mine. She—this is kind of weird, but she knew I knew you, and—well, basically—"

"Is she ugly?" he interrupted, passing the ball between his hands.

"No."

"Is she a mute or something? There's got to be something wrong with her, or why would she send you?"

His head fell back against the wall. A line from one of my favorite Dylan songs came into my head: *Mona Lisa musta had the highway blues, you can tell by the way she smiles.* I'd lain in my dorm room wondering what the highway blues were exactly, but now I knew. How else could you describe the way he looked at me, melancholy and questioning and full of a baited promise all at the same time?

"You've met her," I said. "My friend Willow. I brought her to the summer festival, that one time—" My voice faltered. For a moment Mason's grin vanished, and a deep line appeared on either side of his mouth. I wanted to tell him how sorry I was, but the expression was gone just as quickly.

"The redhead. I remember." He wiped his face with the hem of his shirt, revealing the ridges of his muscled stomach. "I get off at two on Friday. You know that falling-down house on Bloodwort Road near the Laurel Creek trailhead? The two of you meet me there around two-thirty, and we'll go for a drive or something."

"The two of us? But you and Willow could just—I mean, I'm sure she would—"

He shook his head. "I'm too shy. We'll need a chaperone, at least at first."

I didn't believe him about being shy, but I said okay. Mason's grin widened. "Think fast," he said and sprang the ball into the hands I opened just in time.

I wasn't sure how Willow would feel about Mason's plan, but at two-thirty on Friday we were right where he'd told us to be, sitting on an old millstone outside the abandoned house near the Laurel Creek trailhead. It was the kind of place that usually freaked me out. The roof was half-gone, the broken windows foaming with trumpet vine. Though I'd never heard any stories associated with this place, it had an air of old violence—a smell, almost. The mailbox beside the front door swung from one rusty nail, and the door itself was a hair ajar, a black sliver of shadow visible between the lock and the doorframe. Listening to the wind shake the trees made me itchy with nerves, but then we heard the growl of Mason's car coming around the bend, and Willow turned to me and grinned.

Ever since the trip to the bunkhouse, Willow had been so nice to me that she'd made even Caroline seem disinterested and self-absorbed. Willow remembered when my tests were and asked me about them. She promised to stay up all night to help me with my scholarship application for Pritchard College, and though we ended up playing Clue instead of writing the essay, I appreciated the thought. When I mentioned that I wasn't sure how I'd even get to college without a car, she offered to sell me her BMW, Jean-Luc. "It's pretty old, so I don't think we'd have to charge you much," she said. "If you got a summer job, you could probably afford it."

This sounded too good to be true. "But won't you need the car?"

Willow pursed her lips and picked at the polish on her thumbnail. "They'd buy me another one if I want. But sometimes I wonder if I should even bother with college."

I tugged at my braid. Of course I knew lots of people who hadn't been or didn't plan to go to college: Maggie, Clancy, Kayak Boy. In a town like Swan River, you didn't necessarily need higher learning, but Willow was not going to stay in Swan River. We'd already talked about what she was going to study (Visual Arts with a French minor) and I'd thumbed through the brochures, from Emory and Vanderbilt and Agnes Scott, that lay in a jumble at the edge of her desk. "But what would you do instead?"

"I don't know. Just move to New York and get some kind of entry-level job at a gallery maybe."

"But that's not a very good use for your social connections and your Mandarin and all that. Doesn't your dad want you to marry an ambassador or something?"

I meant this as a joke, but Willow didn't seem to take it that way. She'd gotten new contacts that week, and her eyes were a startling purple-blue. "My dad sent me to the Academy for certain reasons," she said. "I did what they wanted, but what I do when I turn eighteen is my own business." She smiled, and I wondered if she was thinking of Mason.

Willow's interest in me was a surprise, but strangest of all, she kept complimenting me in front of Mason. Over weeks, in a series of artful side comments, she led him to understand that I was the only girl she knew who could drive a stick shift, that I had been the best offensive player on the soccer team before I hurt my knee sophomore year, that I had the third-highest GPA in our class after Caroline and Sarah VanDexter. I knew this meant she didn't consider me a threat, but I enjoyed it anyway, and I couldn't help noticing that Mason aimed his melancholy smile at me more often. I started wearing my hair down on Fridays, painstakingly curling the ends with a two-dollar curling iron I found at Goodwill. At another thrift store, I picked up a pair of jeans that Willow said made my butt look tight. Clancy Harp hadn't called me to go to the movies like he said he would, but I told myself I didn't care. I didn't want to sit through some dumb comedy at the Moorefield multiplex. I wanted to be with Willow and Mason, who made me feel that I didn't have to wait for Pritchard College for my life to begin—that here, sandwiched in the front seat of the ugly El Camino, I was already the person I wanted to become.

Most days, Mason took us on what he called the Junk Tour of Swan River. We never went as far as Bloodwort Farm, but we went everywhere else: around the Academy, through the dull quiet streets behind downtown where I had grown up, and finally down to the swampy muddle of the Delta sprawled along the riverbank. We visited old family graveyards, an empty building that used to house a hardware store, the shell of the potato chip factory that had closed last year. There was no discernible method to the Junk Tour, only a common reference to what spoke of rack and ruin, failure and collapse. Along with features of the man-made landscape, Mason pointed out what he called signs—birds or trees or arrangements of cloud that he claimed could be read to tell the future. He said that his mom had learned about these things from her Appalachian foremothers, and that the ability to interpret them was a talent passed down through generations.

After showing us one trailer with a yard full of toilet-bowl planters and another with a dollhouse-size replica of Graceland by the mailbox, Mason had parked at a state-designated scenic location overlooking the car graveyard. The three of us were balanced on the guardrail, Willow and I with our hands punched deep in the pockets of our jackets, hoods turned up against a cold dark mist. "Look at that," Mason said with a mixture of shame and satisfaction. "The government puts up a special sign saying that this is a great view, and then some asshole comes along and fucks it up with a bunch of wrecked cars and a tire dump. Makes me sick."

Below us, the piney slope ran into a declivity that was bare of trees, the land shining with heaps of twisted bumpers and broken shards of windshields. I had heard that Billy Thorpe, who owned this dump along with the Tastee-Freez, trucked in wrecks from as far away as Nashville. The sky filled with flushed crows that seemed for that moment to hang motionless, like a handful of gravel thrown into the air.

"Kate, maybe you should do your environmental activism around here," Willow said. Leaning around me, she told Mason, "After college, Kate wants to go and help out a bunch of third-world countries. Like show them how to build drainage systems or something. She's going to save the world. You should hear our science teacher talk about her—he thinks she's the greatest thing since curly fries."

I knew that this was supposed to be a compliment like all the others, but I caught a mocking undertone. Willow understood why I wanted to get out of Swan River, but she couldn't understand wanting to make the world a better place. To her it was a peculiar, faintly outrageous inclination, like a taste for clove cigarettes or kissing other girls.

Mason picked up a stick and tossed it into the ravine. It was unseasonably cool, but while we were in sweaters and rain jackets—Willow even had a pair of pink cashmere gloves—he was dressed in his usual jeans and T-shirt. Looking back, I'm sure that he wore these clothes because he couldn't afford any others. But because he was handsome, with those goldish eyes and that high-boned, vaguely Native American face; because he had a weight lifter's chest and shoulders from summer construction work; because he kept you on your toes—harsh and mocking one moment, kind and funny the next—because, in other words, he was Mason Lemons, you never questioned what he wore. "She's right," he said to me. "You want to help somebody, help your own people first."

"But these aren't her *people*," Willow said, and I sent her a silent thank-you for not making me say it myself. "They're not my people either. Just because you're born in a place doesn't mean you have to stay there forever. You can go anywhere you want to."

Mason smiled down at the copper-colored carpet of needles below the guardrail. "Not me," he said. "*I* can't go anywhere."

"Yes, you could," I chimed in. "You could go to college. Even if you had to start at MCC, you could transfer after a year or two."

Mason shook his head, smoke drifting around his hand. "Look at that," he said, pointing at a pale silver-plumaged bird hopping from branch to branch in the tree above us. "That's what the old people call a shiver bird. You see one of those in the daytime, it means somebody's going to die."

Despite Mason's gloomy interpretations of clouds and birds, I was happier then and less fearful of disaster than I'd ever been in my life. At the Academy, I was doing less work and having more fun. I even hung out with Willow's friends once in a while. They weren't as boring or as dumb as I'd thought, and I began to feel bad about the names I'd called them: minions, Barbies, Stepford Belles. I had believed that their lives were perfect and had resented them accordingly, but as I got to know them I realized that they got as much pressure from their parents as Willow got from hers. With the exception of Frances, each of them felt the burden of representing not just herself but a whole family line that stretched back centuries. They were not just Matilda and Elise and Lucie; they were Peebles and Seidels and Yateses. Living up to those names didn't involve succeeding in any obvious way; it didn't require getting good grades or getting into good colleges, but there was a whole unwritten list of things that they weren't supposed to do. Matilda Peebles confided in me once that she had wanted to go to culinary school until her grandmother told her that a Peebles would not cook other people's meals for money.

One Saturday Elise and Lucie invited me to go shopping in Moorefield, and the three of us spent the whole day going into discount shoe stores and understocked hippie head shops, buying nothing and making fun of everything. I actually liked them—tiny china-doll Lucie, who cussed like a trucker in a flat Georgia drawl; Elise, who could cut you off at the knees with a field hockey stick and had a funny way of emphasizing every other word that came out of her mouth. Sometimes they talked about the plan to steal Dr. Bell's notebook, laughing about it so frequently that I could tell they were taking it more seriously than they let on. "Figure if we can just get his pants off, it'll be easy to get into his pockets," Lucie said, with a joke-sexy pout and a wink.

If it hadn't been for one discordant note I would have been happy to go on like this all year, but predictably, Caroline didn't like my renewed friendship with Willow. Caroline called her vacant, meaning not unintelligent but emptied, like a vacant lot. She said that Willow didn't really care for other people and only kept them around as long as they were useful, which was why she had friend-dumped me as soon as she got in with Tessa's crowd. I said that Willow had been encouraged her whole life to be shallow, but if she stopped letting her parents make her decisions, she'd have the potential to be a lot more than that. It wasn't an argument I had much hope of winning, and as long as Caroline and Willow stayed away from each other, it didn't really matter if I won or not. But things came to a head a week or two after the trip to the bunkhouse, when Willow caught up with us on our way back from the dining hall.

I was filling Caroline in on Dr. Bell's wild girl story. It seemed she already knew something about it, which probably shouldn't have surprised me. "My dad's really into the Civil War," she said. "Not the way people down here are into it, but in a historian kind of way. He has this book called *The Mountain War* about the campaigns in the backcountry, and I looked in the atlas to see if it had any information about Swan River. It didn't say anything about the wild girls, obviously, but there was a section on the deaths of the Union sentinels. Since there was no explanation, I figured that the wild girls might have been involved."

Willow tilted her head and smiled, curls brushing her wind-flushed cheeks. "Kate told me you want to write a book about the wild girls. Have you figured out anything about why it happens? I mean, why it happens to some people and not to others?"

Caroline looked as annoyed as I'd ever seen her, and I realized that she hadn't heard Willow come up on my other side. "It's okay," I said quickly. "She knows all about them."

"There are lots of theories," Caroline said, ignoring me. "Some scholars think that any girl could become a wild girl with the right influences, but they differ on what those influences are. Can you bring about the state by ingesting certain herbs, or doing certain rituals? Personally I don't find any of that very convincing. I think some girls are vulnerable to it and some aren't, and until it happens you're never going to know who's who."

"Herbs," I muttered. "Maggie didn't eat any herbs. Everybody knows that it's random—that's what's scary about it."

I expected Willow to back me up, but both of them seemed to have forgotten I was there. "So you're seventeen, and you've already started a book," Willow said to Caroline. "That's so awesome. We're the same age, and I don't have a clue what I want to do with my life."

Caroline squinted up at the roofline of Arkwright Hall. "Well, you could just be a hedonist," she said, aiming her words somewhere above Willow's head. "I guess that's always an option."

In retrospect, I should have predicted that Caroline would react badly to Willow's compliment. The fact was that Willow complimented everyone—me, the minions, even Dr. Bell, telling him truthfully that he had the best hair of any teacher on campus. Her genius was that she always began with something that was genuinely noteworthy and, by casting it in the flattering light of her attention, made it look even better. She told Lucie, who sang well but timidly in the back row of the Concert Choir, that she sounded exactly like her mom's old Carly Simon records. She told Monica Sklar, who made funky A-line skirts using rejects from the lost and found box, that we would all see her clothes on the catwalk one day. Her comments were subtle and perceptive and to all appearances sincere, but of course Caroline didn't see it that way. What was the point? she asked. Sucking up to Tessa Cochran was one thing, but what did Willow have to gain from sweet-talking every single person she met? In other circumstances I might have asked myself the same question, but Caroline's prim self-righteousness made it hard to be on her side. The next time we found ourselves alone, I had to call her on it.

"I think it was sort of mean to call Willow a hedonist," I said. "It's not her fault that she doesn't know what to do with her life. She's actually a really talented artist, but her parents are so weird—all they care about is her socializing with fancy people and marrying money. Nobody's ever encouraged her to figure out what she wants to do."

Caroline was folding her laundry, draping a week's worth of ironed plaid skirts over her arm. Shaking her head, she peered at me from under her ledge of bangs. "Did you ever send in that scholarship application for Pritchard College?" she asked. "Isn't it due on the first of the month?"

I sighed. Pritchard was the one school I'd applied to that offered a four-year scholarship that included everything, even a stipend for books, and Caroline knew it. If I blew off the application process, I might end up at Moorefield Community College. "Of course I did," I lied.

"And did you come up with a topic for your research project in Myths and Mysteries? Because Dr. Bell wants a précis from us before winter break."

I shrugged, my eyes sliding to the window. Caroline had lucked into a corner room with two windows, one facing the Lawn and the other the loading dock. I stared blankly for a minute before my brain processed the fact that Mason Lemons was sitting on the edge of the concrete pier, slumped forward, legs hanging over the five-foot drop.

"I have to go," I said. Caroline looked disapproving, and I pushed past her before she could look out the window and have a real reason to wag her finger.

Mason looked up as I approached, sketching a tired-looking wave with his cigarette hand. "I've been waiting here for forty-three minutes," he said.

He had leaned forward over his knees again, and I had to concentrate on the sound of the words to make sure I'd understood him. He ruffled his hair against the part, exposing white, vulnerable-looking patches of scalp. "Were we supposed to meet you?" I asked. "It's Wednesday, not Friday."

"Not you. Willow."

"Oh." The day seemed darker suddenly.

"When I was little and my dad used to whip me," Mason said, "you know which tree he cut the switch from? The willow."

"You remember your dad?"

"Sort of."

"I don't remember my dad." I was stalling now, wondering how to tell him that Willow had left campus with Tessa and Rosa an hour ago. "She's not here, you know," I said finally, bluntly. "Maybe she forgot."

"I reckon she did." Mason scraped the coal of his cigarette along the sole of his shoe. On a normal day, if he had used the word *reckon* it would have been a joke, as preposterously kitschy as any stop on the Junk Tour. This time, though, I had a feeling that the word had slipped out, part of the vocabulary of his thoughts. It made me feel sorry for him. I looked down at the asphalt, at the swirls of rainbow oil left by the delivery trucks.

When I looked up again, he was staring at me. I had dreamed about Mason more than once, and this was the way he always looked at me in my dreams. They weren't particularly sexy or romantic dreams, but that look gave me the same spine-tingly feeling I used to get standing in line for the Tilt-A-Whirl at the county fair. It was a challenging look, as if he were daring me and sizing me up all at the same time. He stretched his arms over his head, smiling. "You want to go for a ride?"

I nodded, and without speaking we climbed into the El Camino. Before I could buckle my seat belt Mason took off, screeching up the campus road to the light at Route 19. My heart beat high in my throat and he was holding my knee like a gearshift, fingers tense with a scorching charge.

CHAPTER SEVEN

I knew what had happened at Bloodwort Farm. I knew that most of the painted cabins had burned, and that no one lived there now except for Mason, Mrs. Lemons, and the Birdman. From Maggie I had heard that even their harsh, hard-living neighbors along Bloodwort Road avoided the commune these days, keeping their children in after dark, locking up their yard dogs. I wasn't the only one who believed that the chaos that infected our town began there, leaching over the dark woods like a stain.

I understood that it would be bad, but I hadn't expected it to be this bad. The ruts in the gravel turnoff would have made it impassable in wet weather, and the brambles on either side were thick enough to rock the car. Now I understood why the El Camino had so many scratches. Gritting his teeth, Mason punched the car forward until it rolled into a rut and wouldn't budge, and then we walked. Compost toilets gave the air a sweet, thick smell. The path we took was littered with old trash: containers of motor oil, disintegrating fried chicken buckets. Most of the cabins were nothing more than piles of cinders and charred beams, and of the few still standing, only one looked occupied. The Birdman sat on the porch, drinking a Coors Light. His face was seamed with scar tissue, and his right hand had been burned into a claw that hung uselessly from the arm of his chair. On the cooler beside him sat a blow-up doll with impossibly round breasts and an astonished expression. He waved at us with his good hand, and when Mason ignored him, I waved back. Though I didn't like the Birdman, I didn't want to be rude to someone who was disabled and likely crazy besides.

Mason's cabin had a narrow bed—a twin, like the ones in our dorm rooms—a desk, and a spindle-legged table. It wasn't as filthy and disordered as the rest of the commune, but it wasn't exactly clean either. The walls and floor were made of cedar logs that probably let in sharp drafts in the winter. Books took up a lot of the space, stretching in precarious stacks halfway to the ceiling. In their shiny cellophane jackets, most were clearly foundlings from the Free Book Box at the library. The majority seemed to have to do with history, with dates stamped below the titles on the spines.

Running my finger up a stack of books on the Mexican-American War, I tried to piece together a picture of Mason's days when he wasn't driving us around on the Junk Tour: coming home, cooking dinner on a hot plate, reading random books on history, working out with free weights and the pull-up bar screwed into the doorframe. I thought of murderers in solitary confinement, keeping to a routine within their cells, imposing their own sense of control on their restricted lives. Of all the weird things at the commune, the weirdest was Mason living in this disaster and collapse as if nothing was out of the ordinary.

I sat on the bed, on a heap of clashing afghans, and Mason sat on the one chair—junkyard-scavenged, he'd told me, the seat patched with mismatched fabric. "This is nice," I said nervously. "It reminds me of the cabins that my mom and Travis talk about renting for vacations. They never actually go anywhere, but every spring they get a bunch of brochures and sit around the kitchen table—"

"Yeah." He stared at the floor. "It could be a lot worse, I guess. But it kind of gets to you, being out here all by yourself. I have strange thoughts sometimes."

The back of my neck prickled. "What kind of strange thoughts?"

Mason leaned forward, elbows balanced on his knees, his uncanny eyes trained on mine. "You know what happened to my sister, don't you? You know what she did?"

I nodded, barely breathing.

"It wasn't her fault," he said. "She was never like that, before—" He stopped himself, rubbing the bridge of his nose. "Anyway, it did happen. And it was just an accident that I wasn't there that night."

"What do you mean?"

A fat-bellied spider scurried between his feet, but Mason didn't seem to notice. "Most nights last summer I crashed in Glen City, but I was supposed to come home on the night of the fire. I'd been seeing signs for weeks—lights floating in the trees, black birds on the windowsill. I saw the skeleton of a vulture on a boulder by the work site, laid out like he'd been crucified, and I ended up getting a six-pack and sleeping in my truck. It was a mistake—I should have come home. I wasn't supposed to live through that fire."

I started to nod again but stopped myself in time. Mason and I both knew that Swan River was a town written in a dark language, incomprehensible to strangers. We were both used to living with chaos, fearing it, anticipating it; after all, he wasn't the only one whose sister had become a wild girl. But there was a difference between dreading the mad violence that threatened us and believing that you should already be dead.

"I'm sure Crystal wouldn't have wanted to hurt you," I said. "I'm sure she'd be glad you didn't come home."

Mason kept his eyes on the floor. "I'm not talking about what she would have wanted. I'm talking about what I deserve."

I waited, but he was silent. "I think you spend too much time by yourself," I said, pulling at a loose thread at the cuff of my uniform blouse. "You really should think about applying to MCC. Isn't there something you'd like to study?"

"Such as what, for instance?"

"*I* don't know." I picked a book off the top of the stack by the bed. It was a biography of someone I'd never heard of. "Isn't there something you're interested in? You've got all these books on history. Maybe you could be a teacher."

Though his face was still set to its expression of careful blankness, I could tell he was listening. "I thought about joining the military," he said. "But most people sign up right out of high school."

"You don't have to do that," I said. "That's what I'm saying. People who join the military, it's because they don't have other options."

"You think I have options?"

"You're smart. Smart people always have options."

He stared at his folded hands, and I began to doubt the truth of what I'd said. It was what I'd been taught, certainly—by my mom and my teachers at the Academy, even by Travis. If you were smart and worked hard, you could make your own destiny. But how many people could I actually think of who had started at a disadvantage and worked their way to success? It wasn't just the former wild girls who were stuck here, treading water in Swan River. "Well, you could at least try," I said. "I can get you an application the next time we're in Moorefield."

"You go to Moorefield? Like all the time?"

"It's not a big deal. It's not that much farther than Glen City."

I was looking down, wondering if it would be disloyal to Willow to suggest that Mason and I could go to Moorefield together, and so I didn't see him stand up and cross the room.

Without warning his arms were on either side of me, hands braced on the edge of the bed. A two-day's beard covered his cheeks, and he smelled of cigarettes and cedarwood. "Are you trying to save me?" he asked.

"I don't think so," I said. It had never occurred to me to try to save him. I was too busy trying to save myself.

The kiss when it came was fast and sweet, like the headache-rush of a cold drink gulped too quick. Easing down beside me, Mason wound a strand of my hair around his finger and tugged, and I felt a jolt of longing so exquisitely sharp that it brought tears to my eyes. I hadn't thought kissing would be like this—it seemed like such a simple thing, lips pressed to lips.

Suddenly he pulled away and rapped at the window screen. Gasping, I looked just in time to see a gray dog slinking off into the underbrush. My skin felt hot from beard friction. "Christ's sake," Mason murmured, kissing the side of my neck.

He was fingering the top button of my blouse, but I put my hands on his chest and pushed him away. If the longing could hit me this hard just from kissing, who could say that going further wouldn't burn me up entirely? And what about Willow? She was my friend, and every minute I spent here was a betrayal. "I can't," I said. "I just— This isn't a good idea."

I turned to fix my blouse and pull my hair into a braid, and when I looked again he was back in his chair—smiling, easy, as if he didn't care one way or another. In spite of myself, I felt sort of insulted.

I was the one who suggested going down to Mrs. Lemons's trailer that day. When Mason asked why, I told him that I wanted to take a walk, but that wasn't the real reason. I didn't want to sit there and be reminded that kissing me was just a diversion for him, a time waster.

Bushwhacking down the trail grown over with underbrush and brambles, Mason asked me question after question about how you applied to college and what you did when you got there. As I recited everything I knew about SATs, and course catalogs, and renting apartments, I began to feel sort of smug. If Mason liked Willow better, that was nothing but what I'd expected, but at least I knew more than he did about almost everything. We groped our way carefully around the rim of the open cave, where he paused, his chest moving with his breath. I felt my pulse speed up. It would be so easy to take a wrong step and stumble through that screen of branches.

"I brought Willow down here once," he said. "Not to see my mom—she just wanted to come back to the cave, because it was the place where we met. We were standing right where you and I are now, and all of a sudden she dropped down, crawled to the side of the cave, and started shouting, waiting for an echo."

"She did?" This sort of spontaneity, not to mention the carelessness about her clothes, didn't really sound like Willow. But maybe she was different when she and Mason were alone. "Did it work?"

He shook his head. "It's like screaming into a blanket—your voice just sounds muffled."

I started to say something about acoustics, but Mason held up a hand, looking tense. "What is it?" I asked.

"Nothing," he said. "I just thought—" Before he could finish, the trailer door swung open and Mrs. Lemons squinted down at us, swaying a little from side to side.

But this wasn't the Mrs. Lemons of three years ago, not the tall, commanding woman with the china-pale skin, a royal visitor from some icebound northern city. This Mrs. Lemons was a bundle of sticks, an outline of a body draped in a dirty white robe. Her long breasts moved loosely under the linen. "Well, look who it is," she said. "Y'all want a drink?" Her face was blurry, and it seemed as if it took an effort to keep her eyes open and to make her mouth move in a normal way. Her stringy blonde hair looked like it hadn't been washed in days.

She let the door open all the way, and I saw the Birdman sitting in the ratty armchair under the mounted head of the yellow dog. He had a jar of clear liquid on his knee. The alcohol smell was stronger now, as if the room were exhaling. It came from Mrs. Lemons too, metabolized by her body into a reeking sweat that turned my stomach. "I haven't seen you down here for a while," she said to Mason. "Days, maybe." Her breath hit my face, and I took a step backward, stumbling into a waist-high patch of poke-weed.

I had drawn her attention; she was glaring at me now, moving her head from side to side. "Who is she?" she asked, and the contempt in her voice would have made me step back again if there had been anywhere to go.

"This is Kate," Mason said. "You know her. Her mother—"

"Shut up, of course I know her," Mrs. Lemons snapped, but I wasn't sure. She kept moving her head, like a fighter trying to avoid a blow. "How is your *mother*?" she said to me, as if there were something funny about the word.

"She's fine."

"Good children are a blessing." Her words were running together. "My daughter's dead, but my baby here—he brings me food, cleans up for me. He's my angel."

Mason's head was tilted back, the tendons in his neck tight as if someone had pressed the tip of a knife against his chin. "All right," he said. "Mom, you go to bed. I'll come by later. Now I have to take Kate home."

Mrs. Lemons smiled, revealing black holes where her molars should have been. "I like her better than that other girl," she said. "That other one's no good for you." For a second her eyes seemed to clear, and she stared at her son as if she despaired of saying everything she meant.

We walked to the El Camino in silence and jostled up the rutted track in silence. Lost in thought, I didn't notice at first that he'd turned right instead of left. We were headed north, farther down Bloodwort Road than I'd ever been, so far that we'd already passed the turnoff for the Academy bunkhouse. With every mile the sky became gloomier, the hedges at the side of the road more thick and tangled, and I envisioned the road closing in on us. The underbrush would squeeze tighter and tighter until the car stuttered and died and we were stuck, pressed together as the windows groaned. Maybe this was what happened to the cars I'd seen at the car graveyard, every one of them crushed, pulped like a fruit.

"Is she always like that?" I asked.

Mason took a long time to answer. "No," he said finally. "Not always. This was a bad day."

I lost track of how many turns we took. How many caved-in shacks and trailers we passed, how many utility poles pulled down and scavenged for copper wire. Where we ended up was a trailhead parking lot, a faded hiking map nailed to the post at the start of the trail. My heart beat hard against my ribs. As far as I knew, there was only one reason why Swan River teenagers ever came to the trailheads along Bloodwort Road.

"I'm sorry about that," Mason said, staring straight ahead. "I mean I'm sorry you had to see it."

I told him it didn't matter, but the truth was that I did feel sort of depressed. Mrs. Lemons had been so different three years ago, when Willow and I had broken into the trailer at the summer festival. I could still feel the firm grip of her hand on my wrist, hear the confidence in her voice as she told me that my life would be different from what I'd dreaded. But how could I trust that drunken, lonely old woman raving in the wrecked trailer? How could I believe that she had any powers at all?

"Umm, I hope this isn't too personal a question," I said. "But where was your mom during the fire? Because she can predict the future, right? Why didn't she know that Crystal was becoming a wild girl?"

Mason rubbed his hands over his face. When he lowered them, something about his expression reminded me of Travis when he'd come back from the destruction at Bloodwort Farm. Mason might not have been there for the fire, but he knew things—things that I wasn't sure I wanted to know.

"My mom slept through it, believe it or not," he said. "They'd been on a bender for a few days, and she was passed out pretty good. To this day, I don't know if she understands what Rondal did to Crystal."

"Rondal," I repeated. It seemed strange to think of him as anything but the Birdman. "What did he do?" I asked, but before the words were out of my mouth, I understood. The way he had talked to Crystal, his voice low as a whisper and sickly sweet. The way he had touched her—the sure, hard hand on the small of her back. "Oh," I said. "Oh. So when he took her away from the cave, he was— Did you and Clancy know?"

"No," Mason said immediately. "I should have known. I should have seen it. She was always over at his cabin, always sitting next to him at the bonfires. If anybody tried to talk to my mom about it, she'd say Rondal was the father Crystal never had." He pressed the heels of his hands against his forehead, and for a shocked moment I wondered if he was trying not to cry. "My mom barely even saw me and my sister back then, because she was all caught up with David Bell. And then when he stopped coming around, that was when she started drinking pretty hard."

I remembered Dr. Bell squatting beside the Birdman as we looked down from the hill, Dr. Bell disappearing up the ridge as the Roman candles smoked and sparked. "Was he sleeping with your mom or something?"

"I don't think anything ever happened, but he knew that she had a thing for him, and he used it. He was always coming by to ask her about different plants and herbs—what does this one do, what does that one do. He was real interested in bloodwort, does it have any special properties, stuff like that."

"Dr. Bell was interested in bloodwort?" I repeated. The herb grew everywhere in Swan River, flowering in ditches and back-yards and on timber-stripped hills; I had seen it all my life without ever giving it much thought. "What did your mom tell him?"

Mason gave me an impatient look. "The leaves can cause hal-lucinations," he said. "And some people use it as an emetic." His accent was coming out again, that familiar twang inflecting the word *properties*, the word *leaves*.

"An emetic," I said. "Gross."

Mason picked up my hand and forced it open, pressing our

palms together and intertwining his fingers with mine. "I'm telling you about my family because I really like you. We're the same in a lot of ways. But there's somebody that I——" He sighed. "I mean, at the cabin, I shouldn't have——"

"It's okay," I said. "I understand." A lock of hair fell onto his forehead, and I resisted the urge to brush it back again.

"She's not like anybody else," he said.

"So you're saying that things are good between you guys?"

"What do you mean?"

There was no way out of it now. "Her parents," I said. "I just didn't think they'd like it—like *you*, I guess. And your mother doesn't seem to like Willow too much either."

Mason gave me a look, and I didn't need a symbol key to know how to interpret it. I had seen his mom. Who in their right mind would take dating advice from Mrs. Lemons? "Jesus," he said, letting his head fall back against the seat. "Willow's the only thing I'm sure about these days."

"That's good," I said—polite, neutral. It shouldn't have been a surprise to me that Mason saw Willow as special, extraordinary, rarefied; I thought of her that way myself. The two of them fit together, and who was I to stand in the way? Still, Mrs. Lemons's words repeated themselves in my brain: *That other one's no good for you.*

We didn't stay much longer at the trailhead. Mason drove me back to the dorm, and then I didn't talk to him for almost three weeks. I stopped eating hot food in the dining hall and lived on frozen yogurt and deli sandwiches. I stopped going up to the abandoned house with Willow on Fridays, and she never said anything about it. Most of the time, I was too busy to wonder what was going on with the two of them. I had bumped my running up to three miles four times a week, and that was just enough to take me down the fire road to the crumbling shell of the Bloodwort mill. Mr. High-tower's class had given me an eye for birds and plants that I would have overlooked before, but agaric mushrooms and red-tailed hawks weren't the only things I was noticing these days. In the woods, I kept an eye out for configurations of sun and shadow that Mason might have interpreted as signs. It was tempting to read the squirrel guts strung along the gravel as an ominous token, but I had no crafty grandmother to train me in the symbology of disaster, no guide in these matters beyond the anxious pounding of my heart.

I sent off my application for the Pritchard scholarship on the day of the postmark deadline, and then there were tests to study for, papers to write. Thanksgiving was coming up and with it the Senior Party, to be held at Frances's vacation house on the last night of the break. When Tessa came around soliciting donations, I gave her twenty dollars that I'd been saving for new running shoes just to keep her from sneering at me.

Tessa had clearly come from the stables, and still wore her riding outfit of jodhpurs and a crisp white button-down shirt. "So," she said, leaning against my doorframe. "Have you seen Willow today? I can't find her anywhere, but I guess she's probably out with her boyfriend."

I shrugged. Lately I went days without seeing Willow, and I was certain that Tessa knew it. "Is he her boyfriend now?" I asked.

Tessa gave me a pitying look, as if she couldn't believe how easy I was to see through. For a moment I wondered if she was trying to make common cause by pointing out that Willow had screwed us both, taking Tessa's position as queen of Swan River Academy, taking the boy I hadn't known I wanted until it was too late. "I'm not sure what they're up to," she said, unrolling the stiff edge of her right cuff. "Probably drinking moonshine and shoot-ing rats in the dump. Isn't that what y'all do for fun around here?"

"Pretty much," I agreed. "When we're not eating roadkill and having sex with our cousins."

Tessa laughed, showing her big square teeth. Horse-Face, I thought, without animosity. Though she would have been horri-fied to hear it, I felt sorry for Tessa sometimes. The ground had shifted beneath her, whether she knew it or not.

CHAPTER EIGHT

As Caroline kept reminding me, one of the things I had to do before the break was decide on a research topic for Myths and Mysteries. We were supposed to pick a theme that showed up in myths across cultures and talk about what its recurrence said about the human subconscious. Caroline was doing wild women, naturally. I had read her précis, which mentioned the *Wilde Frauen* in Germany, the wilis in *Giselle*, and of course the Dionysian revelers of Euripides, tearing and rending in the service of their god. To me the Swan River wild girls lurked behind every sentence, distorted faces peeking between the letters like gargoyles on a cathedral ceiling.

As the wind turned cold and gray and the leaves fell faster, I knew I was running out of time. The thing was, I just wasn't interested in metaphorical interpretations of the supernatural. I didn't care what the belief in witches and gods said about our most primitive selves. How could we be sure that, when the Greeks talked about water spirits or horses with the heads of men, they hadn't actually seen those things? Perhaps they were just as real as the creatures that cursed my hometown. Perhaps in other towns like Swan River, the witches, banshees, goblins, and satyrs had been biding their time, hiding in shadows. The more I thought about the project, the more I resented the whole idea, but I couldn't talk to Dr. Bell about it. When possible, I tried not to talk to Dr. Bell about anything at all.

Out of class it was easy enough to avoid him, since I was not one of his favorites. I was never invited to the Tuesday night tutorials that Elise and Lucie had told me about the day we went to Moorefield. They said that Dr. Bell's office was like an archaeological museum crossed with the Playboy Mansion, all red drapery and objets d'art and plush Oriental rugs. They said that he played opera on the stereo and served shortbread cookies and a smoky tea with the flavor of orange peels. All of that sounded sort of entertaining, but when Caroline offered to get me in, I had two good reasons for saying no. The one I admitted to was that I had enough of Dr. Bell's monologues in class. If listening to him on a daily basis didn't inspire me with great ideas, why would red curtains and shortbread make any difference?

Beyond this, I knew that Dr. Bell was connected to the dark side of Swan River in some way I didn't fully understand. When he lectured, especially about the Greek gods and the frenzy they inspired in their worshipers, his voice took on an unpleasant richness, as if he'd eaten something delicious and wanted to lick his fingers. He was definitely a strange guy, but his creepiness was not, as the minions believed, merely a taste for underage girls. If he had been that kind of weirdo, he would have been a whole lot easier to figure out.

I didn't believe the rumors, but without them I might never have found my research topic. It was early November, and a layer of mist like cotton wool hung motionless over the river. Dr. Bell was lecturing on Hesiod and had gone off on a tangent about Persephone's abduction by Hades. He was talking about how captivating Persephone must have been, how the earth itself had mourned her absence, when Rosa raised her hand.

A charter member of the minions, Rosa was blond and cover-model pretty, with huge blue eyes and teeth that made you contemplate the miracles of modern orthodontia. She was rich, of course; everyone knew she had an elevator in her house, and a Porsche in her name that her parents were keeping for her until she turned eighteen. Like the rest of Willow's friends, Rosa didn't exactly brag about her money, but she dropped references to the Jacuzzi in her bathroom and the trips to Mustique often enough that you got the message. I had come to like the other minions, but it was hard for me to see any depth in Rosa, who sometimes paused her step aerobics videos to check out her own butt in the mirror.

"So why doesn't Persephone get to decide for herself?" Rosa asked. "I know her mom wants her back on the surface and the dead guy wants her with him, but nobody ever asks her what *she* wants."

It was a surprisingly good question, but Dr. Bell didn't seem impressed. "To be frank," he said, "I don't think it's particularly helpful to imagine a Persephone with a will of her own. She had been overwhelmed by the god, subsumed into him. That dark descent to Hades's kingdom, it must have been . . ."

The pause went on so long that people started to giggle. Dr. Bell's gaze had dropped from the ceiling to Rosa—specifically, to her long brown legs sticking out into the aisle between desks. There was a lot to look at. Rosa disdained the regulation kneesocks, shortened her uniform skirts a good two inches above the length stipulated in the handbook, and wore platform shoes that made her look about eight feet long from hip to ankle.

Rosa's cheeks turned pink, but she didn't seem embarrassed. That was the difference between Dr. Bell, with his aging handsome face, and old Mr. Wakefield in the Math Department, who had been accused of pretending to drop his ruler so he could peer under skirts. A lot of girls didn't seem to mind the idea of Dr. Bell looking at them in that way. They had spent nearly four years at boarding school, and at this point inappropriate attention was better than no attention at all. "It must have been?" Rosa prompted gently, with a pretense of naïveté that only spurred the giggling. "You were saying?"

"I—um, excuse me," Dr. Bell said, switching his gaze to the windows as he rubbed at the skin between his eyebrows. "Well, we can't say what it must have been, can we? At the gate of the mystery, language fails us."

It was the end of the hour and most of the class was already packing up, smirking as they slid notebooks into their backpacks. I knew how this story would be told back in the dorms: in the middle of mythology class, Dr. Bell had been so stricken with lust for Rosa Slater that he'd been unable to finish his sentence. For one of our own to provoke such a response was both hilarious and gratifying.

But I had my own interpretation of what had happened in Myths and Mysteries. I'd had a good angle on the side of Dr. Bell's face, and from my perspective it looked like he had checked out completely. It seemed that he wasn't really seeing Rosa's legs, much less salivating over them. His brows were ruffled, his eyes bright but unfocused. He was imagining the Underworld, and I wondered, if when he thought about Persephone's fall from daylight into darkness, he pictured the same thing that I did.

Sophomore year, when Caroline had asked me to tell her what I knew about the wild girls, I'd described to her the cave at the commune. I'd told her about the laurel and bloodwort growing over the rim, and the cold black hole in the center, and the smell that rose from it, like sulfur and moving water. Caroline had listened with breathless attention, her round glasses slipping down to the end of her nose. "It sounds like a portal," she said. "Don't you think?"

"I don't know what that is." The word *portal* sounded nerdy and science fictiony, like a time warp or a wormhole.

Caroline pulled a photo album out from under her bed and showed me a picture of a cave she'd seen on a trip to Greece. It didn't look like much, just an arch of stones and a tunnel leading into a hillside, but she said that it had been a holy site in ancient times. "They believed that the tunnel led down to the Underworld," she said. "And there must be others, don't you think? There's no reason why they would just be in Greece."

She snapped through the album, barely missing my fingertips. On the final page, she had tucked a *Riparian* clipping from June 1, 1978, into the plastic sleeve. It was an op-ed from Reverend Barnett Lipscomb of the Faithful Providence Tabernacle Church, who seemed to agree with Caroline that Swan River was a place where the boundary between our world and the other world stretched thin. According to Reverend Lipscomb, emanations from the fiery pit rose through the surface of the earth, infecting the town's susceptible young women. He never directly mentioned the wild girls, and to someone who didn't know the history of our town, the piece would have seemed a mishmash of Revelations and vague millennial terrors. I had never seen the Faithful Providence Tabernacle Church, but I knew that there were plenty of congregations like it back in the mountains. They popped up like toadstools after a long rain, strung a bunch of religious-sounding words together and set themselves to a rolling and shaking, a bustling and humming and speaking in tongues that threatened to lift the roofs off their one-

room churches. These were people who gave away their possessions every time some televangelist declared the end of days, and
I had no trouble believing that they worked themselves into a fit
when a wild girl swooped down on the county.

I handed the clipping back to Caroline. "I don't understand
why this stuff makes you so happy. He's saying that my hometown
is the gateway to Hell, basically."

"The Underworld doesn't have to be Hell," Caroline said
impatiently. "The Greeks didn't think of it that way. To them it
was just the other world, the lower world. Usually the only time
you get anywhere close to the lower world is when you're dead,
but here, the border is a little bit thinner."

I shrugged. I couldn't understand how Caroline could talk this
way, with such enthusiastic curiosity—as if the land of the dead
were a national park, and Swan River the town outside the gates
that sold maps and souvenirs.

I hadn't thought about that conversation since, but after Dr.
Bell went into a fugue state thinking about Persephone, it came
back to me. What if Caroline and the Reverend Barnett Lipscomb
were right? What if Swan River really was a gateway between one
world and the next? What if we were all subject to what the reverend called emanations, and the girls who went wild were just the
most vulnerable among us?

Practically this new theory didn't make the slightest difference to my life, but I welcomed any distraction from my daily
speculation about Mason and Willow and whether such a mismatched couple could stay together in the long run. I decided that
I would write my research paper on the idea of the Underworld. I
would talk about the Egyptians, the Celts, the Native Americans.
I would discuss cities piled on cities until the lower strata disappeared into myth. I had no idea how I would tie all these things

together or what they could possibly have to say about the human subconscious, but I wouldn't have to worry about the conclusion for a few months at least.

On the day I went over to my mom's office, I was hoping not to see Dr. Bell, and not only for the obvious reasons. I disapproved of him in general, but he had never been creepy to me personally; in fact, when he noticed me at all, he tended to treat me like a little kid. When I talked to my mom at her desk, he sometimes came out of his office to make a jokey comment about how much I must like the new Peebles Library, with its glass atrium and five floors of books. It seemed that the one thing he remembered about me was how, on the night that Maggie became a wild girl, I had seemed more concerned about the fire among the stacks than I was about my sister.

My mom called her space in the administration building an office, but it was really just the hallway outside Dr. Bell's door, and I thought that, if I'd been him, I would have found her an empty room just to rid the hall of her clutter. A pair of galoshes stuck out from under her desk like the witch's feet in *The Wizard of Oz*. Paper from the filing cabinets drifted to the floor whenever the door opened, and the desk itself was crowded with every useless thing you could think of—a windup toy shaped like a duck, a calendar from the last decade, a World's Greatest Mom trophy that Maggie and I had given her a million years ago. Since Mason had pointed it out to me, I'd come to notice that Swan River was full of random junk. There was the commune, the River House Coffeeshop, the car graveyard with its heaps of twisted metal. Sometimes I felt the urge to clean it up, clean it all up, just scour the town from top to bottom.

I could tell right away that Mom was in a bad mood. "If you're here about those fees for your college applications, you're going to have to wait," she said, irritably twitching the knob of her Rolodex. "I told you that I can't send them out until I get paid."

"That's okay." I cleared a file box from the nearest chair and sat down. "The next one's not due until the twenty-seventh. Are you mad at me about something?"

This was always an effective strategy. When she realized that she was taking her mood out on her children, Mom could change from mean to remorseful in the blink of an eye. "Honey, no," she said, pinching the deep wrinkle on her forehead between thumb and forefinger. "I just have a lot on my mind right now."

"Like what?" I still had ten minutes before my next class, so I could afford to act at least a little bit interested.

Mom opened her mouth and closed it again. "It's Travis," she said. "He wants to buy a truck. And not just any truck—one of those huge F-150s that look like they could mount an army. He went up to the dealer in Glen City twice and didn't even tell me."

"Why does he need a truck? He drives the patrol car."

She shrugged. "He says he can afford the money down out of his savings, but I don't know how he expects to manage the payments." She shook her head, her graying ponytail swinging over her shoulder, and I understood why Willow kept bugging me to cut my hair. Mom's was brittle and rough, like an old rope. She was only thirty-nine, which wasn't that old as moms went, but she could have passed for fifty. "Sometimes I wonder why I bother," she said. "It's like having another child in the house."

"You're not thinking of breaking up, are you?" Just the thought of it made my stomach twist with anxiety. Even before I'd seen what had happened with Mason, I'd known that single mothers were not a good thing. The ones who sent their children to the Academy were not as nutty as Mrs. Lemons, but their dependence was almost as frightening. They showed up unexpectedly to take their daughters shopping. They called several times a week, sometimes after a glass or two of wine, wanting to talk about their problems at work or the men who didn't want to marry them. They told stories about their sex lives. They were lonely, and that loneliness could be a greater burden than any angst or worry of your own. It would be the worst luck in the world if just as I was poised to leave Swan River, my mom became one of those clinging mothers.

My alarm must have been obvious, because Mom reached across the desk to pat my hand. "You don't need to worry about me and Travis," she said. "Anyway, what's going on with you?"

A good daughter wouldn't have let her change the subject so quickly, but I was running out of time. "So as you know," I said, leaning forward in my chair, "it's Thanksgiving break next week. And the second Saturday is the Senior Party. And I was wondering if I could go this year."

Mom made a face, which I'd anticipated. In a school where there seemed to be a ritual for everything, from how to walk into the chapel to how to roll your kneesocks, the Senior Party was the tradition that all the adults wished would go away. Academy girls usually didn't have many choices as far as boyfriends went, but for the party, boys came out of the woodwork—college boys mostly, brothers and cousins down from Charlottesville, Chapel Hill, Sewanee. It was a bacchanal for real, even without wild girls.

I'd never gone to the Senior Party, and it wasn't just because I'd never been a senior. You could go as an underclassman, as long as you knew a senior who was willing to give you a ride and assure the others that you wouldn't give yourself alcohol poisoning. But Maggie had dropped out of school before Thanksgiving of her senior year, and I hadn't known any other seniors well enough to ask them to sponsor me. There was also the fact that my mom knew more about what went on at those parties than other parents did. Her usual policy with things she didn't approve of was to pretend they weren't happening, but she was about as likely to let me go to a party where she knew there would be alcohol as she was to pay for a tattoo.

"Whose parents are renting the house this year?" she asked.

"Frances Ortega's family owns a cabin across the river. I'm pretty sure her dad's an upstanding citizen."

"Well, an upstanding citizen ought to know that you can get arrested for serving alcohol to minors."

I decided not to point out that the only people with the jurisdiction to arrest him were Travis and Sheriff McClellan, and they tended to stay away from the Senior Party. "I don't have to drink," I said. "It's not like somebody meets you at the door and forces a beer down your throat. I can just say no."

Mom picked up her stress ball and squeezed it in her fist. "You can go to parties in college. What's the point of driving out in the middle of nowhere just to hang out with a bunch of people you don't even like?"

"But I *do* like them," I said. "Even Caroline's going this year. She told her parents all about it, and they said it was fine because they knew that she would be responsible and make good choices." This was entirely made up—Caroline was going to Scotland for Thanksgiving break.

Mom shook her head. "Maybe I was wrong," she said, "but I always thought you had your eye on bigger things. With your sister, I could tell her high school doesn't last forever, but it was like she didn't know what I was talking about. She couldn't imagine a life beyond what was happening right then, but you could. You wanted things, and I thought that was your best chance of getting out of here."

The calm intensity of her gaze made my heart pound. "I *do* want things. I'm not dropping out of high school. We're just talking about a party, Mom."

Down the hall, Señora Nichols stepped out of the faculty lounge, her gray-black bun sticking up like an ugly hat on the back of her head. The señora taught Spanish and Italian, and was known for turning students in to the disciplinary board for the most minor of infractions—having more than two piercings in their ears, chewing gum in class. She did the same to the staff, reporting them to Dr. Bell for taking too many breaks or smoking behind the post office, and I was sure that she was wondering whether the terms of my mom's contract allowed her to talk to her daughter during work hours.

I stuck out my tongue at the señora's backside as she waddled toward the door. Normally it would have made Mom laugh, but this time I got no reaction at all. She had already turned back to her computer, barely visible behind the fluttering semaphore of old Post-its. "So go to the party if that's what you want."

"That's it?" The stress ball had rolled to the edge of the desk, and I picked it up and pressed it flat between my hands. "First you act like just walking through the door is going to make me a dumb drunk loser, and now you don't care?"

"What do you want from me?" she asked, tired eyes trained on the screen. "You asked me if you could go, and I'm saying go ahead."

"Fine," I said. "I will."

I'm not as harmless as you think I am! I wanted to shout. *I've kissed Mason Lemons! I've drunk strawberry wine in his El Camino, and if you weren't so distracted and tired all the time, you would have noticed that I'm not a kid anymore!* Instead, on my way out, I kicked at one of the stone columns under the archway, and kept kicking until I bruised my toe.

CHAPTER NINE

There were a lot of red sunsets over Thanksgiving break. Every night after dinner I went up to my room and stood by the window, always hoping to catch the moment when the sun sank below the mountains and made it look, for a split second, as if the tops of the trees were on fire. At first the sky was separated into layers—blood red, ketchup red, nail polish red—but as I watched, they blended into a uniform shade that reminded me of the sports car Travis had wanted to buy the summer I turned eleven. It was electric red, brazen, high-octane red. It was like the sky was announcing something, and night after night I tried to read its meaning.

On the night of the Senior Party, I drove Maggie's van over the bridge to the subdivision, called Elysian Acres, where Frances's family had their vacation cabin. The land was flat here, curving toward and away from the river still pulsing with the red heat of the sky. The cabin was one of a handful at the end of the road, each secluded on its own jewel-bright patch of lawn. Most were uninhabited this late in the year, and walking among them was like touring a millionaires' graveyard. They were built of wide pine logs, stained honey-colored and coated with a varnish so shiny it looked wet. Expensive grills sat unsecured on screen porches. It seemed so safe here, so normal and quiet, that I could hardly believe we were only twenty minutes from Bloodwort Road.

I found Willow in the master bedroom. Still in her bathrobe, she was painting her toenails on the white duvet. She was spending the night at the cabin, with Frances and some of the other minions. I probably could have wangled an invitation if I'd hinted, but I knew that that would be pushing my mom too far.

As I stood in the doorway, Willow paused to study me, the brush poised in her hand. "You're wearing jeans," she said. A drop of Passion Purple splatted on the bedspread, and she smeared it in with the side of her thumb.

I looked down at my right knee, with the hole that I'd enlarged with the tip of a pen because I thought it added character. "I almost wore khakis. But I didn't have time to iron them, so—"

Willow shook her head decisively. "Everybody's dressing up."

At the closet, she threw open the doors to reveal row upon row of dresses—short red sundresses with spaghetti straps, long black dresses with plunging necklines, and one weird green satin thing that looked like a reject from some nightmare prom. On the floor were dozens of shoes, in every shade and finish you could imagine. "Jesus, Willow," I said. "How do you fit all this stuff in your closet at school?"

She made a goofy face, as if I'd said something both funny and pitiable. "They're not *all* mine, silly. We decided to hang everything up together so we could pick and choose. Obviously no one can wear Lucie's because she's so tiny, and Rosa has those boobs, but other than that we're all more or less the same size."

I ran my finger along the line of dresses, making them sway on their hangers. "I'm thinking something short," Willow said. "With heels, so you can show off your legs."

After wavering between a black satin sheath and a navy blue cotton A-line, I settled on the A-line as less conspicuous. It was almost as short as Willow wanted it to be, with long sleeves and a deep V-neck embroidered with oversize daisies. It belonged to Matilda Peebles, and when I insisted, Willow went out to the living room to ask her if it was okay for me to borrow it. I stood in front of the three-way mirror, examining myself from every angle. Even without makeup, I didn't look half-bad.

"Matilda says it's fine," Willow said, standing beside me. "She doesn't have the figure for it anyway. I can do your hair if you want."

I smiled at my reflection. I had never cared about clothes, but I could see that just by pulling this piece of fabric over my head I had become older, slimmer, altogether prettier. In this dress I could walk into the tearoom at the Grand Hotel in Moorefield and no one would think twice about whether I was supposed to be there. But my hair didn't match; it was poor-girl hair—lank and dry, unstyled. "Oh, why don't you just cut it off?"

Willow had been winding the sash of her bathrobe around her finger, but now her hand stilled. "Are you serious?"

"That was the deal, right? If I hooked you up with Mason, you'd cut my hair?" As I fingered the heavy braid in the mirror, my heart gave a giant thump, and for a moment I didn't think I could go through with it.

She made me sit on an extralarge towel with another draped around my shoulders. "These aren't great scissors, but they're all I could find," she said, clacking the blades close to my ear. "At home I have a couple of those little tiny pairs, but I was afraid that, if I brought them to school, everyone would ask me to do their hair for free."

"Do you want me to pay you?"

"Shut up."

A soft chunk of brown curls hit the towel, and I looked up just in time to see another piece shear off. I couldn't decide if the feeling in my stomach was excitement or nausea. I had my hair cut at the JCPenney's in Moorefield once a year. Between cuts, I trimmed the split ends with nail scissors. I hadn't worn it shorter than my elbows since age seven, when a boy named Lester Neets stuck a wad of Juicy Fruit on the back of my head in the lunch line. "You know, when I said cut it all off, I didn't mean it literally," I said. "I don't want to be bald or—"

"Look, you have to trust me." The scissors snip-snipped, creating a feathery fringe that swung lightly against the side of my neck, and I decided to close my eyes. "I *am* really good at this," Willow said, looping up one section to hold at the crown of my head while she cut underneath. "Maybe I should go to cosmetology school."

"You can do better than cosmetology school."

"Well, I know I can. The question is, why should I have to? The question is, should I do what other people expect of me or what *I* want to do?"

I started to remind her that I had made this same point before, but Willow talked over me. "It's not like my parents really care. It's not like they're worried about me wasting my potential. It's just that my dad wants to be able to say, *Oh, my daughter, she goes to blah blah blah, she spent the summer doing this and that*—it's another way of bragging about himself."

She blew a stray hair off my neck. A car pulled up outside the bedroom window, and by the time I realized that the engine was too quiet to belong to the El Camino, I'd already convinced myself it was Mason. What if they actually stayed together? I wondered. What if they ended up being one of those couples that went to college together, and rented an apartment together, and stayed smugly content while their friends went through one bad relationship after another? Willow had picked an interesting moment to rebel against parental pressure, just in time to seal the deal with the only guy I'd ever really liked.

"God's sake," said a boy's voice behind me. "Is she a yeti or something? Look at all that hair." I jumped, and the scissors scraped a clean line across the skin of my throat.

"Henry," Willow said, in that singsong voice that girls use when they want to pretend they're mad. "You can't just bust in like that. I'm in my bathrobe."

Henry, whoever he was, lounged in the doorway, hands in his pockets. I knew right away that he had to be the brother of an Academy girl, and not just because I didn't recognize him as a local. The grin, the sandy hair flopping on his forehead, the fine wool sweater with the monogram on the breast all gave him away. On his feet he wore green flip-flops that were intended, I guessed, to show that he was an individual in spite of his cookie-cutter preppiness. He seemed just as cocky as Mason, though with a different brand of arrogance.

Henry bit his lip, looking Willow up and down. "I'm going to give you ten minutes, and then I'm going to drag you out of here," he said. "I'm not afraid of the yeti." His eyes slid to mine in the mirror, and he winked broadly before the door slammed shut.

"That was Elise's brother," Willow said. "He drove down with a bunch of guys from UNC. Tessa thinks he's hot, but he can be kind of a pain in the ass sometimes."

Careful not to dump my yeti hair on the floor, I stood up and leaned into the mirror. The scissors had made a white mark, slicing right across what I was pretty sure was my jugular.

"I'm sorry about your neck," Willow said. "It's Henry's fault."

"It's okay. I don't think it broke the skin."

She patted the top of my head. "Oh, I've been meaning to tell you. Remember when we talked about how you needed a car for college? I talked to my dad over Thanksgiving, and they are going to give me a new one for my birthday. So you can have Jean-Luc if you want."

"Maybe." I avoided her eyes. "It depends on how much you're asking." As I turned for a closer look at my neck, a dotted line of blood welled up, beading the white with red.

For the first few hours, I thought that the Senior Party might turn out to be the best night of my life. Girls kept pulling me into corners, running their fingers through my hair's new layers. These compliments were really for Willow, not for me, but I basked in them anyway. Though I knew that I shouldn't, I found myself thinking of Mason, imagining how he would check me out from new hair to new shoes.

The crowd swelled and spilled into the kitchen. Lucie Yates put a beer in my hand, but I set it down after a few sips. I could feel that something in the mood of the party had shifted, and I wanted to stay on top of it. Bodies crushed me against the wall between the living room and the bathroom. Matilda Peebles was kissing some boy wearing a tennis visor, mashing her face into his with a pressure that was almost violent. My breath raced with panic. I wanted to sit down and put my head between my knees, but suddenly Frances Ortega grabbed my wrists and tried to tow me toward the door.

"Come on," she shouted. "We're going swimming in the river!"

"I don't want to swim," I shouted back, but Frances was stronger and she kept tugging. She was wearing a black bathrobe, and her face was loose and shiny and too close, like a reflection in a fun-house mirror. At the door I finally broke free, pulling with enough momentum to send her crashing backward into a standing lamp.

A few people laughed, and she glared at me as she rubbed her elbow. "You didn't have to push me."

"I didn't push you," I said. "I just don't want to go swimming."

"Your loss, man." As she smacked me on the shoulder, her face came too close again, and I smelled vodka and grape bubble gum. It took all my self-control not to push her for real this time.

When Frances was gone, I fought my way out to the pool and stood in the shadows of the cabana, sucking in lungfuls of air. Other people must have come out here to smoke at some point—butts of gold-filtered Sobranies were bobbing in the shallow end—but now the wind had a bite to it, and the patio was empty except for a couple huddled in deck chairs by the diving board. I pulled my hands into the cuffs of my dress and took a few more long breaths.

A girl rose from the deck chairs and took a step into the shadows. "Kate? Is that you?"

"Caroline?" I said. "What are you doing here? I thought you were in Scotland."

"I got back this afternoon. My mom felt a little nervous about me coming to the party, but we talked about it and she said she knew I'd be responsible." Drawing me into the light, she studied my face curiously. "Why are you laughing?"

"I'm not laughing," I lied. I couldn't explain to Caroline that her story matched perfectly with the one I'd invented. Of course her mom worried about a party where there would be drinking. Of course she put her trust in Caroline's good judgment. The other figure stood up from the deck chairs and moved toward us, into the light.

"This is Oliver Davis," Caroline said. "He goes to Chapel Hill."

Oliver Davis gave me his hand, and though this wasn't something that people our age did in my experience, I agreed to shake it. "Nice to meet you," I said, since that was what you were supposed to say when you shook hands. Oliver murmured that it was nice to meet me too. He was skinny-tall, with the coloring of an Irish setter and a tightness around his mouth that made me think he might be prone to hard judgments.

"We were just talking about Scotland," Caroline said. "Oliver spent last summer on the Isle of Skye, studying Scottish Gaelic."

I had never heard of the Isle of Skye, or Scottish Gaelic for that matter, but I nodded. From this side of the pool we had a prime view of the bow windows at the back of the house, and I was surprised to see Clancy shouldering his way through the crowd toward the kitchen, peering over heads as if he were looking for someone. I hadn't talked to him since the day I'd pulled Mason out of the basketball game.

Caroline reached over and touched my sleeve. "I like your dress," she said. "And your haircut. How was your break?"

"Fine, I guess. I saw a ruffed grouse one day. Maggie and her boyfriend made Thanksgiving dinner."

"They cooked a turkey and everything?"

"Yeah, but—" I looked for Clancy again, but couldn't find him. "It was kind of awful, actually. I mean, Maggie's not much of a cook."

"I had haggis for Thanksgiving," Caroline said.

I made a vomiting noise. Caroline always told me that I should broaden my tastes, but I hated any food that was slimy or had a weird texture or was associated with a bodily function. On Thai curry night in the dining hall, I ate peanut butter crackers out of the vending machine.

"It was good," Caroline said. "My mom and stepdad ordered roast duck, but I didn't see the point of pretending that we could have an authentic Thanksgiving in Edinburgh."

"They don't celebrate Thanksgiving in Scotland?" I said without thinking. Oliver Davis gave a small snort.

"Well, no." Caroline sounded so serious that I knew she was embarrassed for me. "The Pilgrims and Indians and everything, it's not really— Anyway, I don't understand why people get so grossed out about haggis. Sausage is way more disgusting."

I shrugged. On the other side of the windows, bodies were pressing against the glass, blocking out the light. Now that I was on the outside, the change in atmosphere that had seemed so threatening looked like excitement, a reckless energy that I could have been part of if I could have just let go for a while.

A couple came and leaned against the pane close to where I was sitting. I had been cold a minute ago, but now I flushed down to the soles of my feet. I knew that dress, a strapless sky blue silk that matched her new contacts. I knew that hair, the long red curls sticking to the glass. She had thrown her head back, laughing up at Elise's brother. *They're not kissing,* I told myself, *they're just talking.* But even as I watched, Henry Seidel slid his arm around her waist and brought his lips to hers. On the other side of the room, Tessa watched them in astonishment, and I guessed that she had finally clued in to the state of things. Quietly, subtly, without a whisper of open revolt, Willow had taken everything that was rightfully hers.

Caroline had noticed them too. "I saw that Mason guy a while ago," she said, with a weight to her words that made me pay attention. "He was kind of prowling around."

"Really?" I tried to tug at my braid, remembering too late that it was scattered over the bedroom floor. "When was that?"

Caroline tried to answer—I could see her lips moving, but her voice was drowned by the roar of an engine. It got louder and louder, and someone grabbed my hand and pulled me out of my chair just as Mason drove the El Camino onto the pool deck.

I think he meant to drive right through the living room windows, but that side of the deck was too narrow to maneuver, so he parked the car by the diving board, picked up a poolside chair and threw it through the window. Sheets of glass crashed down, making a noise like a piano lid slamming only ten times louder. By then, everyone inside the house had scattered. Through the holes in the windows I could see frightened heads poking up from behind kitchen counters, but nobody stepped forward either to fight Mason or to try to talk him down. I kept waiting to hear his voice—waiting for shouts, threats—but as he hefted each chair and tossed it through the glass, he was as quiet as a hunter stalking a deer.

Crouched in the rhododendron at the edge of the yard, I turned to see who had dragged me off the pool deck. It was Clancy. "Can't you do something?" I whispered. "Can't you stop him?"

Clancy grimaced. My eyes had adjusted to the dark, and I could see that the cut on his left cheekbone looked fresh. "What do you think I've been doing?" he said. "I spent the last half hour trying to talk to him."

"So you're just going to let him destroy the house? He's going to get arrested."

"He's been arrested before." Clancy sounded more irritated than I'd ever heard him. "Look, Kate, I know Mason better than you do. When he gets riled up like this, you can't reason with him."

That might have been true, but I knew I couldn't bear to sit there and watch Mason make his life even worse. Just as I stood up, he put his shoulder to the one remaining pane of glass, slamming it with the weight of his body until it cracked. When he stepped into the light, he was bleeding from his temple and from a cut on his right arm. He stripped off his T-shirt, mopped at the blood, tossed the shirt into the pool. By the time I made it to the pool deck he was down to his boxers, and then they were gone too, kicked through a jagged hole into the living room.

"Willow," he screamed suddenly. "Come out here and talk to me, goddamnit!"

His voice broke. Concealed by shadows, I leaned my forehead against the cabana, dreading the moment when he would see me and I would have to step forward. Of course I wanted to help Mason. But what was I supposed to do—take the shirt off my back and throw it over him? Cover his body with my own?

The words seemed to have taken his last ounce of strength. He stood flooded by light, head bowed, waiting, and I waited too. Ten seconds. Twenty seconds.

"I called the police," a girl shouted in a frightened voice, and Mason took a step backward, nodding. Without a glance in my direction, he jumped into the El Camino, slammed it into reverse, and tore off, the driver's-side door hanging open. A divot of dirt and grass stuck to my dress.

Mason had spared just one deck chair, and I was sitting in it when, half an hour later, Travis and Sheriff McClellan pulled up in the cruiser. Lit by their own headlights, they cut a path across the lawn, the sheriff stiff with gout and moving as if every step pained him. Behind the smashed windows, the girls and boys sat primly on the edges of their chairs, talking in quiet voices about the dullest of topics. The Ortegas had arrived, and the presence of parents had turned the party inside out, from bacchanal to church social.

According to Clancy, there was no reason for me to stay. He had offered at least thirty times to take me home, or at least walk me back to the turnaround where I'd left Maggie's van. But I couldn't leave—I was waiting to talk to Willow. I was mad at Mason for being dumb and pathetic, but what she had done was worse. Cheating was worse, and hiding in the cabin while he screamed his heart out for love of her was worse; it was selfish and cruel. I wasn't about to confront her in there, where the minions and Henry Seidel would line up to defend her, but eventually she would have to come out to smoke, and then I would let her have it.

Indulging my anger at Willow, I tried to distract myself from the image of Mason, swaying in the light that poured through the broken window. Thinking of him just made me sad, but finally I got too tired to fight it, and every time I closed my eyes I saw his slumping shoulders and bare back. Something was wrong with him, I realized suddenly, with the sharp clarity that can come from half-dreaming.

"Thank you for sitting with me," I said to Clancy. "You didn't have to do that."

It took him a minute to answer. The pool's underwater lights glowed blue through the chlorine, Mason's bloody shirt still bobbing in the shallow end. "Well, you seemed sort of upset," Clancy said.

"I'm sorry. I know I was rude. I worry about him, that's all."

Clancy let his head fall back against the wall of a cabana with an audible thump. "Me too."

I looked into the living room, where Frances Ortega's red-faced father was giving Travis a finger-wagging lecture. From the way Travis nodded, slow and rhythmic, I could tell that he was stoned. I knew he couldn't see me, but I drew back anyway, curling up under the blanket that Clancy had scavenged from one of the bedrooms.

Travis shook hands with Mr. Ortega and moved away from him, toward the pool. Frowning down at the serrated edges of the broken window, he took advantage of his posture to loosen his belt. He made a sound like when you pop a paper bag against your palm, and his face relaxed into an expression of relieved pleasure. When I laughed, I must have made a movement that caught his eye. "That who I think it is?" he asked without embarrassment, peering into the dark.

"Mom said I could come," I told him.

"She did, did she?" Travis stepped over the window ledge and onto the pool deck. The words had sounded like a challenge, but I knew he didn't mean them that way. He had a habit of asking questions that weren't really questions, just to fill up conversational space.

"So what happened?" he said, as if he were asking about the outcome of a movie or a baseball game.

"I'm sure you heard it all inside."

Travis nodded, sucking in his upper lip. "That Willow," he said. "She reminds me of a cat I used to have that liked to jump on my lap when I was getting ready to go to work. She'd roll around all affectionate, purring, rubbing up under my chin. Then when I got home and tried to pick her up, she'd claw the shit out of me."

We all exploded at once. When I looked over at Clancy, he was lying on the concrete, the back of his flannel shirt spread behind him like a pair of wings. I felt almost happy. "All right," Travis said, rocking back on his heels. "Back to work, I guess. I'd take you home, Kate, but first I got to find somebody to clear that wreck."

"Wreck?" I said. "Where?"

Travis was quiet for a minute. "You didn't hear about that? It's that boy Mason. He slammed his car into a tree about half a mile down the road."

CHAPTER TEN

The river dream came to me for the first time that night. It was summer and I was skinny-dipping, something I had never done in my waking life. The water was like cool silk against my skin, and the trees bending over the bank left dusty prints of pollen on the surface. The sun, angled through the branches, turned everything the color of copper. I knew I had nothing to worry about; I had a vague sense that there had been troubles in the past but they were all gone now, behind me. But my left foot had caught on something, a strand of algae, an old rope, and suddenly I was pulled down through layers of cold to the bottom of the river.

In the morning I was tired and blurry, my body chilled from the dark progress of the dream. All I'd heard before Travis made me go home was that Mason wasn't dead, and that Mr. Ortega had decided not to sue after Travis pointed out that a trial might bring him unwelcome media attention. I planned to head down to the hospital right after breakfast, but as soon as I walked into the kitchen, I could tell that I wouldn't get away so easily. Mom had taken everything out of the refrigerator and the cabinets, lining up the boxes, jars, and bottles on the table and countertops. Pinto beans cozied up to ketchup; capers rubbed elbows with steel-cut oats. Travis sat in the middle of it, reading the sports section. He raised his eyebrows at me but didn't say anything.

Mom grabbed my wrist and towed me into the pantry, where every shelf was empty, eerie and white in the glow of the hanging bulb. "Look," she said, pressing my palm against the shelf as if she were taking my fingerprints. I smelled rather than saw the layer of soft gray dust, and sneezed into my shoulder.

"See?" she said. "I don't think I've cleaned in here in ten years."

"That's gross, Mom."

"It's disgusting, isn't it? I've let things go for too long."

Globs of yesterday's mascara stuck in her lashes. With her stringy gray hair hanging around her face, she looked like another backwoods witch, Mrs. Lemons's weird sister. She waved me toward the table, and I cleared the peanut butter and horseradish off my usual chair. "Do you want something to eat?" she asked. "I could make eggs."

"No offense, but I don't really want to eat while you're cleaning." I scooted my chair away from the trash can, where a dreamcatcher that had hung on the pantry door for as long as I could remember was draped over a side-split carton of cornmeal. "Anyway, I have to go. I'm visiting Mason at the hospital."

Mom gave me a concerned look, rubbing the heel of her hand against a patch of baking powder just below her right cheekbone. Her fingertips looked pickled, and I wondered if it was possible to come down with obsessive-compulsive disorder overnight, the way you came down with the flu. "Honey, I think it's nice that you're concerned," she said. "But you've never been interested in boys like that. And what did you do to your hair?"

"It's called a haircut," I said. "You should try one sometime. And who said anything about being *interested* in him?"

"Aw, let her go," Travis said to Mom. "She might be the only visitor he gets."

Mom and I both turned to stare, I with surprised relief, she with a hostile weariness that made me remember the F-150 in Glen City. Travis cleared his throat and lifted the paper so it covered his face.

Travis was wrong about me being the only visitor. When I got to the lobby, Clancy was already there, reading an old copy of *Newsweek* with a paper cup of coffee balanced on his knee. "It's his ankle," he said. "He'll be on crutches for a while, that's all."

"Oh, my God, that's great," I said. Clancy raised his eyebrows, and I looked away. It was a small hospital, and at ten o'clock on a Sunday the lobby was empty and echoing. Ficus plants wilted in the corners; a half-empty sleeve of powdered doughnuts lay crumpled on a chair across the room. Maggie's friend Donna Higgins walked by wheeling a mop bucket, and I gave her a tentative wave.

Part of me wanted to go straight up to Mason's room, but I didn't know when I'd get another chance to talk to Clancy one on one. "Look, there's something I've been wanting to tell you," I said. "That night when we walked to the old gym, and I wanted to talk to Mason? Willow asked me to do that."

His bony hand flexed around the coffee cup. On the Junk Tour in the El Camino, I'd told myself that I was glad Clancy hadn't called me like he said he would. I told myself that things never would have worked out with a guy like that, a deadneck with a gun rack on his pickup who wore his camo jacket even on the coldest days of the year, but the truth was that I liked Clancy. Though no one would call him handsome, I liked his freckles, and the spread of his broad shoulders, and his long narrow feet. I liked the way he looked at me, but when I met his gaze, his eyes weren't as warm as they had been a minute ago.

Clancy stretched his legs, the soles of his shoes squeaking on the linoleum. "Let me ask you something," he said. "Why did you come down here this morning?"

I reached up to tug at my braid but had to settle for adjusting my shirt collar. Why had I come to the hospital? It was a good question. On the surface of things, Mason was no more to me than the ex-boyfriend of my ex-friend, a degree of acquaintance that hardly mandated hospital visits.

"I don't want to make a big deal about it, Kate," Clancy said quietly. "But if you're wondering why I didn't call you, that's why."

I didn't know what to think. Had Clancy just given me permission to like Mason better than him? "Well, this is sort of awkward," I said.

Clancy shrugged. "It doesn't have to be awkward. Mason needs all the friends he can get right now. I told you he broke his ankle, but that's just the physical stuff."

"But what else is there?"

"It's not what happened in the accident," he said. "It's what came before the accident that's the problem. When he was coming around the curve, he says he saw a girl in a black robe standing on the side of the road. He thinks it was a wild girl."

"What?" I said. "Wait, that was Frances Ortega—she'd been swimming."

Clancy rubbed his chin with his hand. "He thinks it was a sign, Kate. He thinks the wild girls are out to kill him."

I couldn't believe it. I couldn't fathom how Mason could turn an Academy girl in a bathrobe into the creature of our local nightmares, or why he would stick to his delusion after Clancy explained that he hadn't seen what he thought he'd seen. When I came in, Mason was quiet, his face turned to the window, and at first I took that as a good omen. "Hey," I said, bending into a clumsy hug. "You scared me to death, you know? I saw the chunk you took out of that tree."

"Something's happening." His voice was hoarse, as if he hadn't used it for a while.

"No." I explained it all—Frances, skinny-dipping, bathrobe—but he wasn't listening.

"I'm going to get my own place," he said. "I'm going to change things. Not that it'll make any difference, but at least I won't just be sitting here waiting for it."

"But what about your mom?"

Mason dragged the back of his hand across his nose. "I'm not helping her. I'm probably making things worse, actually."

"You know, they sometimes rent out the apartment over the River House," I said. "If Clancy and I asked him, Kevin might be willing to let you stay there for a . . ."

My voice trailed off, but Mason didn't seem to notice. His eyes were empty, his face slack and dull; he looked years older.

"I knew they would come for me," he said. "I deserve it— I know that too."

"Mason." I lowered myself onto the stool by the bed. "This has nothing to do with the wild girls. You're just making yourself crazy for no reason."

He turned to face the window. The temperature had dropped overnight, the clouds were like pencil shadings on a white sky.

"You don't have to worry about me," he said. "I just know what's coming, that's all."

For those first weeks, Clancy took care of the important things: making sure that Mason had food, keeping the apartment clean. Mason had quit his job at the dining hall, so I only saw him in the evenings when I walked to the River House, the ground frozen now and rucked with cold, a single crimson leaf flashing from a branch in defiance of winter. On those nights, Clancy always manufactured some errands to run and left the two of us together. I felt sort of bad about that, but not bad enough to urge him to stay. I wanted to be alone with Mason. The closer I got, the more my fingertips tingled inside my gloves.

Every time my hopes rose, and every time I had to adjust to the difference in him. It wasn't the sort of change you could ignore. He sat on the couch, bathed in the light of the tiny TV Clancy had picked out of an Academy Dumpster, and watched old black-and-white comedies rented from the library: *It Happened One Night*, *Bringing Up Baby*. I wanted to ask whether it was a coincidence that the only movies he liked were about silly rich girls who had to learn to appreciate the poor men who loved them, but I wasn't sure if I wanted to hear the answer. No matter what Mason had said in the hospital, I was convinced that this depression really had to do with Willow, who hadn't called or stopped by one time in the past two weeks.

I had talked to her about it once. I was heading out for a run, and Willow was coming out of Dr. Bell's office after the Tuesday night tutorial. She gave me an exaggerated smile and wiggled her fingers, but would have kept right on walking if I hadn't grabbed her arm. "What the hell are you doing?" I demanded. "One day you're all over him, and the next you're making out with Elise's brother?"

Willow turned red. "I had to do something," she said. "It wasn't working out. Of course I didn't know he was going to freak out like that, I didn't know he was going to show up drunk and—"

"You broke his heart," I said.

It was an accurate description, but just overdramatic enough to make her pause and examine me more carefully. "Why do you care, anyway? You barely know him."

"That's not true. We're friends."

"Fine," she snapped, pulling her faux-fur collar up around her neck. "Enjoy yourself."

But I wasn't enjoying myself at all. This was not Mason of the summer festival, Mason of the Junk Tour. This Mason was not sexy or dangerous or fun. He had switched to smoking Marlboro Reds because his hands shook too much to roll his own cigarettes. He lived on cheese sandwiches and powdered lemonade, and his beard was growing as long as a woodsman's in a fairy tale. In the first weeks of December I let my visits dwindle to once every other day, then once every three days. I had excuses at the ready, in case anybody asked. December was the season of traditions at the Academy, and as a senior I was expected to participate in all of them. There was Christmas caroling by candlelight, and services in the chapel where we wore white dresses and carried holly branches. There was a gift exchange, and plum cake in the dining hall on the evening of St. Nicholas Day. Like everyone else I made fun of these rituals, but I was realizing now that I loved them too.

Fake evergreen swags and gold foil stars hung in the halls of the dorms. Caroline had started wearing her earrings that looked like Christmas balls. The common rooms were stuffy with radiator heat, and tinkly music spilled from the office where Mrs. Putnam sat knitting when she wasn't enforcing curfew. From Lucie I heard that Matilda had knocked Dr. Bell's notebook off his desk and almost succeeded in slipping it into her bag, but he had spotted it and tucked it back in his pocket. I also knew that Henry Seidel had been up at least twice since Thanksgiving. I'd seen him parking his Mercedes at the loading dock, striding across the Lawn with his hands in the pockets of his regulation khakis. Elise was dating one of her brother's roommates, another floppy-haired Alabaman, and on Saturday afternoons you could find the two couples sharing a table at the River House, the boys talking in drawling voices about the most boring subjects you could imagine—college football, regattas—while the girls listened with glazed half smiles.

All that was fine with me. If Willow wanted to turn herself into some kind of country-club cliché, I couldn't stop her. If she liked Henry Seidel better than Mason, that was her business, but I couldn't brush off her break with me so easily. I could dislike her, even hate her, but I was always aware of her, an agitating presence at the corner of my vision.

On December twentieth, the last day before winter break, I had a harder time than usual dragging myself down to the River House. It was the night of the first real snow, and the palm-size flakes drifted onto the silent Lawn. The international students at the end of my hall were playing board games in the TV lounge; the sound of their laughter came through my radiator, distorted to a comforting hum. I didn't want to go out in the cold, but I had to, because staying would mean that I was tired of Mason. I didn't want to be tired of Mason. I didn't want to be like Willow, playing sweet to people as long as it served my purpose and dropping them without a backward glance, so I put on my fisherman's sweater and two pairs of wool socks and forced myself out into the wind.

Downtown was empty. An orange county truck drove slowly down the center of Jessup Avenue, a fan of salt sifting from the pipe at its rear end. Stepping carefully into the slush-choked gutter, I noticed a bent figure in a bulky coat stumbling along the opposite sidewalk. At the end of the block, the figure leaned into the window of the liquor store, and I recognized her. "Mrs. Lemons," I called, and she hurried away from me, moving so much faster than I'd anticipated that I had to break into a half run to catch up. "Mrs. Lemons!" I started to touch her arm but stopped myself. "Are you here to see Mason?"

I'd been afraid that she was drunk, but the face she revealed as the collar fell back was more troubling than the world's worst binge could have made it. The whites of her eyes were shaded red, her mouth twisted in a rictus of a snarl. I stepped off the curb, ice pellets striking my ankles. "You," she hissed, glaring. "You keep that other one away from my boy."

"Willow?" I said. "But why?"

"Keep her away," she repeated. "She's the one, you—" Her voice dropped to a mumble. "Burn it down, and you—burn it, start again—"

"I don't know what you're talking about," I said weakly, but she was already scuttling down the sidewalk, her scraggly ponytail looking white and more witchlike than ever in the orange glare of the streetlights. At the end of the next block she disappeared, and though I told myself that she'd turned the corner, I couldn't have sworn that she hadn't just vanished into air.

The River House was closed, and I had to knock on the window five times before Kayak Boy got up to let me in. "Hey there, Katie," he said, opening the door with a flourish.

"Not Katie," I said. We had this same exchange almost every time I saw him. "Kate. K-A-T-E."

"Right. Katie, that's what I said." Winking, he put a hand on my snow-dampened shoulder and led me to the table where Maggie was eating a plate of broken blondies. She had been eating more than usual and was starting to gain weight around the middle, something I knew better than to mention.

"I'm guessing you're not here to see me," she said.

"Why else would she be here?" Kayak Boy began, but Maggie gave him a look.

"If you run into Clancy anytime soon," she said to me, "tell him that he still owes us December rent."

I had already reached out my hand for a blondie, but I snatched it back and wheeled on Kayak Boy. "You're charging Clancy rent? He doesn't even live here."

"Well, somebody has to pay for the room," Kayak Boy said.

"It's not like we're fleecing him," Maggie put in. "He's paying fifty dollars a month. We could charge three hundred for that place."

"This is a joke, right? Nobody with two brain cells would pay three hundred. It smells like mildew, and I saw cockroaches last week."

"Like hell you did." When Kayak Boy was mad he put his shoulders back and stuck his head forward, a roosterish stance that reminded me of Travis. "This place has been open twenty years and I've never seen a roach."

"I guess they all moved upstairs," I said. "Maybe you should see if they'll pay three hundred a month."

"Oh, go sit on a nail," Maggie said, but then she stopped, staring over my shoulder. Mason stood in the doorway to the upstairs apartment, barefoot and shirtless. I had to remind myself to close my mouth.

"How's it going?" he mumbled, scratching at the seat of his pajamas. "Kate, you coming upstairs?"

I knew what Maggie was thinking as I quietly followed Mason up the stairs to his room. I knew what she was thinking, and she was wrong, but I didn't feel the need to explain myself. After all, she had thrown herself away on a Swan River deadneck. Why couldn't I do the same?

But when the door shut behind us there was no kissing and groping, none of the frenzy of hands and tongues that they were probably imagining downstairs. Mason went into the bathroom without a word while I lingered in the doorway. A box of half-eaten pizza spread its flaps across the couch; the only chair held an overstuffed basket of laundry. I didn't want to stand there and listen to Mason pee, so without letting myself think too much, I went into the bedroom and sat down on a heap of tangled sheets. Should I tell him about his mother? I wondered. Should I tell him how she'd looked, what she'd said, knowing that it would only make him feel worse?

Light leaked through the blinds, but what I noticed first was the smell, a strong guy scent of sweat and unwashed skin. There were a few clean shirts hung over the chairs, mostly plaid flannels that looked like donations from Clancy. A pile of library books sat at the back of the dresser, lined up so neatly that I knew they'd never been touched. A glinting chain dangled off the top book, and I reached for it. It was the heart-shaped locket I'd given to Willow freshman year. I slid my thumbnail along the crack and pried the two halves apart. It was empty.

The overhead light clicked on, and when I turned Mason was

leaning against the doorframe, yawning. The locket hung between my fingers. "Where did you get this?" I said.

He shaded his eyes. "When Clancy went to pick up the stuff from the impound lot, it was in the bag. It must have fallen off in my car."

My fist closed around the locket. "Are you in love with her?" I asked, my voice higher than I wanted it to be. "Is that why you kept it?"

Frowning, he ran his hand through his hair from back to front, ruffling it into a crest. "I was in love with her, I think. I asked her to move in with me."

"Into your *cabin?*"

"No, I thought we could get a place—I don't know, down in the Delta or something. After she graduated—I wasn't asking her to leave school." He reached for the locket, but I pulled it away and he dropped his hand.

"Willow would never do that," I said.

"Why not?" he asked, almost belligerent. "She's from here too. The other side of the bridge is still Swan River."

I shrugged. The other side of the bridge might as well have been another country, and deep down Mason knew it as well as I did. There were people who were stuck here, like my mother, like his mother, and there were people who weren't. "Is that why she broke up with you?" I asked.

He jerked his head to the side, rubbing his thumb against the bridge of his nose. "I don't know," he said. "Probably. She said the same thing about you, you know."

"She said what about me?"

"We were talking about Clancy. I said he was a solid guy, and Willow said, 'Kate would never hang around in Swan River. She's too good for a shithole like this.'"

I tried to tamp down a smile of satisfaction. "Why were you talking about me and Clancy?" I said. "There's nothing going on between us."

"I know that."

His voice was lifeless, but when his gaze swung back to my face, his eyes seemed to spark suddenly. Without a word, he stepped forward and put a hand on my waist. It was like he was asking me a question, and I didn't say yes, but I didn't say no either. He tilted my head back roughly, bending to kiss the vein that ran from my earlobe down my throat. "All that's over with," he murmured. "She made her feelings pretty clear."

"Wait." My brain felt thick. I had a million questions, but couldn't concentrate long enough to figure out which ones were important. "Where is Clancy anyway?"

"He got another job," Mason said, smiling. "Selling Christmas trees."

"And he won't be back for a while?"

"No." He kissed my neck again. "Not for hours."

But I still didn't feel right. "Wait," I said, pushing him away. "Listen. Have you seen your mother lately?"

He dropped his hands and stared at me for a moment before sinking onto the bed. "Yeah, I saw her. I told her everything I told you. I told her about what Rondal did to Crystal, and the worst part was that she didn't seem surprised."

I put my hand on his shoulder. "You asked me how she could not know that Crystal was going to become a wild girl," he said, raising his eyes to mine. "Well, what if she did know and just didn't give a shit? All these years I've been making excuses for her, trying to make up for the bad men in her life. But I was sitting there, trying to talk to her about what happened to Crystal, and there was this blankness in her eyes, like it didn't mean anything."

I took his hand, rubbing my thumb over the knuckles. "You know, some people think that the cave at the commune has something to do with the wild girls. What if, over time, it had an effect on your mom?"

"What kind of effect?"

I pictured Mrs. Lemons's face when I'd met her on the sidewalk. "Well," I said. "Maybe it made her—you know—kind of mentally ill."

He shook his head. "If she knew what was happening to Crystal and she didn't try to stop it, that's not mental illness. That's just being a fucked-up, evil person."

I leaned my head on his shoulder, and after a moment his arm moved around my waist. "Why did you ask about my mom anyway?"

"I don't know," I said. "Just curious, I guess."

I felt sorrier for him than I ever had, and when he turned to me again, I let him kiss me. Before long my shirt skimmed over my head, and then we were lying on the bed. Frozen rain ticked against the glass. His teeth nipped at my collarbone, and he was fumbling with the button on my jeans. I felt as if I were hanging on to a branch over rushing water, and every time his lips brushed my skin I wondered if I should give in. Give in, and drop under the surface—because he'd had the hardest life of anyone I knew; or because I wanted to prove that I was like Willow, brave enough to take what I wanted without thinking about the consequences; or because it was difficult for me to imagine meeting anyone I liked better than Mason. The gentle-eyed boys I'd seen in the Pritchard College brochures were only phantoms, but this was real, this was right now, and I felt my grip on the branch loosening.

All I can say is that it was nothing like what I'd read about in Willow's copies of *Cosmo*. I didn't bleed, but it didn't feel good either. It was mostly just uncomfortable. What I remembered afterward, more than the moment when I was no longer a virgin, were small things, like the strawberry birthmark under Mason's collarbone. The way he ran his hands over my body as if my skin were tattooed in braille. And the moment after he put the condom on when he hovered above me, asking *are you sure?* and I nodded as hard as I could. Everything about him filled me with tenderness—hair falling into his eyes; skin flushing as he moved above me; and the muscles of his back under my hands. *This is happening,* I said to myself, *this is actually happening.* I felt that I loved every part of him, and wasn't that the same as being in love with him?

When it was over he turned me onto my side and pulled me against him, looping his arms around my middle. Through the slatted blinds, I could see the rail where I'd stood with Willow back in August glinting with blue ice. Mason's breath slowed and steadied, but I knew I wouldn't be able to sleep. Half-closing my eyes, I imagined that this was our apartment, our bed. I imagined him making me the same offer that he'd made to Willow, and me saying yes. He tightened his arms, and I could feel the loneliness in him even as he pressed against me.

At first it was just groaning, low and discontented. His arms tensed again, and my heart pounded when I realized I couldn't break his grip. "Mason," I said. "Let go, you're hurting me."

"Don't," he said into my ear, "don't, don't," his body shaking now, every muscle taut as a tuned string. Suddenly he screamed, and as he fell back against the pillows I was able to turn, take him by the shoulders. I told him that it was just a nightmare. I told him that he was fine, that everything was fine, even while I was trembling all over, sweat slicking the back of my neck.

"I've seen the signs," he said. "Birds flying backwards, fires burning all night in the woods. I saw a dead dog in the gutter the other morning. If I weren't such a coward, I would just off myself right now and get it over with."

What he said was bad enough, but the way he said it, in that blurred, sleepy voice, shook me more deeply still. I had to help him, whether I loved him or not. "Mason, you've got to stop," I said. "You're making things worse."

"I didn't help my sister. I should have died that night."

I wanted to cry in frustration. "Look, I know that Clancy told you about the psychiatrist at the free clinic in—"

"I don't need a psychiatrist," Mason interrupted. "I'm not making shit up. I'm not crazy."

"I don't think you're crazy," I said, only half-truthfully. "I think you're depressed, and they can help you. They can give you pills or something. I can drive you down to Moorefield tomorrow, and at least for the next couple weeks while school's out. Also you have to get some exercise. And you should be nicer to Clancy," I added. "He's not your servant, you know. He's paying fifty dollars a month for this place, and he doesn't even live here."

"I never asked him to rent me an apartment," Mason said in a dead voice. "I never asked you to come down here either."

I snatched up my shirt. "We're just trying to help."

"You want to know how you can help?" he said into the mattress. "Why don't you leave me alone?"

I would have walked back to campus if I could have, but the ice on the road was thick enough to reflect the glow of the street-lights, and I knew I'd be safer in Clancy's truck than on foot. When he got back, Mason and I were sitting in the living room, fully dressed, not speaking. I was playing solitaire on the top of the pizza box. Mason was pretending to read, but he never turned a page.

At the stoplight, Clancy looked at me, his forehead furrowed. "Are you okay, Kate?"

I shook my head, leaning my burning cheek against the window. I hadn't planned to lose my virginity in high school. I'd always thought it would happen later, with a real boyfriend, some sweet, wry Pritchard collegian who could quote poetry in bed. Now I had done what I'd never intended to do, and with a guy who'd told me to leave him alone not ten minutes later. Thinking about it made me writhe inwardly, but there was no one in the world I was less eager to confide in than Clancy Harp.

"I was just thinking about this question on the Environmental Science study guide," I said. "About how cold it would have to get for the Swan River to freeze. I was thinking thirty-two degrees, but I don't think that's right."

Clancy looked at me, but I wouldn't meet his eyes, and finally the light turned green. "It has to get pretty bad for running water to freeze over," he said. "Tell you what, though—I wouldn't want to go for a swim tonight."

It snowed until morning, and after that it got really cold. The radiators chugged and spat, but the drafts that sneaked under the windowsills were still enough to make your teeth chatter. At breakfast the girls from the Deep South wore scarves and gloves, talking longingly of vacation homes in St. Lucia and Puerto Vallarta. I sat by myself, miserable. After what Mason had said, I was pretty sure that I wasn't in love with him. I definitely felt sorry for him, but he was mean and at least halfway to nuts, and I was not going to give up on college for his sake.

In the morning I took an exam in French, then another in Environmental Science. The words made no sense, drifting around the page as my eyes went in and out of focus. I translated the sentence *Qu'est-ce que vous avez appelé?* as *Who would like to have an apple?* I defined *benthos* as an endangered South American tiger. It didn't matter, I told myself. My applications were already in; I'd either get into Pritchard or I wouldn't. The dorms were closing the next day, and as I got ready to leave I could hear suitcases thumping down the stairs. Caroline had gone to the airport that morning. I wasn't sure when the Beckers were leaving on their family trip to Hawaii, but I guessed that I wouldn't see Willow again before break. It was for the best, probably. I wasn't sure that I could hide last night from her.

Coming through the door at the River House, I ran into Clancy. He was pulling on his gloves and his downturned face was tense, almost angry-looking, but when he saw me he smiled. We stood in the entryway, beside the coat rack with its persistent smell of smoke and damp wool. "How did the exams go?" he asked.

I shrugged. "Fine, I guess." I knew it didn't make any sense for me to be mad at Clancy, but that was how I felt. At that moment everything about him was annoying, from the pine tar on his gloves to the shy way he ducked his head when he spoke to me.

Two Academy girls swept through the door in matching black floor-length coats, bringing a blast of Arctic air. I knew them by sight; they were twins, Laura and Pia Rowland of West Palm Beach, and they had a reputation in the sophomore class for being free spirits. One twin wore a pair of star-shaped sunglasses that she lowered to look at me and then, for a longer moment, at Clancy. He kept his face carefully blank, but as soon as the inner door had shut behind them, he took a step closer to me. "You know, it's nice of you to come down here all the time," he said gently. "But you don't have to. Maybe you're stressing yourself out."

Tears of self-pity stung my eyes, and I knew that Clancy was right. Encouraging Mason to get out of the house, to see a psychiatrist—those were things that a grown-up should have done, and I was not a grown-up. I was seventeen; I had my own problems. For a second I thought I'd dissolve into a puddle right there in the vestibule, but then Clancy put a hand on my arm, and suddenly my tears were tears of rage.

"You don't have to be here either," I said. "You don't have to work an extra job to pay Mason's rent. You think you're being all noble or something when you leave us alone together, but it's weak, Clancy—it's just weak." He stepped back, face paling behind his freckles, and I ran through the inner door and up the stairs.

Anger kept me going just long enough for me to get Mason out of bed, dressed, and into Maggie's van with his crutches. He was quiet and surly, and I figured he was still mad at me, but I didn't care. I would take him to the psychiatrist, who would tell him he was depressed and give him pills to make it better, and then I was going to give up on boys for a while.

"Do you remember that time you took me up to your cabin?" I said as we turned out of the parking lot. "You asked me if I was trying to save you, and I said I wasn't, but now I think that might have been exactly what I was doing. And I've realized now that I can't save you, Mason. You have to save yourself."

He slumped against the passenger door, one thumb tapping restlessly against his knee. I had called the sly confidence on his face his highway smile, but he had probably never even been on a highway. He had no prospects, no future. He was a dead end, a gravel turnaround off Bloodwort Road.

When we stopped at the light, Laura and Pia Rowland ran out into the crosswalk, flapping their arms like blackbirds, their coats billowing behind them. Mason sat up and then doubled with a harsh cough that shook his shoulders. I tried to hand him my water bottle, but he shook his head.

Turning onto the bridge, we half-circled the Christmas tree lot where Clancy was loading a ragged white pine into the back of a station wagon. The van's heater puffed in spurts, inhaling and exhaling with audible effort. I flexed my fingers inside my gloves to keep them from going numb. "I mean, clearly it's not going to work out with you and Willow," I said. "Or you and me either. So you have to choose. You have to decide what *you're* going to do to make your life better."

Mason murmured something, his words drowned by the roar of a low-flying plane. It was one of the private planes from the airstrip in Glen City. Rich people, some with daughters at the Academy, liked to pass over Swan River in their five-seater Cessnas, flying low for the best view of the mountains. Mason spoke again, more urgently. "What?" I asked, cupping a hand around my ear.

"Stop the car."

"But we're on the bridge."

"Stop the car!" he shouted.

"Mason, I'm in the middle of the—"

He lunged for the wheel, and I screamed. We went into a slow-motion circle, the sky behind the windshield turning white as milk. The van drifted to a stop facing back toward Swan River and I dropped my head into my hands, shaking with nausea. I felt the draft as Mason opened the door, but I didn't look up.

It seemed like hours that I sat there, my body going hot and then cold again, but it was probably no more than half a minute. When I opened my eyes, no cars had turned onto the bridge from either direction. No one at the Christmas tree lot seemed to have noticed what had happened. Mason was kneeling on the walkway, staring at the vapor trail as the plane dipped over the horizon.

As I fumbled with my seat belt, I saw him rise and hang one leg over the railing. Wind blew his hair back from his face. He balanced there for a moment, half in one world and half in the other. "No," I said, "no, *no*," but he slipped over the side of the bridge and disappeared.

CHAPTER ELEVEN

In the end I was the one who went to the psychiatrist in Moorefield, and spent hours in the file room at the free clinic as she made me describe again and again the moments just after Mason jumped off the Swan River Bridge. I told her how I'd tripped on my seat belt and fallen facefirst on the asphalt, my forehead and palms lacerated by glass I didn't feel. I told her how, as I crawled to the rail, the bridge had seemed to roll and pitch beneath me. By then Clancy was running toward me, and a few people were pointing and staring from the parking lot of the Tastee-Freez. Kneeling on the walkway, I wrapped my arms around a metal post and looked down, but by then there was nothing to see. One hundred feet below the river rolled on as usual, broken sheets of ice glinting in the sunlight.

"But how did you feel?" the psychiatrist asked, her chair squeaking as she crossed her legs.

"I didn't feel anything," I said.

She stared at me, lips parted. She was young, just out of the third-rate medical school at the land-grant college in Glen City, which probably explained why she couldn't do any better than the Moorefield free clinic. Her lipstick was drab enough to blend into her skin, her panty hose laddered with runs. I couldn't help thinking of how Mason would have worked her, staring her down until she spilled her pencils all over the floor.

"Why do you think that is?" she asked, narrowing her eyes. "Your boyfriend jumped off a bridge right in front of you. What's keeping you from feeling your pain?"

"He wasn't my *boy*friend," I said. "Where did you get that idea?"

But I knew where she'd gotten that idea—it had been in the papers. The *Riparian* had printed only the facts, but the Moorefield paper had interpreted those facts in a somewhat whimsical way. According to the *News-Sentinel*, Mason was the son of a charismatic faith healer, a local eccentric who had been accused by former members of the commune of harassment and intimidation. I understood that this was another attempt to translate the darkness of Swan River into something the outside world knew how to deal with—for *faith healer*, read *witch*; for *harassment*, read *turning men into pigs*—but I didn't like it. The paper described me as Mason's high school girlfriend and spelled my name as Katherine Riordan, E-R-I-N-E instead of R-Y-N.

"I don't feel anything," I insisted. "I know that you expect me to fall down sobbing, but I can't do that just to please you."

Her eyes moved to the clock above my head. "Well," she sighed, pulling out her prescription pad, "everyone responds to trauma differently."

She scribbled something on the top slip and handed it to me. Outside, waiting for my mom, I ripped the paper to bits and threw it to the wind.

It was the same dream, but this time I was pulled all the way down to the bottom of the river. There was a town there—not Swan

River as it was now, but perhaps as it had been when the Academy wild girls had slaughtered the Union sentinels. Wagons clattered along the pebbled bed, and people in out-of-date clothes drifted in and out of a tall wooden building with a splintered placard. Giant ferns grew out of the gaps in the walls, and the water lifted off the shingles one by one. I tried to look inside, but it was as if people disappeared as soon as they walked through the door.

No one seemed to notice me. At first the crowd looked old-fashioned and decorous, the women prim as Emily Dickinson, the men tall and grave as Lincoln. But then I saw a girl who I was sure was Margaret Reid, her face blackened by the fire that had destroyed her family's farm. There was Victoria Duvalier with her four friends ranged behind her, all neatly dressed in white linen, all smeared with blood from head to toe. There was Sophia Peabody, still holding the knife she had used to kill her classmates in the one-room schoolhouse; and there was Crystal Lemons, grinning at me through broken teeth. She held out a hand, beckoning me to follow them into the wooden house. *Come with us,* they called, their voices floating thickly through the water.

Then Mason was there, shaking his head with an expression that was part boredom, part amusement. He took my hand and led me away from the wild girls. We fought the tide of people heading for the falling-down house with the black doorway. At the edge of a forest of ferns Mason turned to me and spoke urgently, but his words were broken by the water. "What?" I said, and he spoke faster, bubbles drifting from his lips. But now I was drifting up too, fighting my way through layers of light-shot blue on green until I found myself blocked. It was the underside of a rowboat, and I slammed the heels of my hands against it, convinced that if I knocked hard enough it would open for me like a door.

School was out for four weeks, and I spent every one of them in the haze of the river dream, waking only to eat, brush my teeth, and sleep again. Christmas morning was a blur, and I skipped dinner. Despite the terror of the dream, I found that I couldn't wait to get back to that place—to feel Mason's hand in mine, to listen harder for the words that faded even as they left his lips. I knew that when I told the psychiatrist I felt nothing, she believed that I meant I felt nothing for Mason, and I let her think it. The truth was that I felt nothing for my waking life, no affection for the people around me, no hope for the future.

In that dead month only one or two hours stand out to me, colored snapshots in an album of black and white. There was the day that Travis moved out. Mom forced me to get up, and we stood by the garage watching him haul out the half dozen paper grocery bags that held his earthly possessions. I peeked in one and saw a bong with a base in the shape of a skull sitting on a stack of Allman Brothers CDs; in another, his tackle box balanced a framed photo of Maggie and me at some long-ago county fair. At the end of the driveway sat the apple red F-150, the straw that had broken the camel's back.

Travis put on a good show, but his chin quivered as he said his good-byes. He and Mom had already sat me down and explained that he wasn't moving far, just to an apartment down in the Delta, and I could still see him whenever I wanted to. They had waited until after Christmas for fear of upsetting me, and I didn't have the heart to let them know how little it mattered.

The Friday before the end of break, Mom knocked on my door at eight a.m. I shouted and threw a pillow, hoping that if I made enough of a fuss she would leave me alone, but instead she started switching the lights on and off. "Busy day today," she said. "We're going to Moorefield."

I pulled the covers over my head. "I told you I'm not seeing that psychiatrist again."

"Who said anything about the free clinic?" Mom said. "You're going to help me look for an apartment, but first lunch. I have a coupon for Lily's on the Square."

I couldn't remember the last time we had gone to Moorefield just for fun. When I was in public school, a shopping trip to the mall had been a seasonal tradition, and once a year the trip might include lunch at Lily's, second only to the Grand Hotel in the competition for Moorefield's poshest restaurant. Lily's sat on the corner of the downtown square, across from the statue of Thomas Jefferson that gazed off as if contemplating westward expansion. The walls were exposed brick, the windows hung with fluttering white curtains. I always ordered the same thing, an open-faced roast beef sandwich with a side of garlic fries.

These days, I knew that Lily's was not the four-star dining experience I had imagined it to be. I knew that the tablecloths were polyester, and that the landscapes on the wall were just cheap prints. Even if I hadn't been depressed to begin with, it would have been hard to muster up the old enthusiasm for cheese breadsticks and the chocolate mints that came with your check. Still, I decided to try my best for Mom's sake. She ordered a crab cake sandwich with a side of fruit salad, and every time she swallowed a chunk of cantaloupe, she closed her eyes in pleasure.

"When you come home next year, we can eat out every night," she said. "I heard they're opening an Indian restaurant on Spring Street. It might be fun to try something exotic once in a while."

I decided not to tell her that we had an Indian buffet once a month at the Academy, and I never ate anything besides the rice. "So you're really going to move," I said. "But what about your job?"

"The Moorefield school district is advertising for two positions. Of course I won't quit the Academy until I have something in writing, but to tell you the truth, I can't wait to get out of there. David doesn't need a secretary—he does everything himself anyway. I can't remember the last time he asked me to type a letter."

I swirled a garlic fry in the honey-mustard blend that Lily's called Crazy Sauce. "Why does Dr. Bell write his own letters?"

Mom took a sip of red wine and rolled it around in her mouth. "Well, he's a very private man. I don't think he's found a lot of kindred spirits in Swan River. Travis and I went fishing one time, and out on this little creek in the middle of nowhere we ran into David. He was collecting plants or herbs or something. I think Travis felt intimidated. He kept saying that David looked like those models in the outdoor catalogs."

She clasped her hands around her glass. "I used to think it was such a shame that David never married," she said. "I'm sure he would have made a great husband. But when you have those intellectual interests, the plant collecting and the mythology, maybe they take up too much of your time."

I wondered if Mom had heard the rumors about Dr. Bell and his students. Probably not, I decided. She wouldn't talk about him so respectfully if she thought he might be a secret Humbert Humbert. "But he's had relationships, right?" I asked. "He's not a weirdo or anything?"

"Well, I know that Antoinette Lemons was interested for a while," Mom said. "I don't know if anything ever happened between them, but he might have led her on a bit. You know people say she's a witch, and I think he liked that. He liked the idea of Appalachian folk wisdom. Like those people in the thirties who came down to record murder ballads."

"The WPA?" I felt surprised that she'd heard of them, and then annoyed with myself for being surprised. "Do you think Mrs. Lemons is a witch?"

Mom set her mouth in a hard line. "I think she's the world's worst mother, that's what I think."

"I thought you liked her."

"I did like her," Mom said. "I can't say that we were ever friends, but when I first started going to the commune, I think I related to her in some way. She'd had a difficult life, and your father had just died, and I guess I thought we had something in common. But she just couldn't keep it together. Maybe it was the drinking, or maybe it was men, but you'd notice from year to year that things were getting worse—the buildings were falling down, the fences were broken, and as for those children, they were practically feral. I know that I may have left you and Maggie on your own too much sometimes, but I always knew you had food and clothes—I always knew where you were. With Antoinette, you got the feeling that those kids could have disappeared for days and she wouldn't have noticed."

My eyes filled with tears and I was back on the Swan River Bridge, watching Mason swing one leg over the rail, then the other.

Mom reached across the table and gripped my hand. "I know how hard this is for you, Kate," she said. "I know you're hurting, but you can't ever blame yourself. You tried to help that boy. Whatever was wrong with him, the damage had been done long before you came along."

The waiter paused beside our table, looking self-conscious, and I concentrated on spreading my napkin over my lap. When he was gone, I looked up and met Mom's eyes. "Mason wasn't my boy-friend," I said. "I wasn't in love with him, if that's what you're thinking."

"Well, I have to say I'm glad to hear that." Mom rummaged through her sleeve of credit cards, staring at one for a long time before placing it on the table. "And what about Clancy Harp? You've been seeing a lot of him lately."

"Not *seeing* him, Mom," I said. "It's not like we're going on dates." Clancy had stopped by twice over the break, and each time we'd spent half an hour sitting together in the kitchen. He was the one who told me that they'd dragged the river below the bridge but still hadn't found Mason's body. He told me that when Sheriff McClellan went up to the ruins of Bloodwort Farm to notify Mrs. Lemons of her son's death, he couldn't find her anywhere—not in the old cabins, not in the trailer. They thought she might have left town, and the Birdman too. As I watched Clancy drink burned coffee and pretend to enjoy the cookies I'd served half-raw, I knew that I owed him an apology for the mean things I'd said at the River House, but I was afraid of what might happen if I were nice to him. Clancy would not be satisfied with the simulation of friendship that was all I had to give right now. He would offer his kindness, his interest and sympathy, until it was too much for me, and cracked me open.

Mom slid the chocolate mints across the table. "We don't have to talk about it," she said.

That afternoon we looked at four different apartment com-plexes, each blander than the one before. They had names like Maple Park, Caldwell Forest, Highland Meadows, but there were never parks or forests or meadows anywhere in the vicinity. I thought that I would rather live in the cave at Bloodwort Farm, but Mom kept oohing and aahing, admiring light fixtures in the shape of tulips and built-in microwaves. By the time we got on the road for home, I was exhausted and she was giddy, and I realized that this looked like freedom to her. While I dreamed of Pritchard College, Mom dreamed of a two-bedroom apartment with a washer-dryer hookup and no Travis on the couch.

"I've been thinking about what you said about cutting my hair," she said in the car. "I like yours that way, shoulder-length, but I think I might need a bigger change. What about one of those pixie cuts?"

This was beginning to scare me. "Mom, are you sure you want to change everything at once? Travis just moved out and you stop smoking pot, you're looking for an apartment and talking about chopping off your hair. Those are all good things, but—"

"But it seems sudden," she finished. "I know it does, but I've been thinking about making these changes for a while, Kate. You're going off to college, Maggie has her own life—I don't have an excuse to stay in the same old rut anymore. I want my own space. I want a job that interests me. And then after what happened with Mason . . ."

She took my hand again, squeezing it so tightly that I felt a pain in my wrist. "Ouch!" I said.

She released me, smiling apologetically. "After that, I realized that we probably should have moved a long time ago. You know your dad and I never planned to stay in Swan River."

The pain moved up to my chest. Mom never talked about my father. Maggie said she could barely remember him, and I wouldn't have been able to picture his face if it hadn't been for the dusty photo that had sat on a shelf behind the TV for as long as I could remember. "Where would you have gone?" I asked.

"We talked about Alaska. Your dad wanted to homestead— build our own cabin, live off the land, but then—" She pressed a finger to her upper lip. "When he died, I didn't know what to want for myself, so I just did what was easy. Travis was easy."

Her hand moved to the drink holder, and I guessed that she was feeling for her cigarettes, but then she stopped herself and patted my knee. "I know I haven't done everything perfectly. You girls were both so independent, and maybe I counted on that too much. But things are going to be different from now on."

"I think I'm pretty much okay at this point," I said. "I mean, unless I become a wild girl or something."

I'd meant the reference to sound casual, even jokey, but I'd made it deliberately, to see if my mother had the same fears for me that I had for myself. Though we didn't have much in common, no one could know me better than she did. Was she afraid for me— afraid *of* me, even? Mom glanced my way and looked back to the road, shaking her head. "No," she said firmly. "That's not going to happen to you."

I had heard this before, from Mrs. Lemons. "Why do you say that?"

Mom looked at me again but more quickly, as if the question annoyed her. "I don't know. You're not the type, that's all."

"Well, what about Maggie? She's not the type either."

"Your sister was very lucky. I'm thankful every day that she didn't hurt anyone."

"Mom, that's not my point," I said. "My point is that it happened to her. If it happened to her, it could happen to me."

"But it's not as if it happens to every other girl on the street," Mom said. "You can't obsess about freak things like that."

I sighed and sank back in my seat, rubbing the belt over my shoulder between thumb and forefinger. There was a question that had been on my mind ever since we had talked about Mrs. Lemons at lunch, and if I didn't bring it up now, I was afraid I never would. "Mrs. Lemons told my fortune one time," I said. "She said she used to tell yours too, but after a while you stopped coming to see her."

I paused and waited, but it seemed as if Mom was waiting too. After a moment she glanced over, the angle of the afternoon sun highlighting the crow's feet around her eyes. "That's true," she said.

"But what did she tell you?"

She shook her head, and I gripped the belt tighter. Mrs. Lemons had said that the disaster I feared most would pass over me, but she hadn't said anything about my family, and I hadn't asked. Had she forecasted some other kind of catastrophe—something I hadn't even thought to worry about?

"She said that nothing would change until I changed it." Mom tried for a laugh. "Sounds kind of like a greeting card when you think about it." Abruptly, she swung the car across a lane of traffic and into a gas station parking lot. "Kate, would you pick me up a bottle of water? I'm parched."

She handed me a dollar, and I waited for her to say something else, but she just sat, tapping the steering wheel, not looking at me. I thought about waiting her out, but I'd needed to use the bathroom since we'd left Moorefield.

The convenience store was small and clearly catered to the truckers grinding over the mountain roads between Asheville and Knoxville. There were displays of *Playboy*s and Yosemite Sam *Back Off* mud flaps, and a whole shelf of beer cozies with slogans like *Here's to Another Long One* and *My Truck, My Rules*. The bathroom was locked, so I waited in the hallway with a view of the restaurant advertising chicken salad on white for a dollar ninety-seven. I could tell that Mom believed that Mrs. Lemons had seen down into her, seen her longings and her inertia, but I was skeptical. I loved my mother, but you didn't need the second sight to understand that she wanted more from life. When it came to evaluating Mrs. Lemons's prophetic gifts, I was no better off than I had been.

There were three people in the restaurant, two truckers at one table and a woman sitting alone. The truckers were watching the woman, and she was pretending not to notice them. She could have been in her early thirties, blonde and a little heavy, with too much blue eye makeup. She was smoking a cigarette, swaying as she mouthed the words from the jukebox: *I don't know why I love you but I do.* Her face had a looseness to it that made her look easygoing but not happy.

Then it hit me: Angie Davenport. Travis had pointed her out to me years ago at the county fair. As a high school senior, she had set a car full of her classmates on fire and rolled it into a ditch, killing five. She looked up and straight into my eyes, her gaze tired and uncurious, and I ducked behind a rotating rack of postcards. I had never been trained in Mason's symbol language, but surely this was a sign of some kind. First I had dreamed of Margaret Reid, Victoria Duvalier, Crystal Lemons, and now here was another ex–wild girl. Together, they seemed more malevolent than any floating lights or black bird on the windowsill.

When an old woman with a pink fanny pack came out of the bathroom, I ran inside and turned the lock. Leaning against the door, I repeated the old words like a prayer: *Please, please don't let it happen to me.* But alone here, in the dark, I had to admit that what scared me most was not the thought of Angie Davenport's crimes but the thought of her life today, truck stops and a sad apartment with neighbors who looked the other way when she came home with a different man every night. My prayer was not *May I be kept from frenzy, violence, madness, and murder* but *May I be preserved from a future like Angie Davenport's.* And what kind of god would care to grant such a selfish prayer as that?

CHAPTER TWELVE

The week I came back to the Academy was full of what I took for signs. A leftover leaf on a poplar branch that shivered to dust when I touched it. A salamander on the side of Maggie's van, staring at me as it stuck out and sucked in its bright long tongue. In that first week of February a thaw came over the mountains, the frozen layer of snow bruising and cracking. I had three and a half months to go before Graduation. Sometimes I thought I would make it, but sometimes I thought that the signs spelled disaster for all of us, and I woke up with my chest so tight I could barely breathe.

Caroline had come back to school with a new layered haircut from a salon in Manhattan, where she and her mom and stepdad had spent New Year's. Her round John Lennon frames had been replaced by cat-eye glasses with rhinestones in the corners, and under her uniform she wore colored tights that looked more stylish and less kooky than her old rainbow-striped kneesocks. Over the holidays, when I was stuck in the worst of my depression, she had called to ask if I could meet them, even offering to send a train ticket. I had made up some excuse about wanting to spend time with my family, but it was clear now that she hadn't bought it. "You need to get out," she said on our first night back at the dining hall. "I don't want to sound insensitive or anything, but you need to have fun. It's your last semester of high school."

"Come on, Caroline," I mumbled, hacking at the crust of my sandwich with the edge of a dull fork. "Look at where we are."

She followed the direction of my gaze to the hot line. Three or four of the old cafeteria ladies, Mason's coworkers, stood behind the long counter in aprons and hairnets, gossiping over the pans of corn chowder and potatoes gratin. "Okay, fine," Caroline sighed. "I can understand if you need some time. I just don't want you to wallow, you know?"

Maybe it was the weird state I was in, but something about the way Caroline fluffed up her new hair with her fingers made me suspicious. The difference in her was too great to be explained simply by an afternoon at a high-priced salon. I took a sip of her root beer, watching her steadily over the rim. "So what about that guy Oliver?" I said. "Did you talk to him over the break?"

"We had lunch, actually." Caroline twisted a French fry between her fingers. "He was in Pittsburgh for a conference, so I came in and met him downtown."

"What kind of conference?"

The fry snapped, and she stuck the two halves broken end up in a thimble-size cup of ketchup. "The International Anglican Youth Fellowship."

I'd meant my eye roll to be discreet, but she looked up too quickly. "What's your problem, Kate?" she said, but gently, as if she really wanted to know. "I don't understand why you don't like him."

"He's mean. He's an intellectual snob."

Caroline took off her glasses and rubbed them along her sleeve. She looked genuinely upset now, and I wondered if that was what

I'd been aiming for all along. "He's not a snob. He's shy. You don't know him."

"He laughed at me when I asked if they celebrated Thanksgiving in Scotland."

"Well, you have to admit—" she started, but went silent when she noticed Dr. Bell walking toward us. He was dressed, as always, just a little better than the teachers, in a crisp white button-down and a red silk tie winking with golden triangles. Though he shone his white teeth at both of us, it was clear that he'd come to talk to Caroline.

"I wanted to remind you that we've moved tutorial from seven to seven-thirty tonight," he said, leaning over her. "I do hope you'll be there. I thought we'd take a look at Odysseus's meeting with Nausicaa."

Caroline smiled with a hesitance that puzzled me and said of course she'd be there. Satisfied, Dr. Bell turned to me, folding his hands at his belt. "And how did the Riordan family enjoy the holiday?" he asked, with a solicitous intonation that made me blush. Did he know about Travis moving out, or even my mom's plans to quit her job at the Academy?

"Umm." I kept my eyes on the watch sliding down his hairy wrist. "We enjoyed it fine, I guess."

The dining hall was mostly empty at this time of night, and as he walked away, the shadows of the flags hung in the windows rippled across his back. "Am I the only student from Myths and Mysteries who isn't invited to tutorial?" I asked Caroline, my eyes still on Dr. Bell.

"Rosa and Elise and those girls only come once in a while. I don't think they care much about the *Odyssey*."

"And he never talks about the wild girls, right?"

"Not directly." Caroline picked up her knife and fork and placed them at right angles on her plate. "But sometimes it seems like everything's about the wild girls."

The room was darkening, the shadows of the long tables sliding across the floor. From the kitchen came the sounds of running water and clanking silverware, and when I looked around I saw that we were the only people left in the room.

Three days had passed and we were back into the routine of classes before I even caught a glimpse of Willow. I'd given up on being mad at her by then. Considering everything that had happened, resentment felt like a waste of energy, but I didn't want to talk to her if I could help it. When I saw her sitting in the corner of the Peebles Library lounge with Tessa and the minions, I waved at Elise and Lucie but ignored the rest of them. Willow was playing cards with Matilda, who watched her with adoring bug eyes.

"Hey, Kate," Tessa said in a voice just loud enough to carry. "What did you *say* to him anyway?"

The recycling container I was hauling hit a crack in the wood floor, and while I struggled to right it, I kept the table in the corner of my vision. Lucie slid down in her chair and picked at her fingernails. Elise became suddenly absorbed in the newspaper. Willow laid down a card and peered at it thoughtfully, her lip caught between her teeth.

"Did you hear what I said?" Tessa asked. "I'm just curious, Kate. When a guy has to jump off a bridge to get away from you—"

I closed my hand around a copy of the Swan River brochure, crumpling it in my fist. Tessa was on that brochure, along with other girls who symbolized the Academy as it used to be: Audrey Taliaferro, Cabell Lanier. Until recently, a girl with a name and a high-bridged upturned nose that brought to mind the South in all its antebellum glory would have felt confident enough in her standing not to have to insult a nobody like me. Now Tessa had something to prove, but I had no intention of helping her.

In a couple of strides I had reached them, and I threw the brochure in her face. It hit her between the eyes. When she recoiled, the ball of paper rolled down her neck, one stiff corner catching in the weave of her cashmere sweater.

"You didn't know him," I said. "And you don't know me either. So why don't you shut the fuck up."

In the parking lot of the Tastee-Freez, this would have meant a fight. Though I'd never thrown a punch in my life, I curled my hands into fists. Frances half-rose from her seat, but no one else moved a muscle, and as I dragged the container toward the door, it was only Tessa's voice that followed me. "You think you can just walk away from me?" she shrieked. "You're trash, you know that?"

Outside, I walked slowly and tried to catch my breath. Throwing the brochure at Tessa had felt good. It was what Crystal Lemons would have done, or even my sister. My sister was not trash, but I could see better than ever now that the distinctions that held outside the school gates meant exactly nothing to a girl like Tessa Cochran. When she looked at me, she didn't see that I would be the first one in my family to get a bachelor's degree. She saw a hick in a secondhand uniform, and I thought that I might as well have been a wild girl, bloodthirsty and raving, for all the difference it made to people like her.

I hadn't even gotten to the post office when Willow ran up to me, stuffing her deck of cards into the pocket of her coat. "Hey," she said. "I have to talk to you."

The last time I'd heard this summons had been back in the fall, at the River House. My face burned when I thought of how I'd read her note and run upstairs to meet her, a good little servant. "Well, I don't have to talk to you," I said.

"Kate, come on." She chased after me, one hand clasped to her blue beret. "You think it didn't hurt me? I haven't been sleeping— I didn't get out of bed for three days after I heard."

When I faced her, the recycling can between us, I thought she might have been telling the truth. Her face was white, the skin under her eyes stained blue with fatigue. I started to feel sorry for her, but I told myself that her grief was useless now. Where had she been when Mason needed her, when *I* needed her? "Well, I'm sorry that he ruined your vacation," I said. "In Hawaii."

Willow looked away. With an electric thrill along my spine, I realized that she was crying. "I thought I could talk to you," she said. "I thought you'd understand how I felt. I never meant to hurt him. I went about it the wrong way, I was stupid, and—"

I shrugged and started walking again, dragging the container behind me. I wasn't ready to forgive her, but I wasn't entirely sorry when she followed and grabbed the can by the other handle. "Where are you taking this stuff anyway?" she asked.

"There's a big bin on the loading dock."

"But why? I mean, what's the point?"

"There's this organization I started." I pulled a flyer from the pocket of my coat, and she read it aloud.

"*Clean Up Swan River! First Meeting, Monday, February 6th in the Fallis Hall TV Lounge.*" Instead of throwing the flyer into the bin as I had expected, she tucked it into the pocket of her coat. "So what are you cleaning up—the river or the town?"

I shrugged. "Both, I guess. Eventually I want to do some habitat restoration along the bank, but Mr. Hightower said to start with the recycling."

Willow nodded fervently, though I knew that she was about as interested in saving the environment as she was in quantum physics. Tears were still leaking from the corners of her eyes. They made it hard to look her in the face, so instead I concentrated on the crease of her coat collar. "Mason told me that he asked you to stay with him in Swan River," I said.

Her smile seemed to make the tears brighter. "Sometimes I dream about it," she said. "I come through a door and he's there, you know—sitting in a chair, reading a book. And I think, maybe we could have made it work. Maybe the life I want, the life my parents want for me—I mean, it seems so unimportant next to—"

Willow's voice faded to a whisper. Breaking her gaze, I hugged myself and hopped on one foot, pretending to be even colder than I was. There was no way I would let her know that while she dreamed of Mason living, happy, I dreamed of him dead under the river.

She pushed her hands down in her pockets, looking down at her boots. "Everything seems kind of meaningless now."

The words themselves were ordinary enough. *Everything seems meaningless* was something that teenage girls said, like *If I fail the Calc test, I'm going to kill myself.* No one actually believed that you meant it. But something in Willow's tone made me look at her again. "Well, everything's not meaningless," I said lamely. "It's an awful thing that happened, but—"

"But it was because of me, wasn't it?"

I shook my head. "No," I said. "It definitely wasn't because of you." Until that moment, I hadn't known how sure I was that it was not Willow's fault, nor mine for that matter. Until I looked at her face, exposed by grief in a way I had never seen it, I didn't realize how much I wanted her to understand that she hadn't killed Mason Lemons.

"Well." Willow let out a little puff of breath. "Thank you for saying that, anyway."

On the loading dock she helped me sort everything out, mixed paper in one bin and cans and bottles in the other. Over her shoulder I saw the minions walk out of the library in a pack, without Tessa. The next time I looked back, the minions had disappeared and Tessa was standing on the steps that led down to the Lawn, arms crossed over her chest. Maybe it was sinking in that no one had backed her up when she'd gone after me. Maybe she was putting this incident together with other moments from the past months, and finally cluing into the fact that she'd been deposed.

When we'd finished with the recycling, Willow said she wanted to take a walk, and I followed her across the Lawn and down the steps to the park. Now that I had seen her cry, I could admit that in the past I had sometimes found it hard to tell what about her was genuine and what was an act. Did she really want to be my friend? Were her compliments sincere, or was she as empty as Caroline said she was, as empty as the locket that I had found in Mason's bedroom? I couldn't explain why, but I felt that her grief had answered the question to my satisfaction. She was real, and she was the only person in the world who could possibly understand how I felt about Mason.

We were circling the outer wall of the amphitheater, looking down the marble steps slicked with leftover snow. The park backed up to the real forest and had the same trees, the same cedary, musty smell, but everything here seemed tamed and sanitized. It was impossible to imagine danger or violence here, in this civilized section of the wild mountains.

"I've been a bitch lately," Willow said, as if she were continuing a conversation already begun. "I know I have. It's just so easy for me to run the show around here, and I start getting an ego, I think. I need someone to call me on my shit, and you weren't around. You're my conscience, Kate."

I bit my lip and kept walking. The person she'd described—honest, blunt, full of integrity—sounded more like Caroline than like me; still, I liked the idea that Willow saw me that way. The temperature was only in the forties, but the thaw had taken hold even in the shaded forest. In the scummy wash of needles and bracken, toadstools were brewing, inching their heads out of the ooze as if they wanted to take a look around before they made up their minds. We stopped on a filigree bridge, looking down at the black, half-frozen creek that meandered through the pine grove. I stared down at the creek, where a red leaf floated in a patch of ice. It must have been there all winter, every vein outlined, as bright and out of place as a lost mitten, and I wondered if anyone had ever noticed it before. "I slept with him too," I said.

Willow paused just long enough to make me nervous. "I forgive you." She put her arm around my shoulder and gave me a quick side hug. "If I had to share him, I'm glad it was with you."

Above the curved roof of the amphitheater, the back wall of the administration building was visible, the light in Dr. Bell's office window shining through the bare trees. I rubbed my shoulder; Willow must have squeezed it harder than she meant to. "Whatever happened with my dare anyway?" I asked. "Did anyone steal the notebook?"

"I don't think so." Willow rubbed her cheeks with the heels of her hands. "Frances keeps talking about breaking into his office, but I doubt she'll ever do it. Speaking of, what are you doing for spring break? You can come with us to Frances's cabin if you want."

"Is Tessa going?"

"No, thank God. She's going up to New York for her deb ball."

"I hate her," I said. "Caroline and I call her Tessa Cockroach. Or Tessa Horse-Face."

"It's weird how much she and that horse look alike," Willow said. "Like old ladies and their dogs."

She took out her Balkan Sobranies and didn't show surprise when I held out my hand for a cigarette and a light. The trees closed above us, throwing dark barred shadows across the patches of snow. "I wish we hung out more," she said. "Seriously, Kate. I think we've shared something that—I mean, I don't think anyone else can understand what we've been through."

"Here," I said, fishing out the locket and chain I'd been carrying around for weeks. "Mason gave this to me to give to you. It fell off in his car."

Until that moment, I hadn't been sure what I was going to do with the locket—give it back, or keep it, or throw it off the bridge. But Willow's face lit up, and she snatched the locket out of my hand before I could change my mind. She lifted her arms to fix the clasp, and I watched as the silver heart settled again against the pale skin of her throat.

CHAPTER THIRTEEN

In the weeks before spring break, the envelopes were everywhere. Walking through the dorm lobby, you saw them stuffed into the seniors' boxes—white business size mostly, but some in blue or green, with a big manila envelope or two sticking out like a rolled tongue. The rule was the bigger and thicker the envelope, the better the news, but once in a while you'd see a girl pull out a thin white slip and shriek with excitement. Caroline got into Bryn Mawr. Elise Seidel got into Duke. Tessa Cochran went around telling everybody how totally excited she was about the University of Northern Georgia, though we all knew it was the only place that had accepted her. Lorelei Rice didn't get into Sweet Briar and broke into hysterical sobs in the middle of the dining hall.

I had my share of thick envelopes, but they might have been postcard-thin for all the difference it made. When I looked down to the bottom of the letter, it was always no financial aid, or so little that it seemed like a joke. Caroline tried to talk to me about loans and Pell Grants, but it only made me feel more hopeless. I told myself that I hadn't heard from Pritchard College yet, and kept wearing the heavy fisherman's sweater I'd bought for a cooler climate long after the weather had changed.

I found the letter in my mailbox on my way to Myths and

Mysteries. I held the envelope up to the light—normal business-size, with a frieze of pine trees above the return address. It was neither thick nor thin. Suddenly I felt that I couldn't open it by myself. I had to find Caroline, who could scrape me off the floor if the news was bad.

Today Dr. Bell was lecturing on the Euripides play *The Bacchae*, about the ancient Greek women who worshiped Dionysus. I had always thought of Dionysus as the god of wine, but these women did more than just get drunk. They ran around in the woods all night, tearing animals to pieces and eating the flesh raw. One of them, who had been a queen before the god drove her out of her mind, ripped off her son's head and carried it back to the city in triumph, believing that she had killed a wild boar. Dr. Bell paced between the desk and the window, his shirtsleeves rolled up to show a pair of muscled forearms.

"These maenads," he said, "they represent the side of ourselves that we can't control—the darkness and unreason, or what Freudians would call the sublimated impulse. We may think we've civilized ourselves, but human beings are surprising creatures, full of whims and passions that can't be gratified in conventional society. It's when we believe we've conquered our dark sides that they're most likely to break out and insist on fulfillment, consequences be damned."

I looked sideways at Caroline, but she was writing something on the back cover of her notebook, her hair falling forward to cover her face. It was weird to see Caroline spacing out in class, and I hoped that she wasn't daydreaming about Oliver Davis. I knew that he'd called her once or twice since their Pittsburgh lunch, but she never mentioned him unless I asked.

The windows were open, the drowsy drone of a lawn mower and the scent of heated grass carried in on the breeze. Across the

Lawn, I could see Clancy planting blooming tulips in the mulch in front of Calhoun Hall. Since Caroline was going to Italy to visit her father for spring break, her mom and stepdad had come down this weekend and were taking me along to the Grand Hotel in Moorefield. I should have been excited about the chance to stay in a nice hotel for the first time in my life, but the letter in my bag sent out a distracting hum, like a filled cavity picking up radio signals.

After class, I caught up with Caroline on the steps of Peebles Library and thrust the letter into her hands. "I need you to open this."

For a moment she looked surprised. Though we'd made plans to spend the weekend together, the only times we'd really hung out in the past couple months had been at the meetings of Clean Up Swan River! On our river beautification day, we'd met at six in the morning and spent an hour and a half paddling along the banks, spearing beer cans and plastic bags while mayfly nymphs rose in a cloud around our boat. It was probably the most fun I'd had since Mason started losing it.

"Let's go sit down in the lounge first," Caroline said, turning the envelope over.

"In case it's bad news and I pass out?"

"Or good news," she said. "You could get dizzy either way."

I followed her into the light-filled Bessie P. Seidel Memorial Lounge, and we sat down in two velvet armchairs by the windows. I kept my eyes squeezed shut and listened to the paper rustling. Caroline opened envelopes as neatly and carefully as she did everything else. "Well, you got in."

My eyes sprang open. "I did?"

"*Dear Ms. Riordan, We are pleased to welcome you to the Pritchard class of*— But hold on, it's a long letter. *We would also like to inform you that you are a finalist for the Lila Robinson Porter Scholarship*—"

I didn't need to hear the rest. I pulled Caroline to her feet, and shrieking, we jumped up and down until I felt light-headed. A few girls walked past on their way to the stacks, but nobody paid much attention to us. At this time of year, everyone knew exactly what this sort of happiness meant.

Breathless, I sat down to scan the last paragraph. "*Your phone interview is scheduled for Saturday, April 16th*— That's tomorrow! Do you think I can do it while we're in Moorefield?"

"Sure. I'll hide in the bathroom or something." Caroline smiled a wan smile that made me think of some nineteenth-century girl with tuberculosis—Emily Brontë, or Beth from *Little Women*. "I'm happy for you, Kate."

Though her smile was tired, she did look genuinely pleased, and I realized that there was no one I would rather share this news with. "I guess I should go see my mom," I said. "Not that she knows Pritchard from Harvard, but she'll be excited anyway."

"Look, there's my mom and my stepdad," Caroline said, pointing out the window. "Can I tell them about it?"

The gray-haired, earnest-looking couple crossing the Lawn spotted us and waved frantically. I had met Caroline's mom and stepdad before, but parents in general embarrassed me and I usually tried to get away as quickly as possible. Her mom, who I couldn't stop calling Doctor even after she told me to call her Louise, was prettier than I'd remembered—thin and nicely dressed, with Caroline's narrow face. They broke into smiles when Caroline told them about the interview, and told me I could pick the restaurant that night. They said it would be their treat.

In Moorefield I went with them from art opening to museum to concert, and came to understand that they were exactly the sort of parents I should have had. They were always talking about art, politics, philosophy, all the things I wanted to know more about. Caroline's stepdad, Dr. Blair, said that the soloist in the Aaron Copland piece had a nice mezzo, and I repeated the words in my head: *a nice mezzo in the Aaron Copland piece.* Her mom said that I looked like a Modigliani, and later that day I snuck off to the library to flip through page after page of long-faced, deep-eyed women. This was what it meant to have culture, I told myself, and it made my highbrow classmates' interest in designer labels and deb balls seem even more dull by comparison. I kept a list of the people Dr. Blair mentioned whom I'd never heard of: Ornette Coleman, Martha Graham, Spiro Agnew. The night we went to the Japanese restaurant, I ordered sashimi instead of chicken tempura, and when Caroline gave me a look I stared blandly back at her.

For the phone interview, the Grand Hotel set me up in a conference room with burgundy leather chairs and a speakerphone. The call lasted forty-five minutes, and when it was done I went back to the room I shared with Caroline and flopped down on the mattress. She was on the other bed, reading *Anna Karenina.* "How did it go?" she asked.

"Good, I think." I reached for one of the thousand tasseled throw pillows and laid it on my forehead. "I talked about Clean Up Swan River! I told them that we were planning to do trash pickup on Route Nineteen after the break. They seemed to like it."

"When are they going to get back to you?"

"They said it might not be until the end of the semester. I guess they're doing a bunch more interviews."

Caroline asked more questions, but after a minute I realized that I didn't really want to talk. The more I thought about it, the more convinced I was that I'd messed up the interview. Had I really bragged about starting an environmental club? The other candidates probably started clubs in their preschools, while playing three sports and maintaining a 4.0. "What's that thing?" I said, pointing listlessly to the thick vinyl binder at the end of Caroline's bed.

Caroline turned a page before she answered. Though it was only four o'clock, she was dressed for dinner, in an apricot sundress that I'd never seen before. "It's my research notes for Myths and Mysteries."

I propped myself on my elbows. "It's thick."

"I found a lot of articles."

I moved over to her bed and flipped through the plastic sleeves. Predictably, the nineteenth-century wild girls I'd heard about at Girl Scout camp were not included. Margaret Reid and Sophia Peabody wouldn't have been written up in the *Riparian*, but from 1950 on the wild girls were all there: Elizabeth Jackdaw, Heather Green, Sharon Englehard. Angie Davenport, whose flat face stared out at me from under a fringe of eighties bangs. Jenny Stockton, Misty Greco. Some were convicted murderers; some were dead. A blast of air-conditioning struck my bare shoulder, and I crossed my arms. I could not become one of them, not now. Not when I almost had my ticket out of here.

"I can't believe you did all this work," I said. "Dr. Bell must be really impressed."

Caroline was silent, pulling at a loose thread in the duvet cover. "What's going on?" I asked.

"I want to tell you something," she said. "But you have to promise not to repeat it."

"Oh no." Why hadn't I seen this coming? "Was he—did he try to creep on you?"

"No, it's nothing like that," she said. "Or I don't know, maybe it was, but—" She took a deep breath and pressed her fingertips against her eyelids. "He made me eat these leaves."

"Leaves," I repeated blankly.

"Bloodwort leaves," Caroline said. "But it started before that. A few weeks after winter break, I went to the Tuesday night tutorial and I was the only one there. That happened sometimes, and I was always happy about it, because he was different when it was just the two of us. Not in a weird way," she added, seeing the look on my face. "I mean that he seemed to take me more seriously. We read Ovid in Latin. We talked about my research project, and the classes I should take in college. We never said anything about the wild girls, but I felt like he understood why I was interested in them."

Caroline pulled harder at the loose thread, unraveling an overblown golden rose in the middle of the duvet. "Anyway, somehow he got around to talking about these Dionysian rituals. He's very interested in neopagan mystery cults, and—"

"Wait, what's a neopagan mystery cult?"

"People who are trying to revive pagan worship," she said. "Sometimes they're into worshiping specific gods, and sometimes it's more of a pantheistic thing. Apparently there are a lot of them in England. Dr. Bell was telling me about this ritual where a teenage girl dressed in black goes into the woods and follows all these steps, lighting candles, eating this paste made from leaves and river water. I don't remember all the details, but she was supposed to be able to fly and set things on fire just by touching them. It sounded exactly like the wild girls. And then he took out this packet of bloodwort leaves and said, 'Let's give it a try, just for fun.'"

I felt sick. "You mean he's trying to create wild girls?"

"The file cabinet behind his desk was open, and he had everything ready—candles, and these little vials of water. He must have been positive I was going to say yes."

"But you told him to go to hell," I said. "Didn't you?"

"Well, not in those words exactly." Caroline pulled her knees to her chest. "But yeah, I got out of there."

I shook my head. "Wild girls kill people. Why would he want to create them?"

"I think he sees himself as Dionysus. Like if he calls a wild girl into being, he'll get to control her. There probably is some kind of sexual element. When he told me about the ritual, he was practically panting."

I chewed the inside of my cheek. When Dr. Bell had told us the story about Victoria Duvalier, had he been trying to plant some sort of seed? He had talked about rituals then too—drinking, ecstatic dancing. "I didn't know what to do," Caroline said. "Since then I've just been trying to stay out of his way, but I don't think he's given up necessarily. Last weekend I was coming back from the fitness center late at night, and I saw Willow coming out of his office by herself."

"Willow?" I said. "Are you sure it was Willow?"

"I'm not blind," Caroline said impatiently. "I saw her hair."

"Maybe it was some other redhead. Do you know Hattie Lapham? She could look a lot like Willow from the back."

Caroline rolled her eyes, but I tapped the binder with my fingernail. "You read all these articles. You know where those girls come from. Willow's dad is the mail-order king of the Southeast."

"I know around here people think that being a wild girl has to do with class," Caroline said, "but isn't there another common factor? Those girls had a lot of trauma in their lives. Even Maggie—she was furious about being at the Academy, she was lonely and upset.

What if it doesn't have anything to do with being poor? What if it's just strong emotion that makes it happen?"

"Well, but why would Dr. Bell think it could happen to you?" I asked. "*You* haven't experienced a lot of trauma."

"I complained to him about my parents' divorce one time. I'd been talking to my dad, and I was crying because we'd had a bad connection. Maybe Dr. Bell thought I was more screwed up than I really am."

The phone rang, and Caroline bent forward to reach it, her wide skirt pooling between her knees. "You are?" she said, smiling as she twisted a piece of hair around her finger. "That's great. So where are you staying tonight?"

When I was sure it wasn't Willow, who had already called once to tell me that the Academy was boring without me, I started flipping through the Myths and Mysteries binder. The girls stared back at me, knocked around, downbeaten, and I wondered why I'd ever worried about becoming one of them. I wasn't really that damaged. I had lost my father, and Mason, but next to Crystal Lemons I had no traumas worth speaking of.

The phone clinked onto the receiver. "You know what I think?" I said without looking up. "Remember that stupid dare I told you about, where someone was supposed to steal Dr. Bell's notebook? I bet that's why Willow was in his office. He probably caught her and kicked her out."

"Maybe."

Caroline sounded distracted, and I looked up. She wasn't blushing, but her skin looked warmer than usual. It could have been the makeup, I thought, and then it occurred to me that in four years I'd never seen her wearing lipstick before. "Who was that on the phone?"

She knitted her hands together and looked me squarely in the eye. "Oliver's on his way. He's driving down to meet my parents. I should have told you earlier."

"Yeah, you should have," I said, pulling a pack of Balkan Sobranies from the zippered pouch on my suitcase. "I can't stand that guy, and you know it."

"You smoke now?" Caroline asked, pursing her lips.

"Sometimes."

"Well, I'm pretty sure that this is a nonsmoking floor."

"I'll spray perfume." I moved to a chair, but didn't bother to crack the window. "Et tu, Caroline?" I said under my breath.

"Et tu what?" she said sharply. "I haven't done anything."

"I just can't believe you fell for the first guy who looked at you twice. I like to be a little more picky, that's all."

"Really? Is that why you slept with Mason after Willow broke up with him? Is that what you call being picky?"

I almost dropped the cigarette in my lap. "How did you know about that?"

Sighing heavily, she lifted her gaze to the ceiling. "The way you went on after he died. Like you were ready to throw yourself on the pyre."

Tears prickled my eyes, but I blinked them back. "Why are you being so mean?"

"You're the one who's mean," Caroline said. "Ever since you started hanging out with Willow again, you've been like a different person. I thought that when we were away from the Academy you might be more like your old self, but I was wrong."

"What are you talking about? Different how?"

She still wouldn't look at me. "*One morning Kate Riordan awoke from uneasy dreams to find herself transformed into Tessa Cockroach.*"

"Ouch." Turning so she couldn't see my face, I took a long drag. "I bet you've been saving that up for months, haven't you?"

"I know that you look up to Willow," she said. "But she's not really your friend, Kate. She doesn't have friends. She's an empty person."

"For your information, Willow was really upset about Mason's death," I said. "Anyway, what does that even mean—an empty person?"

"It means someone who only cares about herself. But I don't give a shit about Willow, to tell you the truth. I just think it's sad that you don't appreciate the people who are really there for you."

"Like you, for example."

"Like me. Like Clancy. He feels the same way, you know."

"You talk about me with *Clancy?* What does he say?"

"Well, nothing bad," Caroline said. "He just likes you, that's all. He just wants to know that you're okay."

We could have let the fight end there. Caroline got a bottle of water from the minibar, took a sip, and passed it to me before I could ask. But the water tasted like metal, and it set my teeth on edge. She had hurt me. She had said I was turning into Tessa Cockroach. Now I wanted to hurt her too. "So do you think you and Oliver are like a permanent thing?" I asked, making my voice lively and friendly.

"I don't know," Caroline said. "I mean, I'm going to Bryn Mawr next year."

"Well, I guess it works out for both of you in the short term." I gave a big smile, and she looked back at me without flinching— her face so open, so unprepared for cruelty that I almost regretted what I was about to say. "You know, because he gets laid, and you get to feel normal for a while. You like to come off as a free spirit and an intellectual and everything, but I know that deep down you'd rather fit in. You just don't know how to act like other people."

The words felt thrilling, irresistible, and I told myself that I was giving her a taste of her own medicine. Now we could make up—both sufficiently insulted, both ready to forgive. But Caroline had turned the TV to a news show with men in suits arguing around a table, and every time I tried to speak she nudged the volume higher, until finally her stepdad started banging on the wall.

CHAPTER FOURTEEN

As soon as Caroline's mom dropped us off at the dorm, I went to find Willow. She wasn't in her room or the TV lounge or the dining hall, but when I got back to my room, I'd barely had time to shut the door behind me when she knocked. "Well, Frances was wrong," she said, tossing a creased brown leather notebook onto my bed.

"Wrong about what?" I asked without taking my eyes from the notebook.

"She thought he was writing sexual fantasies about students, or something like that." Willow sat down on the radiator, crossing her legs gracefully at the knee. "But unless *Kalmia latifolia* is some kind of code name, she's way off."

From fieldwork in Environmental Studies, I knew that *Kalmia latifolia* was the scientific name for mountain laurel. "So it's like a naturalist's notebook."

"I guess." Willow jiggled her foot up and down. "Anyway, since you had that theory that he was writing about the wild girls, I thought you might want to take a look."

I turned the notebook over and studied the back. "So how did you finally get it?"

"He left his door unlocked, and Matilda grabbed it. The board of trustees is on campus, so he's in meetings all day, but we should probably try to get it back in an hour or two." At the door, she looked back, and I noticed that her new contacts were a startling ·jade green. "I'm having a party later," she said. "Stop by if you want and tell me what you find out."

I made Willow's deadline by minutes, passing the notebook off to Lucie Yates, who slipped out the side door of Dr. Bell's office just as he came through the front. He was sandwiched between two lady trustees with red suits and matching helmet hair, gossiping and chuckling as if they found him the most charming of companions. Later, Willow and I sat on her windowsill and I told her what I'd put together from the notebook and the conversation with Caroline: Dr. Bell was using his position to turn the girls under his care into murderous creatures right out of myth.

Keeping my voice low so I wouldn't disturb the minions, asleep on the bed and the floor, I explained that most of the notations in the book seemed to be recipes. "We know he's really interested in plants. He's always stopping by Mr. Hightower's office, and Mason told me that Dr. Bell used to ask his mom about the herbs she used in her potions. I think he's trying to find some magic formula that will make somebody into a wild girl."

Willow tapped her cigarette, the ashes drifting down to the privet hedge two stories below. She had asked me to tell her what I'd found, but now she was barely paying attention. "Well, but that's not how it works," she said. "Is it?"

"Nobody knows how it works. I mean, I know my sister wasn't out there in the woods eating bloodwort and mountain laurel. But he's into all this occult stuff, and I guess he thinks it can't hurt."

Willow nodded and blew a stray hair out of her face. I was afraid she was going to change the subject, so I hurried on. I had to tell someone what I'd found, and Caroline and I weren't speaking.

"When you were looking through the notebook," I said, "did you see the initials *VD*?"

"Rosa thought it meant venereal disease."

"Of course she did," I muttered with a glance at Rosa, snoring on Willow's bed with her mouth half-open. "I think they stand for Victoria Duvalier. She was the girl in that story he told us on the Environmental Studies trip, one of the Academy girls who killed the Union sentinels."

He'd headed one page, I explained, with the letters *VD*, and below he'd made a list: first the words *potions? ritual?*, then a series of question marks, and then, on the third line, the word *INFLUENCE*. "Remember what he said about the girl who wrote the diary? When she talked to a doctor after the war, she said that Victoria had controlled her mind. I think Dr. Bell was considering whether one girl could create other wild girls just by manipulating them—you know, through some weird kind of peer pressure."

On the floor, Elise sighed in her sleep. A breeze stirred the heavy branches of the oaks. "Are you sure you should hang your legs out the window like that?" I said to Willow. "I mean, when you've been drinking, it just seems—"

"I'm *fiiine*," Willow sang. She held on to the inside of the window frame and swung her upper body back and forth. "So what do you think, anyway? Your sister was a wild girl. Where do they come from?"

"I don't know," I said. "But if there is some kind of dark force in the universe, then maybe Swan River is—like—an access point."

I had never talked like this to anyone except Caroline. I waited for Willow to laugh at me, but she just stared for a long moment and then nodded seriously. "That's cool. You're a very creative thinker, Kate."

I shrugged and beat my heels in a light tattoo against the base-board.

"No, I mean it," Willow said. "Not to put anyone down, but a lot of the people we know, their lives are kind of scripted for them. They might turn out well or they might not, but they're never going to surprise anybody. But you're so observant—you're always analyzing things. What I'm saying is, when we come back for our ten-year reunion, I think you'll be kicking ass."

"Thanks." I felt suddenly tired of being complimented.

One of Willow's hands slipped from the window frame, and I tensed my body, ready to pull her back in if necessary. "I know I haven't always acted like it," she said, "but I really think of you as my best friend. I think you understand me better than anybody."

"Thanks," I said again, less delighted than I would have expected to be. "I guess you're probably my best friend too."

With the Academy closed, spring break became a mini-version of the summer. In the morning, I read—I was making my way through Dostoevsky, slowly—and in the afternoon I went for a run. When the public library bored me and the movie theater was showing only stupid movies, running was the best way to get out of the house for a while. In the clean pine-smelling mists of early morning, I followed the fire road down to Bloodwort Farm and then through the Delta to the river. In Environmental Science, we had come down here to calculate velocity and the level of dissolved oxygen. We had captured minnows and studied the level of erosion along the bank. Though the river looked clear, I knew that it was threatened by acid drainage by the mines upstream in Tennessee. I knew that in other rivers not far away from here, trout had been caught with two heads or no fins. I always came back with a water-logged bag of chips or a few crushed soda cans in my pocket, as if that made any difference at all.

On the last day of the break, Maggie called me to say that she and Kayak Boy were having a cookout. After a week of eating Hamburger Helper with Mom while she went on about how ter-rific things would be when we lived in Moorefield, getting out of the house sounded like a great idea. Still I hesitated, wrapping the phone cord around my finger. "I won't know anyone there."

"Come on," Maggie said. "You'll know everyone there."

As it turned out, she was right. It was the girls from our Friday night trips to the Tastee-Freez along with their boyfriends and hus-bands, tall bearded guys in hunting caps who seemed slightly def-erential toward the women, as if they hadn't forgotten what these girls had once been capable of. Maggie and Kayak Boy played a set, and as the guests crowded around the makeshift stage, I felt something in the air, the savor of a fierce recklessness. It wasn't that anyone was actually going to do anything violent, throw a punch or a bottle. I could tell that everybody liked Maggie and Kayak Boy, and most of the guests were in what passed for a good mood. But just like at the Tastee-Freez, no one was able to forget what was going on around here. It wasn't just the threat of the wild girls. Swan River was breaking down, and no one seemed able to do anything about it.

After her set, Maggie came and sat down with me at one of the picnic tables. She was sweaty and grinning, a few loose curls pasted to the side of her face. "You should be the mayor," I said.

She dabbed at her cheeks with a paper napkin. "What?"

I shrugged. "Everybody likes you. Maybe you could actually do something to fix this place."

Kayak Boy put a bluegrass CD on the stereo in the living room window. "Listen to that Autoharp!" he shouted down to us, flashing a thumbs-up. I stuck my thumb up too, though I had no idea what an Autoharp was.

"Do you ever wish you'd gone to Nashville with your band?" I asked Maggie. "When you play at the River House, don't you think about what would have happened if you'd really tried to make it?"

"No," she said. "I stayed in Nashville for a while on my way out west. Hated it. Fakest people I ever met."

"But you could have been a real musician."

Maggie pushed her hair back from her face. "Why are you so interested in my music all of a sudden? You never come to our shows."

"I don't come to your shows because they're on school nights," I said. "I've always thought you were talented, though. I know that Kevin didn't want to leave Swan River, but—"

"Is that what you think?" Maggie interrupted. "You think that Kevin made me come back to Swan River?"

She still didn't sound mad, just curious. I looked around and was glad to see that Kayak Boy was too far away to hear us, and most of their friends had gathered around the grill. "I like it here," Maggie said. "I've lived in a lot of places, and none of them felt right to me. You've always wanted to leave, and that's fine, but you don't have to look down on me because I want to stay."

"I'm not looking down on you. But when you came back, that had something to do with Kevin, didn't it? He'd made you hate the Academy, and—"

"What are you talking about? If I hated the Academy, it didn't have to do with Kevin."

"Yes, it did," I insisted. "That semester before you left, you were always sneaking off to be with him. Then your grades got so bad, and you were talking all the time about what a shitty place it—" Suddenly an awful thought struck me and I paused, staring at the toes of my shoes. "Umm," I said, trying to keep my voice quiet, trying not to reveal the agitation I felt. "When you were taking Myths and Mysteries, did Dr. Bell ever—"

"Why?" she said sharply. "He didn't try anything with you, did he?"

"You told me you didn't sleep with him!"

"I didn't!" She slumped forward, resting her chin in her cupped hands. "God, if that had been what he wanted, it would have been so much less creepy. But I started going to those tutorials, you know, because I needed help with my research project. He'd ask me to stay after everyone else had left, and then he'd go off on these tangents about the subconscious and how what you're most afraid of is what you secretly most want to do. At least I thought they were tangents, but then he started describing these rituals he was reading about. He showed me this book that said if a girl went out in the woods and took off her clothes and ate these leaves, a bunch of crazy shit would happen. The moon would turn red— that's the only one I remember."

"Why didn't you tell somebody?"

She folded her arms, laughing bleakly. "Who would I have told? Mom's had a crush on him since day one—she would never have believed me."

A pall of smoke drifted toward us from the grill. "So his ritual things actually worked," I said, mostly to myself. "He turned you into a wild girl."

"No, he didn't," Maggie said. "What, do you think I actually did any of that stuff? I stopped going to class after I figured out that he was a nutjob. What happened to me had nothing to do with Dr. Bell."

"But why then?" I said. "Why did it happen to you?"

"Why does it happen to anyone? It's part of this place. You can't explain it or control it. If Dr. Bell thinks he can make it work the way he wants it to, that just proves he's off his rocker." Maggie looked down and used her thumbnail, hardened by years of picking, to carve a thin line in the wood. "I was so worried about you. That time we had you over for dinner, I wanted to tell you, but—"

"You'd never told Kevin," I guessed. He was walking toward us now, grinning and clutching an oversize spatula. He wasn't so bad, I thought, as he dropped onto the bench and gave Maggie a smacky kiss on the cheek. With Mason, I had caught a glimpse of how hard it could be to keep another person happy. How could I criticize anyone who managed to keep it going, year after year?

"Brats are almost ready," he said, turning his spacy grin on me. "You hungry, Katie?"

I looked at Maggie, who was watching me anxiously. "I'm actually fine," I said.

When I got back to the Academy, it seemed that Willow and the minions had enjoyed spring break even less than I had. They came back tired and listless and, as I realized when I saw Matilda Peebles pass by Rosa in the bathroom without acknowledging her presence, annoyed with each other. When I asked Lucie about it, the worst she would say was that the food hadn't been very good. "Willow wanted to do a cleanse," she said. "So we could only eat salads, and she made us drink this gross tea."

It was an odd choice of words. "*Made* you drink it?"

"Well, you know Willow." Lucie brushed an imaginary piece

of lint off the lapel of her blazer. "It's supposed to be this amazing detox, but it kind of made me sick. The good thing was that I lost like five pounds."

"Oh," I said awkwardly. Lucie was under five feet and probably weighed ninety in snow boots. "Good for you."

Suddenly I was one of them, and I tried to enjoy it. I had never made friends easily, and I knew that part of the problem was that I rarely put in the effort necessary to get past the hi-how's-it-going stage. Even with Caroline, I probably never would have gotten to know her if she hadn't sought me out after Monsieur Barnes's class. Though I had criticized Willow's group, I had also envied their closeness and their power—the way they swept through the halls in a phalanx, chins upturned, the heels of their loafers clicking against the floor tiles. Now the minions came by my room singly or in pairs and confided in me about their parents' affairs, bankruptcies, cancers. Matilda Peebles had a schizophrenic brother. Elise's mother was leaving her father for a holistic healer named Wayne. The only ones who avoided me were Tessa and Frances. Lucie told me that Frances had refused to do Willow's cleanse, saying that if she wanted to sit around drinking tea all day she'd join the damn Junior League.

It was a perfect role for me. I had always been a listener, a sideline observer, but after a while I got tired of saying *Uh-huh* and *Really?* and *What happened then?* One evening at the end of April, I was sitting on the porch of Fallis Hall with Willow and Elise, who was complaining about her mother's new boyfriend doing nude calisthenics in the breakfast room. Since Willow clearly wasn't paying attention, I had to be the one to nod and make sympathetic noises at the appropriate times. The sign in the flower beds had been changed to read Phallus Hall, the seniors' usual April Fools' joke, which none of the staff or faculty had bothered to correct this year. On the other side of the steps, Clancy was kneeling in the peony bed, up to his elbows in mulch. The scent of the cedar bark reminded me of Mason, his sad cabin at Bloodwort Farm, his blank face as I drove him toward the Swan River Bridge.

"Excuse me," I said when Elise took a breath. "I just—it'll only be a second, okay?"

Clancy looked up as I approached and gave a half smile, wiping his ungloved wrist across his forehead. "Hi."

"Haven't seen you around much lately," I said.

"I've been here," he said. "I've been here pretty much all the time."

"I guess what I mean is that you haven't tried to talk to me or anything. And that's all right," I added hastily. "I know I was acting weird after Mason died."

"I don't blame you for how you acted after Mason died." Clancy picked up a stalk-snapped blossom and held it for a minute, his head bent. "Do you want to go for a drive this weekend?" he asked, looking up at me. "There's something I'd like to show you."

"Sure," I said, though I felt anything but sure.

At nine the next morning, I stumbled down to meet Clancy at the loading dock. Unlike Mason, he didn't drive too fast or play the radio too loud. He didn't stop for a bottle of gas station wine. Instead of heading north toward Bloodwort, he went south, taking the curving ridgetop roads that overlooked the river. This was a part of the county that I didn't know, different from both the violent, sharp-edged landscape of the high mountains and the walled sanctuary of the Academy. We were getting closer to Glen City, and some of the new brick ranches with boxy SUVs in the drives clearly belonged to commuters. Still the land looked rural, with rocky fields grazed by uncurious cattle and a church on every hillside. The churches were mainstream for the most part, not the mad, factional sects of the more isolated valleys, the Tabernacles of Holiness and the Wells of the Prophecy of Christ. The hills were gentler here, and old women stomping out to the mailbox waved at us as we drove by.

The drive might have seemed aimless, but on the way back we stopped at a picnic area overlooking the land that Clancy was thinking of buying. He called it a farm, but it was only five acres, owned now by an old man named Currans, whose kids were putting him in a nursing home. "The way they run the landscaping at the Academy is so stupid," Clancy said. "They buy a bunch of fully grown plants to put out for Family Weekend and Graduation, and the rest of the time all we have to do is mow and trim the hedges. I've got to get my own place, where I can do what I want."

"Such as?" I asked, yawning into my fist. "Plant corn or something?"

"I don't know about corn," he said seriously. "I was thinking about tomatoes, peppers, root vegetables. Any variety with a weird name, summer people will pay through the nose for it—I guess they think it's healthier or something. I figure if I plant what they want, I can run the farm the way I want. I've been reading about crop rotation, no-till farming. I mean, I don't want to sound cheesy or anything—" He dipped his head, tucking his hair behind his ears. "But I want the dirt to be happy, you know?"

I didn't know. "How can dirt be happy?"

"Either you pump it full of chemicals—" He made a flat sweeping motion with his hand, taking in the farms along the river. "Or you treat it with care, with love. Happy dirt, happy vegetables. Happy people."

This didn't sound too bad really. Apart from the good-looking boys, the main thing that had attracted me to Pritchard College

was all the talk about organic farming and sustainable agricul-
ture on the brochure. Clancy didn't know about my interest in
Environmental Science, but I could already imagine the ardent
look he would give me if I started talking about soil erosion and
renewable water resources. It would be a bond between us, and
that was precisely why I kept my mouth shut. He was just a hippie, I told myself scornfully. How much could anyone really
know about ecology who had never been to college and didn't
plan to go?

I looked down, toeing the dirt. "What would you do in the
winter?"

He cleared his throat, squinting at the hills. "I'd read. Do some
carpentry. I don't know—I'd like to have kids someday. I could
take care of them if my wife had a job."

"Did you know that my sister's pregnant?"

Clancy turned to me, his smile friendly but cautious. "Kevin
told me. Congratulations."

"It was an accident. I don't think you say congratulations when
someone gets knocked up by mistake." Maggie had announced
the news at a family dinner a few days ago, and the drama still
hadn't died down. Mom had started talking about abortion, and
when Maggie said it was too late for that, Mom accused Kayak
Boy of using an expired condom on purpose to keep Maggie tied
to Swan River. Maggie shouted back that Mom was the last person in the world who should give anybody advice about relationships and children. She'd been a terrible mother and a terrible
partner to Travis, and now he was living in a two-room apartment in the Delta with a single set of plastic silverware. Both
sides had demanded my opinion and then shouted me down halfway through what I thought was a nuanced response, and in that
moment I'd missed Travis with an intensity that surprised me.

If he'd been there, we could have at least rolled our eyes at each other.

"I don't know why anybody has children," I said to Clancy. "It's like, 'Well, the world's in horrible shape, what should we do? I know, let's make more people!'"

Clancy cleared his throat again, stuffing his hands in the pockets of his Carhartt. "I was thinking about goats. We used to have them at the commune back in the day. Then you have milk and cheese, and they're good company—kind of like dogs in a way."

"I hate goats," I said. "Our neighbors up the hill used to have them, and sometimes they'd chew the fence wire and get onto our property. Travis would yell and wave his arms, and they'd bleat at him like he was the one in their way. Sometimes one would get on my mom's car and just stand there."

"Okay." Clancy looked down at me with a tired but not unfriendly expression. "Okay, I get it."

"Well, I'm not trying to offend you," I said, following him to the edge of the slope. "I just really hate goats."

He'd turned his body away from me, a muscle twitching in his neck. "Not to change the subject," he said, with a mild edge to his voice that I recognized as his version of sarcasm. "But there's something I've been wanting to talk to you about. You remember the day Mason died, when you said I was being weak?"

My chest tightened. "I'm sorry. That was totally out of line. I—"

"No, you were right. I thought that if I hung around and kept showing you what a great guy I was, you'd change your mind. That *was* weak. And ever since I've been thinking, What if I'd told you how I felt? Maybe you wouldn't have been in the car with him that day. Maybe everything would have happened differently."

Afraid to meet his eyes, I kicked a bald spot in the grass, decapitating at least half a dozen violets. "That sounds like you're blaming yourself for Mason's suicide. Maybe I wouldn't have been in the car with him, maybe he wouldn't have gone over the bridge. That's just crazy, Clancy. That's—"

I didn't finish that sentence, because Clancy took me by the shoulders and kissed me hard. Holding his mouth against mine, he pulled my body closer, and I felt a sharp twist in my stomach that was almost painful. This was the rush I'd had with Mason, the nerve-tingling body-fireworks that I'd never expected to feel with Clancy Harp. When he drew away, I leaned into him, hoping he'd do it again.

"Kate," he said, stroking my back. "I know I haven't gone about this the right way, but if you'll let me, I want to spend every single minute of this summer with you. Think about it."

I stepped back and tilted my head so our eyes met. Though his words were gentle, there was a harshness in his face that thrilled me, even scared me a little. Since Mason's death, I'd been living in my head more than ever, dreaming, wishing, dreading. After I turned eighteen and the threat of becoming a wild girl was behind me, could I let go of all that for a while? Could I have a summer like the ones they sang about in country songs, back roads and bare feet on the dashboard? I closed my eyes and willed myself to relax into it—the sun on my hair, Clancy's hand firm on my back.

"I'll try," I said. "I mean, I'll think about it."

CHAPTER FIFTEEN

The invitations came at the beginning of exam week. *Mr. and Mrs. John P. Cochran request the pleasure of your company at a party to honor their daughter, Tessa Jane, on the occasion of her graduation from Swan River Academy. Friday, May 21st, 7:00 p.m., The Cedar Tree Inn. Formal dress, regrets only.* The paper was a heavy cream card stock with a design of embossed lilies. "Like a *wedding*," said the girl behind me at the mailboxes, and she and her friend cackled like witches.

Everyone thought it was tacky, but everyone was going. The chatter in the halls was not about French conjugations, or the date of the Battle of Hastings, or even where the parties would be on Graduation night. Academy girls missed out on most of the rituals of normal teenage life, and this party felt like both compensation and an entry into a larger, brighter world. Tessa went around with her nose in the air, dispensing advice about the proper lingerie to wear under a cocktail dress. She would never again be the queen of the school, but her parents had bought her a memorable send-off.

I was late for the party, and since I didn't want to show up at the Cedar Tree Inn in Maggie's Volkswagen, I asked my mom to drive me. She had spent the whole day packing up the house and kept sneezing into the crook of her elbow. I sat on the far edge of my seat, the skirt I'd borrowed from Matilda Peebles tucked under my thighs.

I had told Mom the party was just for students, and I was afraid that if she looked closely enough, she might notice that half the people drifting between the buffet table and the gazebos were mothers—cool half-drunken mothers in silk suits, desperate single mothers in dresses made for girls half their age, a few serious-looking mothers with unplucked eyebrows like Caroline's mom; but no mothers like my mother, in jeans and a too-small Tar Heels T-shirt, with a thin whisper of dust on her upper lip. I felt guilty for excluding her, but I didn't want to think about it too much.

When I opened the car door, she put a hand on my arm. "Kate, I want you to know how excited I am about your scholarship. For you to have this opportunity—it just makes me so happy."

She was smiling, but *happy* wasn't the word for the expression on her face. In fact, when I looked back over the past couple months, I thought that she might not have been happy for a while. In that moment, I regretted showing her the letter that had come that morning from Pritchard College. It was what she'd wanted for me, but there was no doubt that my departure would make her even lonelier than she was.

"You know, I don't have to go to this stupid thing," I said. "We could just go home. We could get Chinese, rent a movie."

"No, no." Mom sneezed again and pointed at the tear leaching from her right eye. "Allergies," she said. "You have a good time tonight."

I wanted to have a good time. The party spread out on the lawn before me was like a Gatsby party—breezes and fluttering curtains, Chinese lanterns floating in the trees. Inside, the dining room had been made into a shrine, with one long table lined with pictures of Tessa from infant to debutante, and another table piled high with white-ribboned presents. I had only brought a card, and I slipped it under a Chanel gift basket when no one was looking.

For such a big party, the inn needed extra staff, and Clancy had been hired as a waiter. He was wearing a white uniform, his ponytail tucked discreetly into his collar, and as he passed champagne flutes to the parents, he caught my eye and gave me a can-you-believe-this look. By the bar, Willow's parents were standing with the Cochrans, laughing as if there were no one else in the room. I caught the words *villa* and *St. John's*. Tessa stood beside them in a long shell-pink dress, looking bored until her mother turned and put an arm around her shoulder. Mrs. Cochran had Tessa's long face, but she didn't look like a snob; she was pleasantly ugly, like pictures of Eleanor Roosevelt. She said something in her daughter's ear, and Tessa broke into a wide, goofy smile.

Willow was at a table by the window beside a tall blond boy with magazine looks and a disdainful expression. Someone whispered that he played the bad seed on a soap called *Days and Nights*. He was Nellie DeLong's cousin, and he had come down with his family for Graduation weekend. Next to me at the buffet, Elise said, "*Shit*fire, does she have to pick up some dude *every*where she goes?" I made a sympathetic face, but I didn't want to get into a big conversation about Willow's dumping of Henry Seidel.

During hors d'oeuvres, Willow waved and smiled at me, but she never beckoned me over. I tried not to mind. I talked to Elise and Lucie for a while, but when they started on hunter-jumper horse shows, I got bored and wandered over to the hallway behind the gift table, where Clancy found me. Pulling me back into the shadows, he pressed a champagne flute into my hand. "Champagne makes my nose itch," I said.

"This stuff tastes like money," he said. "Just try a sip."

I stuck the tip of my tongue into the glass. "Wow."

Clancy slid his arm around my waist and, looking furtively over his shoulder, pressed his mouth to mine. We were in a corner, but it was still risky, and I was glad when he wiped my lip gloss off on his hand and headed for the kitchen.

I stepped out of the corner and leaned against the wall, feeling the blood pulse in the tips of my fingers. The kiss had made me thirsty, and without thinking I tossed off the rest of the champagne.

"Look at you, Miss Goody Two-Shoes," said a voice from one of the tables. It was Frances Ortega all done up in her Abilene best, with caked-on makeup and long red fingernails. In a black lace dress, with a probably-for-real diamond choker at her neck, she looked older than some of the mothers. I glared at her, and she rolled her eyes. "Oh, come on." She patted the seat beside her. "I don't give a crap what you drink."

I didn't want to sit with Frances, but the champagne had made me wobbly, and I wasn't used to high heels. "Where are your parents?" I asked. They should have been easy to spot; Frances's mother was reportedly a former Miss Texas, and I had never seen her father without a bolo tie.

"They're not here yet. The state legislature's in session, so my dad can't leave until tonight. It's a good thing for Tessa—if my dad were around, everybody would pay attention to him instead."

She said this matter-of-factly, without arrogance, and I liked her slightly better than I had a minute ago. Our chairs were turned so we had a perfect view of Willow, seated with her back to the window. Nellie DeLong, a waifish junior with snaggleteeth, was whispering in Willow's ear while the soap star cousin leaned in from the other side. Willow said something that made him laugh, and I could tell by her smile that she knew every eye in the room was on them. "Well, forget about my dad," Frances said, crunching the ice cubes in her Coke. "Looks like Tessa's been upstaged already."

Tessa's father tapped the microphone and made an amplified cough. "Thank you all for coming out tonight."

A lot of people clapped. Willow's dad stuck two fingers in his mouth and gave a loud whistle. Frances nudged me and opened her purse, revealing the top of a pack of cigarettes. "I'm going to get some air. Want to come with?" I shook my head. Frances shrugged, and I watched her push through the crowd, the lace on her dress pulled tight across her broad back.

A chair scraped along the floor, and I turned to see that Tessa's dad had pulled up a chair for her beside the gift table. "I'm so proud of my Tessa," he said into the microphone. His voice was quieter than I'd expected. If I hadn't known that he owned a plantation and could write a check to fund a fitness center, I would have thought of him as just a nice old man in a tie that seemed too tight for his neck.

"I don't want to brag," he said softly, "but most of y'all already know that Tessa came in second in the Hunt Seat Rider competition at the IEA nationals last year." He paused for scattered applause. Tessa's eyes shone as she looked up at her father, and as he talked on about her accomplishments and prospects, I could see her as a real person, with a history and a future I knew almost nothing about. I could never be friends with Tessa Cochran. She had called me trash, after all. But suddenly I regretted putting so much energy into hating her.

The Cochrans seemed to expect everyone to stand still and ooh appreciatively while Tessa opened her gifts, but it wasn't long before the rest of the room turned back to their own conversations. Since I didn't have anyone to talk to, I kept watching while Tessa plunged her hands into nests of tissue paper and pulled out silver picture frames, gold bracelets, and at least a dozen jewelry boxes. After dismantling Rosa's Chanel gift basket, Tessa opened the card I'd bought at the dollar store. "*May the road rise up to meet you, and may the wind be always at your back,*" she read, aiming her toothy smile in my direction. "*Thank you, Kate.*"

"And this last one's from Willow," Mr. Cochran said, speaking—inadvertently, I guessed—into the microphone. She had come to stand beside Tessa, folding her hands at her waist.

"It's not anything amazing," she said, speaking loudly enough for everyone at the front tables to hear. "It *is* personal, though."

My first hint that something was wrong came from Tessa's hands, trembling as she unwrapped the square box. Another picture frame, I thought, but when Tessa pulled it out I could see that the frame contained a watercolor picture of a horse. "Oh," Mr. Cochran said. "It's a picture of Taffy, isn't it? Did you paint that yourself, Willow?" Willow nodded and said something inaudible to Mr. Cochran, moving her hands as she spoke. The sunset light gleamed in her bright hair, and it seemed natural that she would be the center of attention. At the bar, her father beamed his approval.

I was the only one watching Tessa, still staring down at the watercolor with a nauseated expression. It was not a picture of Taffy at all. The long jaw might have been his, but the close-set eyes and pursed mouth were more human than equine. It was a caricature of Tessa Horse-Face, done with such subtle precision that it would be unmistakable if you were looking for it, and nearly impossible to see if you were not.

I decided to walk back to the Academy that night, and had almost made it to the bridge when a black Town Car pulled up beside me. Willow rolled down the window and smiled. "I'm skipping out," she stage-whispered. "Hurry up and get in before anyone sees you."

"No thanks," I said and kept walking. The driver started to pull out, but Willow spoke to him sharply and he slowed to inchworm speed.

"Hey," she said, "did you ever figure out where you're working this summer?"

It was such a strange question that I stopped, crossing my arms over my chest. "It depends. If we're in Swan River, I'll probably apply at the Tastee-Freez."

"I just wanted to know if you had a plan. Because I still want to give you Jean-Luc, you know. I don't want you hitchhiking to college."

I stepped off the curb and leaned down into the window, bracing my hands on the sill. "Don't you think I've noticed that you only bring up Jean-Luc when I'm mad at you? Don't you think I know what you're doing?"

Willow yawned and peeled the false eyelash off her right lid. "It's going to rain."

"I don't care," I said. But I looked at the gray mist rolling off the mountains, and then I looked at the bridge. About two-thirds of the way toward the Swan River side was the spot where we'd spun to a stop after Mason grabbed the wheel. No skid marks or dents in the guardrail marked the place, but I knew it was there, and I climbed into the Town Car.

The rain started almost immediately, solid drops clicking against the windshield. "Why did you do that to Tessa?" I asked quietly.

"Oh, so you're on Tessa's side now?" Willow let her head fall back against the seat. "It was a joke, Kate. She'll get over it."

"Well, I think it really hurt her feelings."

"She hurt my feelings a time or two," she said. "Christ Almighty, she treated me like her damn maid. *Willow, get me a Diet Coke; Willow, let me copy your homework.*"

"You didn't have to be friends with Tessa in the first place. Just because your dad wanted you to make contacts didn't mean you had to do it. You could have made your own friends."

"Coulda, shoulda, woulda." Willow pulled a mostly empty bottle of champagne from under her jacket. It seemed to be filled with the same sunset light that had slanted across her face in the dining room, and just looking at it made me feel warm. "There are a lot of things I wish I could have done," she said. "I wish I could have hooked up with Nellie DeLong's cousin, but I don't think his boyfriend would have liked it."

"Nellie's cousin is gay?"

She tilted the bottle over a plastic cup. "We sure made a cute couple though, didn't we?"

We brought our cups carefully together. "To the end of finishing school," Willow said. "To being finished."

"What would that mean anyway—to be finished?" I thought of things that had a finish: desks, dining room tables. After four years at the Academy we were like good furniture, lacquered with a fine veneer.

"Maybe it's really a Finnishing school. Like a school that makes you want to eat lingonberries and tiny meatballs."

"I'm pretty sure that's Swedish." I looked at her sideways. I wanted to explain why her gift to Tessa had bothered me so much, but it was hard to find the words. "Are you still upset about Mason?" I asked.

She laughed. "Mason," she said. "Like that would have worked out."

We didn't talk much after that. The car went fast on the wet roads, the driver inscrutable under his black cap, his shaved neck very pale in the dashboard lights. When he turned through the brick gates between the magnolias, I opened the window and poured out the rest of the champagne.

By the time Clancy arrived, it was almost one and Fallis Hall was shaking as if rocked by a small earthquake. Girls ran up and down the halls, laughing and shrieking. I kept hearing snatches of the school song, *friendships true, mountains blue,* and then more laughter.

Clancy walked in with his baseball cap in his hand, ducking his shoulders as usual. "It's weird out there. Some girl came out of the bathroom and flashed me."

I shrugged. "Graduation's on Sunday. Everybody's going loco right now."

I sat on the bed, and after considering for a minute, Clancy sat beside me. "When I got hired on landscaping, they gave me this letter saying that going into a girl's room for any reason was cause for immediate termination. They made it sound like they'd have you arrested."

"Oh, come on," I said. "The security guards never even get out of their trucks. Who's going to arrest you, Travis?"

"Good point," Clancy said, putting his hand on my knee. I wasn't used to panty hose, and the friction of his palm on the nylon sent prickles up and down the inside of my leg.

When I'd called the Cedar Tree Inn and asked Clancy to come by after work, I'd known that he'd think I was agreeing to be his girlfriend. I had called him anyway, because I didn't want to spend the night alone. Willow's cruelty to Tessa had left a bitter taste in my mouth that even her stolen champagne hadn't been able to wash away. There would be no sleep for me that night, so why not spend it with Clancy? But first I had to make sure that we understood each other, so when he angled his body toward me, I scooted to the end of the bed. "I have something to tell you. I found out today that I got this scholarship. To a school in Minnesota."

"That's great," Clancy said. "I'm proud of you."

"So I'll definitely be leaving," I said. "What I mean to say is, I know you want to buy your farm and everything, and I think that's cool. But I'm going to college, and I'm not coming back."

He stopped smiling and hunched forward, long hands hanging between his knees. "Kate, you don't have to worry about me trying to hold you back. Like I said, I'm proud of you."

"Really?"

"Yeah, really." He slapped his cap against my leg. "It's cold as hell in Minnesota, isn't it? What do you want to go up there for?"

Reaching for my college folder, I pulled out the Pritchard brochures and gave him the pictorial tour of the working farm, the ecofriendly dorms, the wooded trails along the blue ice of Lake Superior. I showed him students making their own bread and stoking a fire in the campus smithy. Outside, girls were running down the hall, pounding the doors with their fists. Clancy kicked off his shoes and lay down on the bed. "It says on there that the fall semester starts on August twenty-second. It's only the third week of May."

I lay beside him, keeping my arms at my sides. "That leaves June, July—"

We kissed then, and I waited for the rush of heat, the sharp near-painful feeling in the pit of my stomach. I waited to lose myself in sensation, but it didn't happen this time, and after a few minutes I pressed my forehead against Clancy's shoulder. When I tried to apologize, to explain that I was just in a weird mood that night, he said, "Shh, don't worry about it."

He held me and stroked my hair, and I thought that maybe it really didn't matter. Maybe he liked me so much that he didn't care if we made out or not. That was nice and everything, but then I thought of Mason, who had asked Willow to change her whole life for him. I didn't want Clancy to control me, but I sort of wanted him to want to.

It doesn't seem exactly accurate to call what happened next a dream. Part of the problem is that I don't remember falling asleep. The transition from one reality to another seemed instantaneous, like one minute I was lying in Clancy's arms, staring up at the radiator-stained ceiling, and the next I was speeding over the bridge in Willow's Town Car. In the middle the driver stopped, opened the back door, and hoisted me over his shoulder. It was the Birdman. I just got a glimpse of his dead eyes and his withered hand before he tossed me over the railing. Wind roaring in my ears, I fell down and down, barely slowing when I hit the water.

My feet sent up explosions of silt and my hair lifted off my shoulders, rising into a fright wig. I didn't see the wild girls this time, but as usual Mason took my hand and led me away from the dark house and the people streaming through its shadowed doorway. When the crowds around us had thinned, he turned to me and spoke, blood blooming from his lips. *"Gibdow,"* he said. *"Gebbow,"* he said. "Get out. *Get out.*"

I woke up choking, water in my lungs streaming out of my mouth. Clancy tried to hold me again, but I sat up and swung my legs over the side of the bed. In the sky above the Lawn, clouds hovered like pastel balloons.

"You have to go," I said, trying to make my voice sound normal. "I'm supposed to meet Maggie at the River House."

Clancy yawned into the side of his fist. "Bluegrass Jamboree tonight. Will I see you there?"

I picked the skirt I'd borrowed from Matilda off the floor and tried to shake the wrinkles out. I was afraid to look at Clancy— afraid of what he'd see in my face if I did. "I'll try to make it," I said.

By the time I got down to the River House, the Saturday morning crowd had claimed most of the tables. Except for two old couples, Academy girls were the only customers, and of course they weren't behaving the way you're supposed to behave in a restaurant. They stuck their legs out into the aisles and scattered sugar grains around the rims of their saucers. The minions were all there, sans Willow. It seemed like no one had taken a shower, and their makeup looked strange, smudged and bleeding. Teased hair had been mashed into matted halos, and they were so loud that the old people by the door winced at every laugh.

I waved to Elise and Lucie, Matilda and Rosa, but sat down by myself at a two-top table by the window. From this angle I couldn't see the river, but I had a perfect view of the opposite bluff, and if I leaned all the way to my left I could just catch a glimpse of the Becker family gazebo. I wondered if Willow's parents understood what she had done last night, thumbing her nose not only at Tessa and the Cochrans but at their entire hierarchy. It was what I'd been waiting for Willow to do for years, so why did I like her so much less now than I had before? I was chewing on a fingernail, wondering if I would even keep in touch with her after Graduation, when the table jerked to the left. Tessa had taken the seat across from me, and Frances pulled up a chair to sit between us.

"I need to talk to you," Tessa said.

"It's about Willow," Frances chimed in. I tore off a piece of my cuticle and tasted blood.

"Frances, tell her about what happened over spring break," Tessa commanded.

"Well, first I think we should establish a couple things," Frances said. "To begin with, Tessa and I know about your sister."

I looked around, making sure that Maggie was in the back. "What does my sister have to do with anything?"

Tessa laid her palms on the table, her businesslike manner contrasting with eyes that were red from crying or sleeplessness. "Willow told me. Freshman year, right after it happened. She came by my room one night and said that Maggie had jumped out the window, that she'd set a fire in the library. I'd never heard of the wild girls—honestly, I thought Willow was high or something. But after what Frances told me about spring break, we started to put it all together."

"Started to put *what* together?" My voice was rising, and Frances kicked me in the shin. From across the room, the other minions shot us curious glances.

"Frances, tell her," Tessa said again, and this time Frances nodded obediently.

"Remember at the bunkhouse, when we played that game? Willow put me up to it. She told me to get everybody to play Truth or Dare, and then to dare you to steal Dr. Bell's notebook."

"Me specifically? But why?"

Frances turned up her palms. "I guess she thought you would do it."

The saltshaker had a crooked lid, and I unscrewed it with

unsteady fingers. "So she wanted Dr. Bell's notebook for some reason. So what? When Matilda brought it to her, she barely even looked at it."

"How do you know that?" Tessa said.

"Because she told me. She said there was nothing in there but lists of plants, and she gave it to me."

"And why did she give it to you?" Tessa asked with rhetorical solemnity. "Because you know about the wild girls. She wanted you to read it and tell her what it meant."

"When Dr. Bell talked about them, we thought they were like mythical creatures or something," Frances said. "But they're real, aren't they?"

My hands were trembling so much that the shaker tipped, dumping half the salt onto the table. I swept it to the floor, remembering too late that I should have thrown a pinch over my shoulder.

"She wanted us to do these rituals," Frances said. "At my cabin, over spring break. We'd go out in the woods and stand in a circle and do these long chants, calling on goddesses and stuff. She had a script. And she was making us drink this tea, made from bloodwort leaves—she said it was a cleanse, but I've been to a detox spa and it didn't seem like a cleanse to me. It made everybody puke their guts out."

I looked at the other table. Lucie met my gaze and then leaned in to say something to Rosa. "Nobody told me about any of this," I said.

"Willow told us not to talk about it," Frances said. "I swear she had some kind of mind-control thing going. I dropped out halfway through and went back to eating regular food, but the rest of them—it's like they were her own little cult."

"If they weren't that already," Tessa said under her breath.

I pushed the saltshaker away from me. "You're one to talk,

Tessa. I know what this is about. Willow took over your group, she embarrassed you at your fancy party, and now you're getting back at her."

"Look, I don't like you much either," Tessa said, "but those girls over there were my friends before they were Willow's, and if she's planning some kind of human sacrifice or something, I'm going to do what I can to stop it."

"Noblesse oblige, bitches," Frances said, and Tessa nodded seriously.

"Human sacrifice," I said. "Jesus, Tessa. I don't know what the fuck you're talking about."

I couldn't look at them. As I scanned the room, my eyes settled on the last person I'd expected to see. At the table tucked in beside the counter, Caroline was drinking out of a gigantic tea mug, and across from her, close enough for their knees to touch under the table, Oliver talked energetically, using his big hands to make grand unnecessary gestures. With his passionate expression and ungainly body, he looked like a creature out of its element, a landlocked waterbird, and I could see that some of the girls at the next table were laughing at him. Typically, Caroline didn't seem to notice. She listened with careful, focused attention, the way she had always listened to me.

I told myself that if I could just go over there and pull up a chair, all of this would go away: Tessa's accusations, the threat from Dr. Bell. If I could sit down with Caroline, tell her about the Pritchard scholarship, eat half of her banana bread without asking, everything would be normal again. We would graduate tomorrow, and leave Swan River, and the great disaster I'd waited for my whole life would hold off at least a little longer.

I might have done it, but before I could move there was a loud crash from a table near the door. Elise Seidel had jarred an old woman's purse with her elbow, pushing it to the floor. Hairbrush, keys, and a pack of mints scattered in different directions, and Elise and Lucie giggled behind their hands. In the silence, the woman's husband stood and faced the table of minions, hands working convulsively at his sides.

"You girls," he stammered. "You think you can come down here and do whatever you please, but I'm not going to put up with it. I'm not—"

Suddenly he went white, and his mouth opened and shut without a sound. His wife pulled him back into his seat. Rosa and Matilda were laughing, and Elise gave the old man the finger. Her skin had a green, unhealthy radiance, as if lit by the glow of storm clouds.

Tessa tried to grab my arm, but I jerked away and knelt in the middle of the floor. A pack of tissues, pictures of kids in clear plastic sleeves—I fit each of them carefully into the purse. *I'm sorry,* I repeated in my head, *I'm sorry,* though I wasn't sure what I was apologizing for. After a minute I noticed that Caroline was kneeling beside me, and then someone touched my shoulder. Maggie stood above me, her shawl knotted over her belly. I was pretty sure she had missed the whole thing. "Are you ready to go? I only have an hour before the lunch rush."

I looked at Caroline, who nodded without meeting my eyes. "Go ahead," she said, scooping up a half roll of breath mints. I didn't even look at Tessa and Frances on my way out the door.

A poster of a smiling, nonpregnant Maggie hung on a sign in the parking lot, advertising the Bluegrass Jamboree that evening. The poster made it sound like a big event, something that people would come from miles around to see. *Saturday May 22nd, Maggie Riordan On Banjo And Guitar!* "Are you coming tonight?" Maggie said, striding into the parking lot without even looking to make sure I was with her. "I mean, why would you, since you never come to our shows, but I just thought I'd—"

"Can you not?" I burst out. "Can you just give me a break for once? Seriously, Maggie, I have enough on my mind right now."

"Oh, you have enough on your mind," she repeated, smiling mockingly. We walked down Jessup Avenue, where the brick storefronts were slowly opening for the nonexistent Saturday shopping crowd. The dusty used bookstore stocked with how-to guides and Erma Bombeck; the florist, her window filled with dusty plastic flowers and a sign that read *Congratulations, Graduates*—the whole town looked as if it hadn't slept well. The sun glare and the prickly heat made me feel like I was moving at half speed.

Maggie stopped to fix her shawl in the window of Nathan J. Lockhart, Certified Personal Trainer. I leaned against the glass beside her, taking deep breaths and trying to banish the panic that curled like a fist inside my ribs. Nathan J. Lockhart had been out of business for years, but the office equipment was still there— desks, chairs, file cabinets looking as functionless as if they'd come from an archaeological dig. On the ledge in front was a plastic block with the label *5 lbs. of Unsightly Fat!* The fat, yellow and marbled with red veins, was the most disgusting thing I had ever seen.

"I don't want you to think I'm making fun of you," Maggie said, touching the blue circles under her eyes with her fingertips. "You're graduating tomorrow, and I know it probably seems like your world is ending, but trust me, you're going on to bigger and better things."

"Thanks," I mumbled. We had crossed the railroad tracks and turned onto River Street, a meandering two-lane that led through the Delta until, at the edge of town, the street became Bloodwort Road. *I shouldn't be here*, I told myself despairingly; I had to find

Willow, I had to do something. "Look, I can't stay long at Travis's," I said.

"Oh, come on," Maggie said. "Have you visited him once since Christmas? Did you even invite him to Graduation?"

"I didn't *invite* him. I mean, he can come if he wants to."

"He helped raise us, Kate."

"He didn't raise me," I muttered. "He was just a guy who lived in the same house."

Maggie sighed. We were walking between trailers and one-room shotgun houses, some with junked-up cars in the yard, others with Tibetan prayer flags waving in the breeze. On one screen porch, a wide-legged couple in matching jean shorts rested in folding chairs, petting a golden retriever. They didn't look familiar to me, but they waved at Maggie as if they knew her.

A few driveways down, we stopped in front of an empty gravel lot so Maggie could tie her shoe. "I've been thinking about what you said at the party," she said. "About me running for mayor one day. I've been thinking maybe I should do it."

"Really?"

"Yeah, really." She opened the mailbox, revealing an empty Dr Pepper bottle and a rusty nail. "I know you think I'm just some flaky deadneck, but you're not the only one in the family with a brain."

"I never said you were a flaky deadneck."

"You didn't have to say it."

I pressed the heels of my hands to my temples. Maggie gave me an annoyed look, and I lowered them again. She was right, of course; I had thought of myself as the smart one compared to my sister, who'd had enough intelligence and ambition to get out of Swan River but not enough to stay away. I owed her an apology, but it was hard to keep my mind on it right now. If Tessa and Frances were right; if Willow had succeeded in creating a wild girl, or many wild girls, then everyone I loved was in jeopardy.

"Hey," I said to her back. "If you knew someone was becoming a wild girl, what would you do to stop it?"

Maggie had walked ahead, but now she stopped and stared back at me. "Mom told me that you talked about the wild girls the day the two of you went down to Moorefield. Why is this stuff on your mind all of a sudden?"

"Why were you and Mom talking about me?" I countered. "I didn't even know you were speaking."

"Of course we're speaking," Maggie said impatiently. "You thought she was going to stay mad at me when I'm having her grandchild? But listen, Kate—you're not the type."

I nodded glumly. Of course, Maggie herself was not the stereotype of the wild girl. Neither was Victoria Duvalier. But if the defining characteristic was not poverty but rage at her own powerlessness, nearly every girl I knew was at risk.

"Look, I swear to you that I'm not talking about me," I said. "It's just a hypothetical, okay? It's just something I've been thinking about."

Maggie looked at me for a long moment and then sat down heavily on the steps of a stilt-legged shotgun shack. "If I knew someone who was becoming a wild girl, I would tell her to add up everything that matters to her—the people she loves, her hopes for the future. Put that on one side of the scale and, on the other, put the satisfaction of destroying what you hate."

I sat down beside her and rested my elbows on my knees. This didn't feel like enough of an answer, but when the pause stretched on, I knew that it was all I was going to get. A door opened at the top of the stairs, and the aroma of barbecued brisket wafted down. Pushing her palms on her thighs, Maggie stood up and held out her hand to me. "You don't need to help me up," I said. "*I'm* not pregnant."

"Then that's one thing you don't have to worry about." Maggie shaded her eyes and smiled up at Travis, who stood in the doorway in a meat-stained apron, waving us in with both hands.

The house looked better on the inside than it did on the outside. The living room was clean, and I wondered if Travis, like Mom, had decided to turn over a new leaf. He was almost embarrassingly glad to see us, grinning and rubbing his hands together as he asked if we wanted coffee, lemonade, iced tea? I picked up a miniature motorcycle and spun it across my palm. "I didn't realize at first that this was your place," I said. "I didn't see the truck outside."

"Oh." Travis scratched the top of his head. "Tell the truth, I sold that thing. I started thinking, What do I need a truck for when I always drive the patrol car?"

We were following Maggie into the kitchen, but in the doorway I stopped short. A girl about Maggie's age sat at the table, drinking coffee from a Western Carolina mug. She had brown dreadlocks that fell between her shoulder blades. A tattoo of a snake decorated her neck, its forked tongue darting behind her right ear.

"Hey Trish," Maggie said, picking up a slotted spoon and stirring vigorously at a pot of baked beans. "Kate, do you know Tricia Leggett? She lives next door."

Tricia Jo stared at me from under her unibrow. "Kate and I go way back, actually."

"Maggie, I need my basting brush," Travis called from the back porch. Maggie gave the beans one last stir and followed him, and I sat down in the chair across from Tricia Jo. It was plastic, and seemed like it might collapse if I leaned all my weight against the back.

"So I haven't seen you for a while," I said. I felt a crack on the underside of my seat and wiggled the two pieces with my thumb and forefinger. "Umm, what have you been up to?"

Tricia Jo slumped down in her seat and crossed her feet at the ankles. "Well, let's see. I worked on the line at Hammond Snacks until it closed. Now I'm on the night shift at the Stop N Go down toward Moorefield."

"Oh," I said. "So do you and Travis hang out a lot?"

"Do we hang out a lot?"

"Yeah," I said. "I mean, I know it's none of my business, but are you—you know, a couple or anything?"

Raising her eyebrows, Tricia Jo spun in her seat and leaned into the refrigerator. "My girlfriend and I are both friends with Travis. Donna Higgins. She's at work up at the hospital right now, but she's coming by later." I opened my mouth to say that I knew Donna, but Tricia Jo didn't wait. "Hey," she shouted out to the porch, "either of y'all want a beer?"

"I'm pregnant, you idiot," Maggie shouted back.

"Oops." Tricia Jo grinned at me. "I forgot. What are you having again?"

"We're not finding out," Maggie said. "But I hope it's a girl." A piece of the seat broke off in my hand.

I looked at Tricia Jo, kicked back in her chair with a Bud Light on her knee. She had never been a wild girl, but she had been best friends with one. "So I guess the last time I saw you was at Bloodwort Farm," I said. "I'm sorry about what happened to Crystal."

With the bottle halfway to her lips, Tricia Jo paused and shifted in her chair. She set the beer on the table, rubbed the back of her neck. I thought that I'd made her uncomfortable, but when she spoke her voice was tight with anger. "I'm not sorry about what happened to Crystal. If she was sitting here right now and you asked her if she had any regrets, you know what she'd say? She'd say she wished she'd taken that asshole Rondal with her. That's it, end of story."

"Well," I said. "He's gone now, anyway. Clancy told me that when Sheriff McClellan went up there to tell Mrs. Lemons about Mason, he couldn't find anybody. He thinks they've both left town."

"Rondal didn't leave town. He'll be there till he dies, trust me."

Her face contorted. She rose and bent over the sink, gulping water out of her cupped hand. "It's hard to talk about," she said, looking out the screen door. At the other end of the porch, Travis was poking at the brisket, Maggie seated beside him fanning herself with her hand.

"Mason told me what Rondal did," I said. "He didn't go into the details, but—he raped her, didn't he?"

Tricia Jo's head dipped suddenly, and I wondered if she were crying. "Her mother wouldn't do a thing about it. If it weren't for Donna, I'd go out there with a shotgun tonight."

"I'm sorry," I said again, more softly this time. Tricia Jo shrugged and wiped her nose on her hand.

I waited a minute or two, but then I felt that I couldn't wait any longer. "I know you said it's hard to talk about, but I have to know—did you notice any signs before it happened? Was there any way to know for sure that she was going to . . ." I let my voice trail off, thinking of Mason with his stories of untended campfires, shiver birds, dead dogs in the gutter.

Tricia Jo turned to me, crossing her arms over her chest. "Yeah, I noticed a sign," she said, her tone not exactly friendly. "There was this look she got right before it happened. It was like she was lit up from the inside—glowing, kind of."

"Glowing," I repeated, and then my whole body went cold. I thought of the old man at the River House, how he'd scanned the minions' faces, each with that faint feverish glow that I'd attributed to late nights and too much makeup. *It was happening,* I told myself. It had started already.

CHAPTER SIXTEEN

Maggie got mad when I said I couldn't stay for the brisket, but I told them that I had a last-minute paper to write and left before anybody could ask questions. Back at the Academy, I went looking for Willow, checking the dorms, the library, the stables, even the fitness center, though I'd heard her say that StairMasters were for people who liked to be bored stupid and in bodily pain at the same time. No one had seen her, or the minions either. Finally I left a note on her door, written in her own cryptic style: *Very Important! FIND ME.*

I could have called Clancy or Caroline, but I decided not to for the same reason that I hadn't told Maggie or Travis: because I still didn't want it to be happening. I paced my room for a while and then lay down on the bed, staring at the Dylan poster I'd inherited when Maggie left the Academy. It was hot, and I hadn't slept well the night before. As I dropped in and out of consciousness, I listened to suitcases and cardboard boxes being dragged toward the elevators. Everything seemed so normal. "Sweet Home Alabama" was playing on a second-floor stereo; the smell of Dino's pizza drifted down from the TV lounge. The clock on my desk said 8:30, which meant that up the hill at the headmaster's house, Dr. Bell was hosting a cocktail party for major donors. The Cochrans would be there, and the Beckers, talking about their upcoming sailing trip to the Virgin Islands. Their daughters could not be wild girls. The world didn't work that way.

I closed my eyes and I was back under the river with Mason, who shouted at me as blood clouded the water: *Get out!* I sat up gasping, and went to the mirror to make sure that my skin wasn't glowing. My face was dull and tired; there was a patch of acne on my left cheek, and I went down to Willow's room and pounded on the door. No answer. My note was where I'd left it, wedged under the corner of her message board. The board had been wiped clean, but when I looked more closely, I could see the afterimage of Willow's handwriting: *Amphitheater. 9:00.*

It was five to nine now. I grabbed a cardigan from the lost and found box and pushed through the lobby, through the crowds of parents kissing their daughters good night. The Lawn was deserted now, and I ran as fast as I could across the damp grass, but at the top of the stairs I stopped, peering down at the white marble stage that shone in the moonlight. It was empty, and I leaned against the outer wall, my knees gone weak with relief.

I took the back way to the dorm, cutting around Calhoun Hall. As I crossed the faculty parking lot, I saw someone hurrying around away from the administration building with an armload of books. "Mr. Hightower!" I called. "Do you need a hand?"

He paused at the curb. The halogen light turned his prematurely gray hair pure white, and there was a strange scorched smell about him. "Kate, I have to go," he said.

"Are you going to Graduation? I'm glad I caught you, because I wanted to tell you that I got the scholarship. I just wanted to thank you for writing my recommendation, and helping me with Clean Up Swan River! and everything."

"That's wonderful, Kate. It's a great opportunity for you." He took a deep breath that turned into a cough. Had he been fired?

I followed him as he hurried toward his sad-looking sedan. "Mr. Hightower, did something happen? You can tell me."

He leaned his forearms on the roof, shaking his head from side to side. "You're going to think I'm crazy."

"I won't," I said. Though he was a good six inches taller than me, his rounded spine made him look weak, even childish, and I tried to sound reassuring. "I mean—I think I might already know what you're going to say."

He laughed with a rising note of hysteria. "I doubt that," he said, rubbing his hand over the back of his head. "I was at that reception for major donors. Bunch of boring old farts eating tiny crab cakes—I couldn't wait to get out of there." His country accent was stronger than usual, and for a moment he reminded me of Mason. "David left early, so I figured that I could leave too. I picked up some books from my office, and I was cutting through the Lawn on the way to my car when I saw a light on in the administration building. I looked in the window. It was David's office. Willow was in there. It looked funny to me that he'd be meeting with a student so late, so I watched for a minute, and I saw her touch an orchid on his desk. It went up in flames. There was no lighter in her hands, no match. I must have moved, because she looked out the window and saw me. The air heated up, and then—"

He held out the books, and I could see that the cover of Audubon's *Ornithological Biography* had been charred black. The cuff of his shirt was burned too, the skin of his wrist blistered. He took a quick fearful glance over his shoulder and opened the car door. "I have to get out here," he said. "I don't know what this is, but I have kids at home—"

"Were they still in Dr. Bell's office when you left?"

He nodded, and I set off running. "You should get your wife and the kids in the car," I called over my shoulder. "Leave town."

I took the steps to the administration building two at a time, my breath shuddering in my chest. When I opened Dr. Bell's door, he was standing at the window in shirtsleeves, a silk tie loosened at his neck. The air was filled with the same carbon scent I'd smelled on Mr. Hightower. On the desk was a pile of ashes under glass. I looked around for Willow, wondering if she might have been hiding behind the curtains, but they didn't stir.

"Come in, Kate," Dr. Bell said, gesturing with a manic looseness that made me wonder if he were drunk.

He led me into the inner office. It was just as the minions had described it, a cross between an archaeological museum and a fantasy suite at the Playboy Mansion. The chairs and sofas were upholstered in lush silks and brocades. Above them, on dark lacquered shelves, round-bellied figures that didn't look quite human stared out with blank stone eyes. My mother had sat at the desk outside this office for years. My mother had worked for this man, and had a crush on him, and never had the slightest inkling what he was up to. The good adults—my mom, Travis, Mr. Hightower—had done what they could, but no one could help me now.

"Are you here about your research project?" Dr. Bell asked. "Because you'd been so strong in class discussion, I gave you a B for the course, but I must say I was rather disappointed by your paper. You present all these examples of underworlds, buried cities, but then your argument ends in the middle. There's no conclusion."

I sat on the edge of a chaise longue upholstered in Chinese silk. "I'm not here about my paper," I said. "I know everything, Dr. Bell. I know what's happening, to Willow and the others, and I want to ask you to stop it."

For a moment I watched him waver between his two selves. "What a strange idea," he whispered, his eyes glittering. "Why on earth would I want to stop it? I've been waiting for this—waiting for years now."

I could hear the girls screaming, long bright screams that ended and began again like a song in rounds. "Willow went behind your back, you know. She's been working on her own. Your little rituals and spells and whatever—they don't even work."

"I think that's open to debate," he said, leaning back in his chair. "Antoinette Lemons suggested to me years ago that blood-wort might cause a kind of ecstatic frenzy, but whether the leaves had an effect on the girls, or whether it was merely the strength of Willow's hold over them, a sort of cult of personality—I'm not sure it matters. The point is that we succeeded in the end."

On the shelf above his head, a Priapus peeked out from behind a Russian icon. "When you took the job here," I said, "you already knew about the wild girls, didn't you?"

"I'd heard things," he admitted. "There was some interest in occult circles. Of course I was intrigued."

"And when you spent all that time at the commune," I contin-ued, "was it because you'd heard that Mrs. Lemons was a witch? Did you think she'd be able to help you?"

"Antoinette," he said absently. "What a disappointment. She knows a bit about homeopathy, I'll admit, but when it comes to anything esoteric, she's a complete fraud."

He moved to the window that looked down on the amphithe-ater, and I followed. "Can I ask you one more question?" I said. "Why not me?"

"Why not you what?"

"Why did you assume I wouldn't be a wild girl?"

He gave me the look he gave the not very bright students when, reading aloud, they stumbled over *Lycaon* or *Ganymede*. "Because you don't want to be."

"You think that all wild girls *want* to be wild girls?"

"Yes," he said, turning back to the window. "I think on some level, they do."

We had a perfect view of the stage, filled with what looked at first like black fluttering shadows. Then I picked out Rosa's long blonde hair, Lucie's small frame—it was the wild girls, wrapped in their graduation robes. Dr. Bell's face looked like Travis's thumb the time he hit it with a hammer. "You'll have to excuse me," he said with strained politeness.

"The wild girls kill people." My teeth were chattering, and I tried to lock my jaw. "You can't control them, Dr. Bell. You can't make them do what you want them to do."

He was breathing fast, his face beaded with sweat. "Don't be ridiculous. It's not as if this has never happened before. The Greeks had their maenads, medieval Europe had its witches. This sort of madness is always containable, tamable, if you know what you're doing."

"But those are just parallels. The wild girls aren't like anything else."

The screaming outside was louder now. Dr. Bell ripped off his suit jacket and kicked his shoes into a corner. He took his pants off too, and I looked away. I was shaking all over.

"Don't go out there," I said. "Dr. Bell, don't—"

"Shut up," he barked. He ran down the hall and out to the side porch, and I followed him. At the top of the amphitheater, he paused, chest heaving, while I crouched behind the wall. The girls were frenzied now, rolling over the stage. Elise, her mouth distorted in a scream; Matilda, clawing at the skin of her face; Rosa, Lucie, but not Willow. I looked again, counted again: not Willow.

Holding out his arms, Dr. Bell descended the steps to the stage. *"Dancing in the mysteries I've established,"* he intoned hoarsely, *"making known to men my own divinity!"* It was a quotation from something we'd read, I couldn't think what, and he followed it with a few words that I was pretty sure were Greek. The wild girls answered him with a chorus of shrieks, and he dropped to his hands and knees. I couldn't help looking at his naked body now, and it was hairier than I'd imagined, hairier than any human body should have been.

He prowled among them, and Rosa reached out to caress his shoulder. As if on cue, they circled him, their black robes hiding him from sight. I heard one scream, guttural and rattling, as if he were choking. The wild girls were screaming too, and streams of blood blackened by moonlight ran from under their robes, spilling over the edge of the stage.

The pickup came around the curve and swerved toward me just before I reached the safety of the trees. I jumped off the bike, letting it skid into the road where the driver clipped it and fishtailed, tires screeching. Crouching in the bushes, I tried not to breathe.

Men hollered from the back. "What the hell was that?"

"Just some kid on a bike."

"Did you hit her?"

"If I didn't, I'm about to."

Once I heard that, I didn't care how much noise I made. I ran blindly down the side of the hill, throwing my body through briars that cut my face and arms, sometimes falling on my skinned palms and breathing there, stunned, until I remembered to run again. I kept thinking about the bike, which I'd found leaning against the rear wall of Calhoun Hall, and wondering stupidly how I could find the owner to apologize. But it seemed unlikely that I would ever go back to the Academy, or ever again live in a world where taking someone's bike without permission was a thing that mattered.

The River House parking lot was packed with cars, the spiny new trees by the door strung with colored lights. Music throbbed against the glass. Maggie was onstage, and the room was dark except for an overhead light that shone on her and Kayak Boy. At the last moment I glanced in the mirror over the umbrella stand and wiped the dirt off my face, but then I didn't know what to do. How could I warn people? What could I say? As I waited by the entrance, my mind blanking with panic, the band wound up an instrumental number and Maggie looked right at me. "Clancy," she said, "could you turn on the light by the door?"

In a moment I was lit up, an amoeba under a microscope. "There," Maggie said. "Ladies and gentlemen, this is my baby sister. I used to change her diapers, and we've been playing here— how long now?"

"Eight months," shouted a voice from the audience.

"Eight *months,* and she's never ever been to see us." Maggie shook her head sorrowfully, and a few people in the audience made tsk-tsk noises. "But she's graduating from high school tomorrow, so I want to dedicate the next number to her. Because it's like when that boy in the Bible finally comes home and they kill all the cows."

"The prodigal son," someone yelled.

Maggie's fingers swept over the strings and Kayak Boy went to work with his bow, a beatific smile on his face. I felt someone touch my arm and looked down: Clancy. Finger to his lips, he pulled me toward the kitchen, Maggie's voice following us. She was singing a ballad called "Katie Dear" about a girl who kills herself when her parents won't let her marry her sweetheart. She'd told me once it was the only song she knew with my name in it, but it seemed like a gruesome choice for a dedication.

"Are you okay?" Clancy asked when the door had swung shut behind us. "When the light was on you, you looked kind of—"

"It's happening," I said. "Wild girls. Rosa, and Elise, and Matilda Peebles—all of Willow's friends."

In the light filtering through the one high window, Clancy's face had hardened. "My truck's in the lot. We'll head for Moorefield."

It was what I'd told Mr. Hightower to do, but he was an outsider, with no ties to the town outside the Academy gates. Clancy and I had responsibilities. "We have to warn people," I said. "We have to find my mom!"

Before he could answer, the lights went out. The music stopped, and the audience murmured uneasily. I pushed through the swinging doors, stumbling against a mannequin that Kayak Boy had positioned to point the way to the bathrooms. Falling back, I bumped against a table, and looked down to see Caroline and Oliver.

"Kate," Caroline said, reaching out to steady me. "What's going on?"

Her glasses were off, and she was wearing a white peasant blouse that showed the delicate bones of her shoulders. *Gamine*, I thought—a word the two of us had once spent a week trying to use in a sentence. "You look nice," I said. "You look like Audrey Hepburn." Caroline stared at me blankly.

The exit sign seemed to have brightened until it lit the whole room. "Folks," Kayak Boy called from the stage, "if you'll keep your seats, we'll have this sorted out in a minute or two." Then I saw Clancy up on the stage, whispering in his ear. People were already pushing toward the door, and the hum of voices had gotten ten louder.

Outside a red glimmer lit the sky over the Academy. The polite evacuation was halfway to becoming a panic, but Caroline was still beside me, brows peaked over wide eyes. There was already a backup on the driveway leading to Jessup Avenue. "You can come with us," Clancy was saying to Oliver. "The fire probably won't cross the river."

Clancy put a hand on my back and led me toward the green truck. The people in the cars we passed looked deliberately calm, like strangers on a boat in heavy seas. "What about Maggie and Kevin?" I asked, craning my neck for a glimpse of my sister.

"Kevin wants to make sure that everyone gets out," Clancy said. "They'll meet us in the parking lot of the Tastee-Freez."

I started to protest, but Clancy gripped my arm harder. In that moment, he was almost unrecognizable. The red light cast a fierce spark into his eye, and as I let him guide me, I felt that I had entered a state of eerie calm. Shock, I told myself: this must be what shock felt like. "I saw them kill Dr. Bell," I said, and Caroline shuddered.

"Don't think about it," Clancy commanded. "Keep your mind on—"

A crash, like thunder but louder, canceled his words. Tiny red cinders rained down on the parking lot, and a woman darting through the cars ahead of us cried out in pain. I glanced at Caroline and Oliver in the backseat. She was gripping his hand, and his face was tense with nerves.

The cars were bottlenecked all the way through downtown, and at the last moment Clancy swung left, onto Bloodwort Road. "What are you doing?" I cried.

"There's too much traffic. I'm going to take the fire road and come down on the other side of town."

I sat on my hands to stop their shaking. I knew that Clancy was right; there would be no traffic on the fire road. But going through the woods would take us near the cave at Bloodwort Farm.

Driving fast, not talking, we passed the bunkhouse. The fire glow in the sky was fainter now. We were driving through a tunnel of black trees, our headlights reflecting off the trunks. "Tell me what you saw," Clancy said in an undertone.

I told him about the girls writhing across the stage and Dr. Bell crawling out to them. "Shit," he said quietly, flexing his hands on the steering wheel. "And you said it was Willow's friends. What about Willow?"

"I don't know where she is," I whispered. Clancy turned to the right, and as the lights shone against a wall of close-growing oaks, I saw a black shadow drifting across the road. We were hit by a sudden blast of hot air, and then one of the oaks exploded, split straight down the middle, revealing heartwood of fire and ash. The tires went off the track, the truck lurching over root and stone before rolling to a stop. A cloud of cinders hit the windshield with a dry hissing sound.

I kicked open the door and crawled into the middle of the road, where I lay on my back coughing so hard that I wondered if this alone could kill me. In the sky the stars and sparks swirled together and there was the red firelight too, a bloody light that made the trees stand out like veins.

Suddenly I felt myself lifted, pressed against Clancy's shoulder. He carried me to the side of the road and laid me under a tree. When I turned my head I could see the truck, still steaming a little, though the smoke seemed to have blown away. I tried to raise myself on my elbows. Caroline was sprawled beside me, and down the road I could see Oliver's shadow retching into the underbrush. "Are you all right?" I whispered to Caroline.

"I'm fine. Oliver?" she shouted, raising herself on her elbows.

When he stepped back into the light, I could see that his arm hung limply from his shoulder. "I fell against the door," he said, looking down at the arm as if it belonged to someone else.

Clancy put his hand on Oliver's back and felt along the forearm until Oliver cried out. "Once we get where we're going, I think I can set it," Clancy said.

"You can set a broken arm? Where'd you learn to do that?" I couldn't resist asking.

Clancy gave me a look, as if the answer should have been obvious. "Mrs. Lemons," he said.

I watched him walk back to the truck, keeping his body stiff so we wouldn't see him limp. The dome light clicked on as he poked around in the glove compartment. After a minute or two he came back, boots creaking on the loose stones, a flashlight shining down the length of his pant leg. "Follow me," he said.

We walked for a while on the fire road before turning onto a ghost track through the woods. Stumbling in every rut, Caroline kept rubbing at her bare arms, and after a minute I took off my cardigan and put it around her shoulders. "But I'm not cold," she mumbled.

"Well, I don't want it." Wind swished through the poplars above our heads. I kept thinking that I saw the black fluttering thing silhouetted against the sky, and I counted silently in French to keep myself calm.

I'd made it all the way to *quarante-sept* when the trail faded at the edge of a briar patch. "Do you even know where you're going?" I called to Clancy as he plunged off the path into the brush. He gave me an annoyed look and shone the flashlight into the clearing, revealing two picnic tables and two matching kayaks upside down on sawhorses. I breathed a sigh of relief. Kayak Boy's cabin wouldn't offer any protection from the wild girls, but at least it was somewhere.

Clancy found a key under a watering can and let us into the living room, hitting the light switch with his elbow. "The design is based on the four classical elements," I explained to Oliver. "My sister's boyfriend did the decorating."

Caroline sat on a chair decorated with velvet flaps that resembled flower petals, while Oliver sank into a beanbag chair that had been painted to look like a mushroom. His knees came up to his chin, and after a minute he pushed himself off with his good arm and sat on the floor. "It's nice," he said, looking up at me politely, as if I were his hostess. "It's very clean."

I nodded awkwardly. "Well, my sister's kind of a neat freak, actually."

"Kate, do you know where Kevin keeps his guns?" Clancy asked.

"His what?"

"His guns," he repeated. "Squirrel guns, shotguns, whatever."

"I don't think he has any," I said, but I followed Clancy into the bedroom, where he disappeared into the closet. After a minute he came out holding a box of shells, which he tossed on the bed. A shotgun was tucked under his arm.

"Are you going to shoot at the wild girls?" I asked.

He stood up, and I thought that this hard-eyed man, blood streaking his cheek, could not be Clancy Harp—mild, gentle Clancy, who had taken shit from me all year and asked for seconds. "Do you have a better idea?"

"Willow's in charge of this," I said. "I want to go back to the Academy. If I can talk to her, maybe I can—"

"No," Clancy said.

I glared at him. "You can't tell me no."

"I am telling you no. You think that shooting at them is a bad idea? Talking to them is the dumbest idea I ever heard."

Tears were spilling down my cheeks, and suddenly I was mad at myself as well as him. "You don't understand. She can make those girls do anything, Clancy. The whole town could be dead by morning."

Clancy cracked open the shotgun and reached for the box of shells, undulating on the water bed. "I can't let you go out there, Kate," he said. "If we just wait it out, this might all blow over."

"Fine," I spat. "Fine, I'll just sit here like an idiot." But when Clancy looked down to load the shotgun, I reached for his flashlight and slipped it into my pocket.

I trailed after him back to the living room, where Caroline and Oliver were sitting together on the log-shaped couch. She was examining his arm while he watched her with a warmth that livened his whole face, making it almost handsome. It was possible, I admitted, that I'd been wrong about him—as wrong as I'd been about Kayak Boy. It was possible that what I'd felt had been less reasoned disapproval than jealousy. But it was too late to do anything about that now.

"I'm going to make tea," I announced, but no one seemed to be listening. Clancy was in the bathroom, the shotgun leaning against the wall outside.

In the kitchen, the orange flames painted on the walls leaped almost to the ceiling. I turned on the faucets and bumped the teapot against the sink, just in case anyone was listening. Then, under the cover of rushing water, I eased open the door to the side yard.

"Wait," Caroline whispered. She tiptoed into the kitchen, a finger to her lips. "I heard what you said to Clancy. I'm going with you."

"I can do this myself," I hissed.

Caroline set her mouth in a firm line and shook her head, hair swishing against her cheekbones. "You're not going alone."

CHAPTER SEVENTEEN

We didn't really need the flashlight. As Caroline and I trudged up the fire road, the glow in the sky brightened until it lit the undersides of the leaves. I pictured the Academy burning, leaded windows cracking and melting, and at that moment I heard the moan of sirens—fire trucks from Moorefield or Glen City. Had the flames spread to downtown? Had the people from the River House made it across the bridge in time? Neither of us seemed to feel much like talking, so I tried to distract myself by picturing Mom and Maggie, Travis, Clancy—holding each of their faces in my mind, and saying in my head the words I might never get to say in person.

When the slope to our left got steeper, I could tell that we'd reached the border of Bloodwort Farm. Caroline looked shaky, and we sat for a minute while she wiped her face with the hem of her sweater. I don't know if I can do this, I thought, but wasn't aware that I'd said the words aloud until Caroline turned to me.

"It's kind of late for that," she said, smiling. "Don't you think?"

"I'm going to confront her," I said. "It's just that I don't think of myself as the kind of person who—takes action, you know what I mean? That's the thing that was so great about Willow—she actually went after what she wanted, while I just sort of thought about it."

Caroline shook her head. "It's not like the choice is between being a wild girl and being a spineless blob. I know you, Kate. You're a lot stronger than you think."

It was close to what Mrs. Lemons had said to me back before she'd lost it completely: *you're different than what you think you are.* "Besides, you know I'm a tough bitch," Caroline said.

It was exactly the wrong time and place for it, but we laughed anyway, and kept on until the smoke got in our lungs and the laughter turned to coughing. "From the top of this hill, we'd have a good view of the Academy," I said.

Caroline nodded, and we started climbing, grabbing on to roots and the trunks of saplings. A sharp rock tore a patch out of my bad knee, but when the blood ran down my leg, I kept going. At the top, I climbed up on a boulder that rose above the trees. The sky had turned bright orange over the Academy. As far as I could tell, the fire hadn't spread—not yet, anyway.

Caroline offered me her shoulder, and I held on to steady myself as I jumped to the ground. The smoke was drifting north now, shrouding the moon above the trees. "When you were doing all that research," I said to her, "did you read anything about a wild girl being talked out of killing people? Has that ever worked?"

"Not that I know of. I'm not sure that they're human, precisely. So when you think about it, talking to them would be kind of quixotic."

I picked up an egg-shaped pebble and zinged it at a nearby trunk. She was right, of course. Caroline and I couldn't fly or start a fire just by looking at something. We didn't even have a squirrel gun. All I could do was try to convince Willow that she didn't want to destroy Swan River, and the only advantage I had was that I understood her in a way nobody else ever could. I knew that she felt responsible for Mason's death. In her mind she was already damned, so why not go all the way with it? Why not make the most of her power? Maggie had said that a wild girl should balance what she loved against the satisfaction of destroying what she hated, but Willow had already done the math. The life her parents had planned for her looked like a bad joke, and she didn't love anybody.

Except maybe me. I was her conscience; she had told me so. If anyone could stop what was happening, it was Willow, and if anyone could stop Willow, it was me.

Something moved in the bushes halfway down the slope. I scrambled to my feet and swept my flashlight in a wobbly arc: tangled brambles; pale blooms of rhododendron, shuddered as if by wind. Everything was quiet. But as the glint of the flashlight reflected off a pane of glass, I realized that I was looking at the commune trailer. Kudzu and bloodwort wrapped it in viselike loops, spreading their wide leaves over the door and windows.

The noise I'd heard could have come from one of the animals that roamed the state forest: coyote, bear, catamount. It could have been the wild girls circling, closing in. But when the rhododendron blossoms trembled again, I thought of Mason, and felt a jolt of longing so intense that I had to stop, breathe deep. They had never found his body. It hadn't washed up in a mesh of branches, or snagged on a rock in the downriver rapids. What if my gloomy dreams of the river bottom were only dreams and the flesh and blood Mason was here, come back for me?

A figure stepped out of the bushes, and I felt a raw scream tear from my throat. Caroline was screaming too. I dropped the flashlight, and it rolled a few feet before coming to a stop, illuminating two dirty feet and the hem of a white robe.

The figure let out a wry cackle. "Company at last," it said in a high cracked voice. "Miss Kate, I've been waiting. I knew you'd be back here one of these days."

"Mrs. Lemons?" So she'd been up here all these months, keeping her useless watch over the gateway to the Underworld, getting crazier and crazier.

She reached out and grabbed my wrist, the hood of her robe falling forward to cover her face. "I have something for you. It was Mason's, and I know he'd want you to have it. I'll just need a minute to find it, if you'll step inside." Caroline moved forward too, but Mrs. Lemons waved her away. "Not you, missy," she said.

Leaving Caroline on the other side, Mrs. Lemons dragged me through the tangle of rhododendron. She put her shoulder to the trailer door and shoved hard—once, twice. By the wavering candle on the worktable, I saw that the room was trashed, the floor stained black with spilled potions and glittering with broken glass. A heap of blankets filled one corner. The air had a half-sweet smell, like something rotting in swamp water.

The door shut with a bang, and the skin on my arms prickled. "Maybe I should go," I whispered.

"Come on, now," Mrs. Lemons said. "You wouldn't leave an old lady by herself on a night like this, would you?" Slow as nightmare, I looked down to see that the hand on my arm was a blackened claw.

The whine was gone, abraded to a rough rasp. "*Got* to be my lucky day," the Birdman said, throwing off his robe. "Wild girls in town, and now a little present shows up right on my doorstep." When I tried to run past him to the door, he slapped me and kneed me in the chest, pushing me to the floor. The broken glass stabbed and scraped the skin of my back, but I forgot it when he was on top of me, fumbling at my clothes. He bit my chin so hard that I felt the skin tear.

"Don't fight me, girl," he shouted, using his knee to push my legs apart. "We're going to die anyway. Might as well go out right!"

I thought I heard someone pounding at the door, but it was all mixed up with the roaring in my ears and his panting breath as he fumbled with my jeans. He had been holding my hands above my head, but now I was able to pull my left hand free. My fingers scrabbled over the floor until I found it: a knife-shaped shard ending in a point. I raised it in my fist and with all my strength drove it into the side of his neck. The door blew open and the Birdman rolled off me, his body sheathed in flames. Within them, it jerked and buckled, collapsing in a heap of ash and bone.

Willow leaned against the worktable. "You're welcome," she said.

I turned on my side and threw up. Blood, mine and the Birdman's, dripped from my face and pooled among the shards of glass.

Willow held out her hand. "Get up." Her touch was surprisingly cool, and I felt a sudden urge to press her palm against my forehead and hold it there until the nausea went away.

She put her arm around my shoulder and guided me out the trailer's broken door, down the steps and into the snarl of rhododendron. I stumbled, looked down—an orange crate, a broken bottle: the remains of the shooting range. "Why are you doing this?" I asked numbly.

"Why am I saving you from being raped and murdered?"

The pain from the cuts on my back hit me then, sharp enough to make me catch my breath. "I'm pretty sure I'd already saved myself," I said.

She pushed the branches aside like a curtain and I saw the cave, vines latticed around a black open mouth. The branches to our left began shaking, and the minions emerged: Rosa and Elise, Lucie and Matilda. They were still in their graduation robes, and like Willow they all seemed to be lit from within, radiating a light as beautiful as it was terrifying. Each of the pairs carried a body

255

between them. One was in jeans and a white sweater, with a pair of glasses crushed in her hand. Caroline. Rosa dropped her to the ground, and she rolled over, gagging. I tried to run to her, but Willow held me back.

"Leave her alone," Willow said to the minions, her tone almost peevish. "I don't care about her." She dragged me over to the second body, dressed in black slacks and a frilly white blouse open at the neck. One foot wore a black kitten heel; the other was muddy and bare. Willow grabbed a branch and poked at Tessa until she stood up, rubbing her eyes. Her face was dirty too, and scratched as if she'd been dragged through the bushes headfirst. As bad off as she was, her eyes widened in horror at the sight of me.

Willow made a sweeping, game show hostess gesture. "All right," she said to me. "Kill her."

The Birdman's blood had run into my right ear, and I thought at first that I must have misheard. "What?"

"Kill her," Willow repeated impatiently. "However you want to do it, I don't care."

I held up my hands, most of the nails broken, the backs bleeding from a hundred cuts. "I'm not a wild girl, Willow. Didn't you notice that I'm not glowing?"

Willow looked at me for a long moment. "Maybe it's not too late," she said. "You have it inside you, Kate—I know you do."

Rosa gave a sharp cry. Caroline had hold of her ankles and was trying to pull her down while she kicked at Elise and Lucie, who circled around her, snarling.

"Hey!" Willow shouted. "I told you to leave her alone. I didn't want her here in the first place."

Lucie, who had reached out to touch Caroline's hair, pulled her hand back into her sleeve. "Well, what do you want us to do?"

she asked with a mutinous edge to her voice, but Willow ignored her. She had turned back to me, looking into my face with something like pity. Little snakes of flame curled along the underside of her hairline, flickering up and dying down again; the backlighting gave her face a warm glow, like heated copper.

"You're telling me that if you had the chance to destroy Swan River, just raze it to the ground, you wouldn't do it? I *know* you would."

Burn it down, Mrs. Lemons had said. *Burn it down and start again.* Dr. Bell had said that I didn't want to become a wild girl, and Willow had assumed that I did. In a way, they were both right. But when Willow waited for me to step forward and join her, I didn't move.

Willow hesitated for another moment and then wheeled to face Tessa. She had collapsed into Matilda's arms, but as Willow approached, Tessa straightened, and for a moment I saw on her face the old habit of command. "This is ridiculous," she declared. "Stop it right now." For a second I thought that she might actually stomp her foot.

"Stop what?" Willow asked. Taking one step closer, she reached out and used her fingernail to slit Tessa's body from throat to navel. The white blouse turned black, and with a surprised expression, Tessa dropped to her knees and fell heavily to the ground.

The minions shrieked with pleasure, their voices so much louder than my own that I didn't know I'd screamed until Willow slapped me. The others watched over her shoulder, their faces animated by a feral hunger. Dr. Bell had thought he was Dionysus, but I knew it would take only a twitch of Willow's little finger to make them tear me limb from limb.

"Please," I whispered between clenched teeth. "This isn't you, Willow."

Our eyes locked, and for a second I thought I'd gotten through to her. "Why do you think I planned to burn the town?" she said, almost pleadingly. "We were going after the Academy and Dr. Bell anyway, but the rest of it—that's for you, Kate. You can still have it, I know you can, if you'll just admit that you want to be one of us."

We were standing so close that I could feel her cold breath on my cheek. "If you were going to burn Swan River for me," I said into her ear, "then you can stop it for me."

Her hair brushed my lips. She leaned even closer and hissed, "But I don't *want* to stop it, Kate. Why should I do what I don't want to do?" She pushed me away, shaking her head in disappointment. The empty heart locket swung at the base of her throat.

Shivering violently, I tucked my hands into my armpits. "Poor baby," Willow said. "Are you cold?" She put a hand on my shoulder, and suddenly my shirt was on fire.

I smelled singed cotton, singed hair, something that could have been my own flesh burning. Willow fell on top of me, laughing. The laurel snapped with flame. The minions ran toward us, teeth bared, screaming, and I rolled us into the cave.

EPILOGUE

I lay in the cave for almost twenty-four hours. The arm I had fallen on throbbed with pain. I fell in and out of sleep, watching the clouds of smoke slowly dissipate. The sky turned white-blue, orange-yellow, and finally the cooler blue of late afternoon.

All through that long day I was aware of Willow, the body beside me on the cave floor, but it wasn't until the sky went blue again that I managed to turn over and look at her. She had fallen on a piece of jagged rock that pierced her back just below the left shoulder. Her mouth and eyes were open, legs and arms falling to the sides. I knew that she was dead, but it didn't stop me from talking to her. I told her that the Underworld wasn't too bad, all things considered. I told her that I was sorry for pushing her into the cave, but there really wasn't anything else I could have done under the circumstances. Unseeing, she stared up through the laced branches to the sky slowly darkening to evening. At some point, I unfastened the locket from her neck and fit it around my own throat.

Voices whispered to me from the river that day; lights without a source flickered over the floor. If I spent another night there, I knew that I would die too. Though from a distance the cave's gray walls looked papery as wasps' nests, I could feel the rock-cold seeping into my bones. I lay my body against Willow's and put my arms around her, but I might as well have hugged the stone itself.

Then I remembered the cigarettes in her pocket, and after four or five false starts, I managed to spark the lighter. I held it up, illuminating the pile of cloth and bone that lay at the far end of the cave, close to the ledge of the underground river.

Mrs. Lemons. Without the white robe and the strands of yellow-gray hair still affixed to her skull, I wouldn't have been sure it was her. Her body must have been down here for months now; there was no way to know whether she'd jumped into the cave or been pushed, and I guessed it didn't really matter. With my good arm, I rolled the robe off her body, tugging when it snagged on a shoulder or finger bone. I tucked it around my own shoulders and stuck my head out over the river. The water was black, and fast, and judging from the spray that stung my face, colder than the stone it carved through.

It took me a long time to lug Willow's body over next to Mrs. Lemons. The voices of the river hissed and sang to me. The water would carry them to my underwater dream city, where Mason was waiting. They were slumped side by side, black shadows on the stone, and I rolled them one by one into the river. Willow's hair caught on a rock, and I thought for a moment I'd have to jump after her, but then the current claimed her and swept her around the bend, into the tunnel that connected the cave to Swan River. Tightening the robe around my shoulders, I lay beside the water, hoping that when I died I would tumble off the ledge and follow them into that green river-world. I could already see it—the tall ferns swaying and bending, the leaning house with its dark doorway. And Mason the way he'd been at the last summer festival—Mason whole again, with his golden eyes and highway smile.

And then I was opening my eyes on the beam of a flashlight. A man's face poked through the hole that Willow and I had made in the undergrowth, his mouth open in a funny-looking O. "Travis," I mumbled. "Is that you?"

I spent the summer after the fire, after what should have been my high school graduation, at Mom's new apartment in Moorefield. Reporters called once in a while, but the story of the teenage girl who spent twenty-four hours in a cave didn't get as much media attention as you would expect. Most of the newspaper articles and TV segments concentrated on Tessa and Willow. The minions remembered just enough of their wild night to accuse Willow of stabbing Tessa before pulling me into the cave, and I went along with their story. The newspapers didn't know exactly what to make of the whole thing—was it a satanic ritual? a love triangle gone deadly?—but there were no satisfying answers, and after a while they stopped asking the questions. It didn't matter to me what people said, as long as Willow took every bit of the blame.

The newspaper and TV people didn't know how to connect the deaths at Bloodwort Farm to the destruction of the Academy, so those stories focused on the discovery of Dr. Bell's body, found facedown on the stage of the amphitheater. Despite the oddness of his position, most of the stories suggested that he'd died trying to save the girls under his charge. They gave him credit for the orderly evacuation of the dorms, for the miraculous fact that none of the students had died in the fire, and strangely, I found that his undeserved reputation for heroism didn't bother me that much. His death—pathetic, brutal, and ridiculous—was punishment enough for his delusions.

Though the board of trustees didn't make a final announcement until July, the closing of the Academy seemed inevitable long before that. Whether you blamed the fire on faulty wiring or a rogue cigarette, no one wanted to send their daughter to a school charred and gutted down to the last chunk of Gothic masonry. And what girl would want to go to a school where fourteen horses had been burned alive in the stables, screaming, beating their hooves against their stalls?

In August the washer at the apartment complex broke down, and I was shoveling diapers into the dryer at the Laundromat when I saw Clancy coming through the door. "You look good," he said, staring down at his hands. "Your arm and everything."

I had raised my knuckles to thump my cast before I remembered that it wasn't there anymore. Like my braid, it had been part of me for so long that I sometimes missed it.

"How's Agnes?" he asked.

"Great. She's almost two months old now. I mean, she wakes me up a lot, but it's been fun living with them." After the fire, it seemed that everyone who didn't have a house to sell had left Swan River, and business at the River House had been so bad that Kevin had been forced to close. Maggie had wanted to stay in their cabin while they regrouped, but he had insisted that they come to Mom's new place in Moorefield, and I had been on his side. Maggie might have been the leader who could have saved what was left of the town, but she was also the mother of a daughter who would one day turn sixteen. For everyone's sake, I hoped that Agnes would celebrate that birthday somewhere far away from Swan River.

Clancy gave me a tepid smile, and we were silent. The only other people in the Laundromat were a fat mother and her toddler, who was sitting on a washer and laughing at the way it jiggled. The mother folded clothes with her eyes on the TV. She had beautiful red hair that made me think of Willow's, and a tired, disappointed face. "Are you still planning on buying that farm?" I asked.

"I'm working on the financing. I'm thinking about bringing in some guys to work with me. They'll make payments toward the mortgage and get a share of the profits. It'll be a real community business—everybody will have their own plot, but we'll collaborate on planting the fields, building fences, whatever."

It sounded sort of like a commune, but I knew better than to say so. "Happy dirt," I said.

"Right," he said with a glum face. "Happy dirt, happy vegetables. Look, Kate, I know I was an asshole that night. I just didn't want you to get hurt."

"It's not that." I took his hand, but then I didn't know what to do with it. "Clancy, you saved my life. If you hadn't called Travis, no one would have had any idea where to look for me and Caroline. And you were right about everything you said, but you don't understand what I saw that night."

I looked across the street, the river invisible past the slope of the bank. They hadn't found Willow's body either. She and Mason were still under there—snagged on tree roots, perhaps, their bodies bloated, eyes pickled and picked by scavenger fish. "I'm just not over it yet," I said.

Clancy pulled his hand away, grimacing. "I've got to get to the credit union before it closes." Though he hadn't asked me to walk with him, I followed him out the door.

With the river breeze, the heat didn't feel as bad as it had inside the Laundromat. Couples and families with kids were walking toward the farmers' market, and pretty hippie girls in long silky skirts stared at Clancy from under their bangs. I tried not to be jealous. I had no right to him; I knew that now.

We stopped beside the credit union, under a green awning that flapped drily in the breeze. "Well," he said. "This is it, I guess." I could tell that he would have liked to sound casual, but the pain in his face made me want to close my eyes and walk home blind. I kissed him quickly and ran across the street to a gallery that specialized in Appalachian crafts. I hid out there for half an hour, until I was sure he'd gone, and then I went back for the diapers.

On my last day at home, as I packed my suitcases into the van Maggie had given me for my eighteenth birthday, Travis watched from the patio, Agnes in her infant seat beside him. I knew that Mom had let him move into the new apartment only because she was grateful to him for getting me out of the cave, and to the casual eye, he wasn't any different here than he had been at home in Swan River. On weekends, he still liked to sit around all day in boxers and an undershirt, reading the paper from front to back and drinking Miller High Life. But he had found a job right away, at a private security company, and worked overtime so Mom and Maggie could spend more time with the baby. Though Travis came home late and left early most days, Agnes seemed to like him the best of any of us. When I looked over to the patio, she was staring up at him with a blurry grin.

"You be careful," he called, tilting his beer in my direction. "They've got a lot of wildlife up there, don't they? Bears and wolves and everything?"

"I think so," I said. "But it's a college campus, so I'm sure it's pretty safe."

Mouth ajar, Travis seemed to consider commenting on the idea that campuses were safe places. Instead he used the bottle to scratch the side of his nose. "Saw a mama bear come down to the river once when I was a kid," he said. "I was fishing. She could have reached out her paw and knocked me right out of the boat, but it was like she didn't even see me."

We nodded at each other. "You say good-bye to your mother?" he asked.

"I said good-bye to everybody this morning." Maggie had to work the early shift at the Mermaid Café, and she'd woken me before she left, sitting down on the end of my bed and talking about everyday things: the strawberry-rhubarb pie she was going to make next weekend, and Agnes's appointment for her vaccinations, and her own plans to enroll at MCC for a degree in public administration. When she was already late, she'd hugged me so tight I couldn't breathe and left before I could say a word. An hour or two later, Mom said she had to go to the DMV, slipped me a check for two hundred dollars, and gave me the same kind of hug, this one so hard I thought she'd bruise my ribs. I was sort of glad when they were gone. I knew now that I'd taken them for granted, and their joy at my deliverance was for me an itching kind of shame.

I slammed the back door of the van and faced Travis, searching for the right words, twisting my hand in the hem of my T-shirt. "Thank you," I said.

Travis squinted down the bottle like there might be a prize in the bottom. "You go on and do something with yourself. That's all the thanks I need."

I'm sure that Travis didn't intend to make me feel guilty, but those words stuck with me better than any inspirational speech I ever heard, and were at least part of the reason why, after four years of environmental studies at Pritchard College, I turned down offers from Greenpeace and the Sierra Club and took a job with Appalachian Natural Resources out of Knoxville. I had thought that I'd travel, but instead of going to Africa and Nepal, I spent most of my time on the road to places like Hangdog, West Virginia, and Mudstone, Kentucky. I worked on natural gas rights and mountaintop removal. I saw a lot of small towns that could have been Swan River without the Academy, without the cave to the Underworld, without the madness that simmered just below the surface. Sometimes I hated the town I was in and everyone who lived there, but I stuck with it, organizing meetings and protests, working with a kind of penitential fervor. As Mason had said, these were my people, for better and for worse.

Through those hectic years, I kept up with Caroline better than almost anyone, probably because she always made the effort to keep up with me. She had gotten a PhD in neuroscience and married another professor, a tall blond-bearded man who passed his long-jawed face on to their three boys. She came to visit me once when I was working with some rangers at a state park in north Georgia, and we spent a weekend on a white-water rafting trip down the Chattooga. But no matter how much we laughed and reminisced, no matter how much wine we drank around the campfire, we never talked about Willow and the minions. Caroline never mentioned the ethnography she'd been planning to write, which would prove to the world that divine ecstasy still lived among us. I had seen the dazed, hopeless look that sometimes flashed across her face when she thought I wasn't paying attention, and I knew that what she had seen that night had changed her just as much as it had changed me.

Only once did we come anywhere near the subject of the wild girls. We were sitting on a log with our feet in the river, and I had begun to feel sort of tense, the way I often did in the woods at night.

"I saw Oliver on the news one time," I told her. In his clerical collar, he had been sitting just to the right of the president at the Easter prayer breakfast. I had recognized him immediately, though he looked different in some ways: easier, friendlier. His arm still seemed stiff, but he didn't. "If it hadn't been for everything that happened," I said, "do you think you guys would have stayed together?"

Looking out toward the river, Caroline folded her hands on her knee. "He wasn't that bad, you know."

"I know," I said, but she shook her head.

"You didn't give people a chance. You thought you had everybody's number, and then you couldn't handle it if anyone turned out to be different than what you expected."

"That's probably true," I said. "I'm sorry."

I had to raise my voice to be heard over a chorus of bullfrogs tuning up on the riverbank. We sat in silence for a few minutes, listening, and then Caroline slapped her palms against her thighs. "I didn't mean to go off on you like that," she said. "I'm just tired." I told her it was fine, but that night, as I lay listening to rain dripping down the sides of the tent, I thought about what she'd said. I'd called Oliver judgmental, but if Caroline was right, it was a case of the pot and the kettle. Had I been too ready to make up my mind about Oliver and Caroline, Mason and Clancy and Maggie and the minions—and Willow? If I'd been smarter, more clear-sighted, would I have figured out sooner what was happening to her? Could I have stopped her—helped her—before it was too late?

I never saw the minions again, but I heard that some of them had a pretty hard time. Lucie Yates spent the summer before her freshman year at Mary Washington in a private psychiatric facility. Elise Seidel tried to commit suicide, and ended up dropping out of college after three semesters.

I did see Frances once, at the wedding of two of my coworkers. The reception was held at an inn on the South Carolina coast, three days after a hurricane that had destroyed a nearby barrier island but left the inn miraculously unscathed. Though I hadn't known that Frances was a friend of the couple's, somehow I wasn't surprised to see her there. She was sitting in an Adirondack chair at the edge of a green lawn, and I took my drink and went to sit beside her.

She glanced at me and raised a pair of perfectly arched eyebrows. "Kate Riordan," she said. "Is it still Riordan?"

I nodded. "I hear you're in Atlanta now."

"In a sense," she sighed. "Of course I travel six days out of seven. My therapist says I'm in a long-distance relationship with myself."

She slid her foot most of the way out of her champagne satin sandal, hooking the strap over her toes as she gazed out at the ocean. The water was littered with debris, fence posts and pieces of smashed boats. A palmetto stuck out like a giant splinter from the dock to our left.

"You know," Frances said, "sometimes I'll see a woman with red hair on the street, and I'll wonder what her life would be like if she'd lived. I used to think that she would have done something amazing, but now I think she would have married just the kind of guy that her dad wanted her to. Not right out of college, of course, but eventually she would have found some stock market shark with a hard-on for redheads and a little place on the Outer Banks.

And right now she'd be pacing around her house in Charleston or Birmingham, bored out of her goddamn mind."

"I don't think you even believe that," I said.

Frances pushed her glasses down her nose, meeting my eyes for the first time. She was in gold from head to foot, her haircut chic and expensive, all the Abilene oil money refined right out of her. "So you've still got it," she said dryly.

"Got what?"

"Your girl crush. Whatever, that's probably not the right word for it. We always just said you were in love with her."

I felt the heat rising to my face. "I stood up to her," I said. "Tessa and I were the only ones who did."

Frances smiled, but it wasn't the superior smirk I'd anticipated. She looked as if she felt sorry for me—as if, in her blunt way, she was actually trying to help.

"Some people hit their peak at seventeen," she said. "Willow was one of them, and she knew it. You'll be happier when you realize that she really wasn't that special."

Though I felt a little annoyed with Frances for ruining a party where I'd planned to have a good time, I knew that she was right about Willow. I loved her, but I saw her faults better than anyone realized, and I can't blame her, or Mason either, for the shape my life has taken.

It seemed too late to change, but then, on a night when I'd dragged myself home from failed community organizing in a failing mining town, there was the message on my answering machine. From Clancy. He had seen an article about me, and called my mom to get my number.

It was a strange coincidence that Clancy and I had ended up

moving in the same circles. He was everywhere these days, on the radio and in the newspaper, and he didn't talk about happy dirt anymore. He talked about organic conversion and food security. If a photo of protestors agitating for subsidies for small farmers was going around the office, I was sure to find Clancy's face in the crowd. Half a dozen times over the years, I'd go to a conference or a meeting to find that he had been there the day before, or was coming the following day, but somehow we'd never met. Maybe that was intentional, at least on my part.

"Anyway," he said, clearing his throat. "I've been thinking about the time when we knew each other. About how sure you seemed to be about everything. You knew exactly what you wanted, and you were going for it. I don't know if you realized, but coming from where I did, it was important for me to see that. So I wanted to say congratulations. You're doing good work. And I wanted to say that if you're ever in the area—or if you'd ever like to come to the farm—" His voice got louder, until he sounded almost angry. "I'd like to see you. I'd like to make you dinner." He gave his number and hung up quickly, without saying goodbye.

I let the message play twice, and then I stood for a minute with my finger on the delete button. I wished there was some way to explain that it wasn't that I didn't want to see him. I knew what a good man he was, and understood that he'd given me more chances than I came near deserving, but I was afraid of what might happen if he got close to me. I was afraid that if he saw what I really was inside, he'd hop the first train out of town and never look back. Perhaps this is always the danger of intimacy, but I have, I think, more reason to fear it than most.

When I left my mom's apartment in Moorefield and drove off to start my freshman year at Pritchard College, I went the wrong way, passing over the interstate and continuing north to Swan

River. The town was even more desolate than I'd imagined, the last remaining businesses on Jessup Avenue shuttered, half the houses in the Delta abandoned. I parked at the front gates of the Academy and tried, without the buildings for markers, to find my way to the Lawn. The cranes of construction companies hired to clear the rubble lifted their heads above the piles of charred wood and ash. Finally I found the sidewalk and fought my way through debris to the middle of campus. Fallis was a black hunk of stone to my west, and the other two dormitories simply weren't there at all. I thought of what Mr. Hightower had taught us about ecological succession—how, in nature, one community makes way for another. The town torn out of the dark wilderness was returning to it, and I was not sorry. I would never belong anywhere but Swan River, but it wasn't a place where people ought to live.

As the day dimmed and the moon rose into the branches of the blackened oaks, I tried to talk to the wild girls. The day we'd walked in the woods, Willow had said that I was her conscience, the voice inside her head. That night, sitting in the rubble of Swan River, I promised them that they would be the voice inside my head. I told them that I would carry them wherever I went, my secret dark self lurking below the surface of my daylight life, and I've kept that promise. The wild girl is with me always; she is my rage and my hunger, and if I live what passes for a decent life in this world, it is because I know to say no to the thing inside me that yearns, even now, to burn it all down.

ACKNOWLEDGMENTS

Thanks, and more than thanks, to all of the following people, so necessary to the novel and to me:

Five years ago, Aimee Mepham met me for drinks and encouraged me to expand a long, weird story about angry girls who could fly. Paul Graham, Mika Perrine, Cynthia Lindstrom, Erin Saldin, and Drew Johnson provided thoughtful and generous critiques as I worked through draft after draft. Anna Teekell Hays gave me the word *deadneck,* and Matt Fluharty brought a little country to the urban Midwest. My agent, Denise Shannon, offered invaluable guidance when I wasn't sure where to go, and the phenomenal Alexis Gargagliano helped me find my way through to the end.

Finally, my heartfelt gratitude to the family and friends who made the years I spent writing *Wild Girls* a happy and fulfilling time in so many ways. Special appreciation is due to Mary Welek Atwell, Sarah John, and above all Charlie and Henry, who I simply couldn't do without.

ABOUT THE AUTHOR

MARY STEWART ATWELL's short fiction has appeared in *Best New American Voices* and *Best American Mystery Stories*. She grew up in southwest Virginia and now lives in Missouri.

RADFORD PUBLIC LIBRARY
30 WEST MAIN STREET
RADFORD, VA 24141
540-731-3621

DISCARD

3-13

F   Atwell, Mary Stewart
        Wild girls.